Saving Saskya

Saving Saskya

SIMON GESCHWINDT

ISBN: 978-1-874682-04-2 (paperback)
ISBN: 978-1-874682-03-5 (ebook)

Printed in the United Kingdom

Infonet Publications
Registered office:
67-69 Chancery Lane
London WC2A 1AF

Simon Geschwindt is a journalist and linguist specialising in media communications, ethics and eastern philosophies. Born 1949, he is married with five children, and lives in Cape Town, South Africa. Former editor of *Environment Matters International*, Simon has written numerous magazine and newspaper feature articles on ethics and the environment. He is author of the novel *Lost Identity* and the non-fiction works *Plastics Recycling – Cradle to Grave* (with M. Ward) and *Am I Right or Am I Right – an Introduction to Ethical Decision-Making*.

For Karin, my parents, children and grandchildren.

Saving Saskya is an exciting, challenging and moving philosophical story of enduring love while one man's inexorable slide into corruption is matched by another's redemption.

Saskya joins her father, a visiting scholar in ethics at the University of Cape Town, to do voluntary work in township schools. Appalled by the corruption, lack of resources and extremes of corporal punishment, she decides to return to Europe with her father. On their return journey, they cross South Africa by train to one of the world's most dangerous cities – Johannesburg – an error of judgement that has terrifying consequences.

Wir zwei, lieber Freund, sind Sonne und Mond, sind Meer und Land. Unser Ziel ist nicht, ineinander überzugehen, sondern einander zu erkennen und einer im andern das sehen und ehren zu lernen, was er ist: des anderen Gegenstück und Ergänzung.
Narziß und Goldmund, Hermann Hesse, 1930.

We are sun and moon, dear friend; we are sea and land. It is not our purpose to become each other; it is to recognise each other, to learn to see the other and honour him for what he is: each the other's opposite and complement.
Narcissus and Goldmund, Hermann Hesse, 1930.

Johannesburg

1

The morning sun was already warming the geckos basking on the mustard-coloured stone wall around the raised vegetable patch. Each morning during summer, the man who called himself Guido van Rensburg, wearing black to absorb the heat, sat beneath a towering jacaranda tree, drank his first cup of coffee and felt the sun's warmth penetrate his bones – a life-giving natural heat that relaxed his lanky body and energised him for the day ahead.

He took off the first layer, a black woollen jumper revealing a black silk shirt tucked into black jeans. The passers-by on the street beyond the spiked gate were still dressed in coats and scarves and woollen hats. Mothers had their babies strapped to their backs, completely covered in brightly-coloured blankets.

Shielding his eyes against the rising sun, Guido made out a black dot – a bird of prey soaring hundreds of feet above in the clear, fiercely blue sky. The watchful bird spiralled down to the point where Guido could make out the white part of its body and huge black wings. With a slight movement of its feathers, as though beckoning him to follow, the majestic bird headed south-west towards Soweto.

Guido nodded to his tall, gangly gardener and guard, Innocent Jentile, raking leaves in a patch of sunlight. The fading full moon, still high in the fresh morning sky, seemed to smile down at Innocent benevolently. As a man almost two meters tall thanks to his Zulu father, he was taller than most people from Limpopo.

Guido reflected on how dependent he'd become on this streetwise chancer, and how Innocent's quiet humility masked a toughness that underpinned his saintly forbearance. He was brave, but not for the sake of applause. Innocent was no such hero. With a complete absence of histrionics, without playing to any audience real or imagined, he went about being brave with a quiet dignity. His god had given him life and would take it away when the time came. That's how it was. To try preserving life at any cost was an insult to the god that gave it to him. Whether he consciously knew this was hard to tell. But Guido felt that somewhere at a deep instinctive level, Innocent seemed to understand it with a solid certainty that formed the cornerstone of his courage.

Innocent was not only the gardener but also protector and fixer in Guido's rented mansion on the edge of Johannesburg's Little Congo district. His tools included an odd assortment of stolen police-issue eight-shot pistols, a stun gun, a switch-blade and a pair of handcuffs. His sister, Precious, cleaned and cooked. Both brother and sister understood that life is war, and that careless talk costs lives.

That morning Guido had been thinking about 'home'. Where was it? Amsterdam, where his parents' ashes were entombed? No. Home had become wherever he found himself. And now that was Johannesburg. His father had died over thirty years before. His mother followed soon after. There was no one else. Even if it had been possible to return, merely to stand in the tiny graveyard and stare at the grey, plain plaque, and wonder why tears wouldn't come, would have been pointless. He could never see their graves again. His forged identity had trapped him within Southern Africa's borders.

'Mr Guido, you're in the paper. Look!' Innocent held up

2

the front page of *The Tribune* he'd bought from the street vendor. 'Hah! They make you look young.' His deep voice raised a tone or two. 'You get nice women when you look like that.'

Innocent laid the paper flat on the table. The headline was *English girl disappears at Hillbrow petrol station*.

'It's you, but it's not you, Mr Guido.'

Guido studied the photo. Despite the horn-rimmed glasses, it looked amazingly like him. A distant memory stirred. Then his eyes rested on the caption, and the name Christian Kettermann. He froze, holding the newspaper in a tight grip. For the first time in a long time, he felt an overwhelming sense of unease verging on vertigo. Perspiration soaked the back of his silk shirt. The old world had beaten a path to his door.

He read the text about the disappearance of the man's daughter from a petrol station near the city's Hillbrow district, notorious for its thieves, kidnappers and murderers. The poor soul must be desperate, he thought.

Innocent stared at the soft pink of the palms and insides of his long fingers in silence and wore a typical absent look that could have been mistaken for insolence or indifference. He looked down at Guido, waiting for him to continue.

'Thank you, Inno,' Guido said, by way of dismissal, and watched his tall, slim protector leave the room in a few loping strides and enter the garden.

Guido wandered aimlessly around the room, dragging on one of his pungent French cigarettes. Christian Kettermann, his cousin last heard of in Europe decades ago, was now in Johannesburg and trapped in a nightmare of the most awful kind. *What was he doing here?*

Guido's heart seemed to rise in his throat. Conflicting emotions battled with each other – profound pity for his

3

cousin's awful predicament and the desire to protect him versus the urge to run.

He knew that this more basic reaction was similar to what he expected to feel if he were ever caught – as an illegal immigrant, as a forger, as a murderer. And at that moment, he experienced a single flash of perfect understanding of why this had come about – a sense that this had been brought to his door to set in motion a new stage of life that he had unconsciously been hungering for – one that would somehow consolidate the previous stages of his life, and perhaps bring about a fitting conclusion.

This would involve going against the self-centred street survival instincts born of bitter experience during about a third of his life. This poor man – this cousin whom he hardly knew – needed the kind of help that people like he and Innocent could provide; the kind of help that recognises no boundaries of legality or petty moralising.

Action was required, but first he needed to think. He launched himself at the drinks cabinet. Pouring himself a generous glass of Dutch gin, he put on his headphones, selected a string quartet by Dmitri Shostakovich, and nestled himself into the vast leather sofa. He closed his eyes and tried not to breathe while he called up an image of a petrol station, a frightened young girl and her terrified father.

He refilled his glass to the brim, lit a cigarette and sank back into the sofa, his lean, handsome face wreathed in the heavy smoke that thumped his chest and made him even dizzier. The rhapsodic music fuelled emotions that were already in overdrive, and he switched it off before he felt nauseous. A fly caught between the curtain and the window buzzed irately and fell still. He would ask Precious later to make him a pipe.

His mind drifted back to Christian Kettermann, a cousin

4

on his father's side, whom he hadn't seen for at least thirty years. He was roughly the same age as Guido. Whilst Guido's mother was French, Christian's was Irish. Guido remembered little about him, except that he used to joke that his Catholic mother believed that the good Lord would be more favourably disposed towards a Christian than, for example, a Kevin. He remembered smiling politely and hoping that Christian would eventually cotton on to the fact that it really wasn't funny enough to keep repeating. One other point he remembered was that despite their having different parents he looked startlingly like Guido. Judging from the press photo, he still did.

To dodge the temptation of the drinks cabinet, he went back outside, then back in again to make a cup of *rooibos* tea. He sat on the *stoep*, warming his hands on the steaming cup, and absent-mindedly watched his Alsatian dog named Tsotsi, meaning 'urban gangster', chase its tail, and charge back and forth between the swaying jacarandas that had turned to a lighter, brighter shade of green as they waited for more of the summer rains.

Apart from his one catastrophic mistake decades before, Guido considered himself a non-violent man. He believed in peaceful protest and civil disobedience. *When you are as skinny as me*, he used to think to himself, *the best solution to conflict is diplomacy*. However, anger can change even the most phlegmatic of characters.

Guido reminded himself that most people's complicated characters have their extreme side and that he was no different. When diplomacy fails, more extreme solutions are necessary. And the most extreme solutions were going to be essential to help his beleaguered cousin wrestle his way out of this nightmare.

He entered through the French doors and crossed the

living room to the CD player on the TV cabinet. He pulled out a CD of Miles Davis' *Kind of Blue* album and put on the wistful ballad *Blue in Green*. He lowered himself into the armchair in the other corner, his legs stuck out in front of him, one foot resting on the other. The music did what it always did. A form of osmosis, it penetrated his skin and spread through his entire body as though carried through his veins and arteries by the irresistible force of its own emotional content. Life itself was a form of imprisonment, but if the chakras, like windows to the soul, were ever in danger of flying open and letting in a gentle consecrating light it was at moments like this, especially when such moments were accompanied by the tranquilising effect of one of his pipes.

Once the music had drawn to a close on an ambiguous, inconclusive chord that left him emotionally suspended, he pulled himself to his feet, freshened up his tall, wiry body with a shower, rearranged his curly grey hair, and stalked back to his room feeling energised by clarity of purpose. He took a pad of paper, a black felt-tipped pen, three gold Krugerrand coins and a well-worn copy of the *I-Ching*, the Chinese *Book of Changes*, from his chest of drawers. He tossed the coins on the table top six times until he had completed a hexagram on the pad. He looked it up in the book. It confirmed the need to 'strictly persevere for a favourable outcome'. His mind was already made up. He just needed to confirm it.

He rang *The Tribune*'s editorial office and asked for Blessing Molokwane, the journalist whose name was printed below the headline. He got put through, and explained that he was Christian Kettermann's cousin, and wanted to help. She refused to give him Christian's number, but took Guido's and promised to pass it on.

Cape Town

2

'Dad?' It was a bad line. 'Dad. Can you hear me?'

Christian Kettermann took a deep breath. 'Sas. How are you? Where are you?'

'London. My application to schools on the Cape Flats has come through. *Wahoo!* doesn't begin to express what I'm feeling.'

She explained that her Child and Youth Studies course required her to observe in schools. Because Christian was in South Africa, she approached Cape Town schools and had just obtained special permission from her course leader.

She sounded breathless. 'I've booked a flight. To Jo'burg. Then onto the Cape.'

'A flight?'

'To join you next week.'

As a visiting scholar at the University of Cape Town, Christian's days were jam-packed with working with staff and students, attending seminars and little time for anything else. A second longer and the pause would be hurtful. 'Yes.'

'I'll stay with you.'

He stared at the phone and saw her brilliant, bright-eyed face. 'No problem. But – '

'But what, Dad?' Her voice was losing its cheerful lilt. If his reaction hurt, she bravely hid it. 'I promise to be quiet,' she pleaded.

'But I'll be going back to Lisbon soon.'

She couldn't see him ruefully shake his head.

'Please. Pretty please!'

He tried to put an ironic smile into his voice. 'I'd love to see you, Sas. You can stay at my flat. So looking forward to – '

He was on the point of asking how long she wanted to stay but thought better of it.

'Love you, Dad. You might actually enjoy having me along.'

Love you, Dad. It gave him the kind of warm feeling that *Love you, Christian* could never match. He'd managed to divert his former wife from the fashionable, smart idea twenty-odd years before that children should address their parents by their first names. The idea had been to close the gap between parent and child and between generations. But nothing could beat the sense of protectiveness that *Dad* engendered in him, and the sense of protection that he hoped it gave to her.

And at this precise moment, it was the issue of protection that nagged him deeply. The moment he hung up, while his thin hand was still resting on the keyboard, he felt a wave of apprehension wash over him. He sensed even then, that he was making a dreadful mistake, the results of which would be unforeseeable.

He hadn't even asked about her studies or boyfriends. He cast his mind back to the last time he'd seen her, his eyes still burning after a sleepless journey from his flat in Lisbon before his departure from Heathrow to Cape Town – her flat, its tiny bedroom filled almost entirely with a double mattress on the floor, tangled sheets and duvet. He couldn't wait to leave that cramped, damp, clammy country, with its level of prosperity that spawned the type of whinging and whining rarely heard in poor parts of the world. He never got warm and could hardly wait to heat his bones in the Cape's spring sunshine. He hated London.

Saskya breezed into the arrivals hall, dressed in black and white. The thought that wearing a full-length, black leather coat might be inappropriate for that beautifully warm climate – the best in the world as any South African would tell you – had apparently never occurred to her.

They hugged – hers warm and rounded, his, bony and angular. 'I'm so glad to be here,' she said. 'And so pleased to see you, Dad.'

She grabbed his stick and did a brief Charlie Chaplin impression, her curly auburn hair bouncing on her shoulders. 'This was a journey where I've covered thousands of miles in a short space of time, and now I feel like I'm cruising down the highway with streamers on my bumper and bubbles coming out my exhaust. And it's not like me to exaggerate, eh, Dad?'

They headed for the car park, to the clippety-clop of her case on wheels and the dull thud of his walking stick. They looked an odd couple. He was sixty-something, gripping the stick's round handle, shaped like a shepherd's crook, curly-haired, grey-bearded and bespectacled and with a skin-and-bones physique.

His companion was easier on the eye, thanks to her strikingly handsome Scandinavian grandmother, rather than her mother. Tall, long-legged, beautiful, she was the sort of girl that girls love to envy, but the sort of girl that he loved to love, even when her hormones got the better of her, and her moods swung from manic self-assurance to the deepest gloom of self-doubt.

He unlocked the doors and put her case in the boot. He turned the ignition key, and the ancient navy-blue and rust-coloured Toyota from Rent-a-Wreck spluttered into life.

'So, what's new?' she asked, pulling the top of her white jumper away from her neck, as though it were already too warm for her.

'The news is still dominated by crime and politics, which

9

are often seen as the same thing,' he replied, peering through the scratched windscreen.

Within a few minutes they were out of the airport, and on the busy freeway heading towards the city centre set at the foot of Table Mountain. She pulled a face at the acrid smell coming from the miles of sprawling shacks at the side of the road.

'So, you're still that crazy, shy, absent-minded, lone hermit on the hill?'

'Yep.'

'Not over the hill?'

'No.'

'You don't get lonely?'

'No.'

'You don't find yourself becoming monosyllabic?'

'No.'

She smiled. Not one of those purposeful smiles that look like circuit training for the embouchure, but a genuine involuntary smile that was accompanied by sparks of pleasure that danced from her eyes. He felt as though his soul were basking in the warmth of that smile.

'Where are we?' she asked.

'Forest Hill. Staff accommodation.'

They waited for the electric gate to slide open and drove through to a parking lot outside the apartment block. He locked the car, waved to the guard, and led Saskya with her case up the outside steps to the second floor.

'One step at a time, Dad,' she teased.

He paused for breath and leant on his stick while searching in his trouser pocket for the keys. She closed the door behind them, and explored the lounge and two bedrooms, while he put the chain across, and secured the locks.

'What've you got in here, the crown jewels?'

'I never completely relax until I've locked the front door behind me and put on the chain. But that's me, eh?'

He joined her in the lounge. She was frowning. 'What are you afraid of?'

'The constant fear of being robbed. There are times I just don't know what to do for the best. I've huge doubts about my familiarity with the culture, so I play it safe.'

'Trust you. You said the same about Portugal.'

'Trust is the issue. Colleagues have warned me that you can suddenly find yourself in a dangerous situation with no easy way out. In the street, if I see someone coming towards me I tense up. Can I trust them or not? I never have anything of value on me.'

'Apart from your life.' She paused for a moment. 'I never imagined you getting like this. You, the closet communist revolutionary.'

'I'm concerned for my own personal safety. And yours.'

She looked away suddenly as if to dismiss the subject and walked through to the balcony.

He tucked his pale-blue cotton shirt into his neatly ironed fawn slacks, limped into the kitchen, and put the kettle on for a cup of tea.

She stood up in one easy movement and followed him. 'I'll make it, Dad.'

He nodded, returned to the lounge, parked his stick, and sank down into the brown sofa adjacent to the portable TV in the bookcase. Waiting for the kettle, she remained standing in front of him, hands in the pockets of her black jeans. Her green eyes surveyed the room critically.

'So, where's the Forest and where's the hill?' she asked, hands now on hips.

'The hill's up there,' he replied, pointing at the lounge

11

wall. 'Devil's Peak; and the forest up there probably reached here a long time ago.'

'Talking of forests, why have you grown a beard, Dad?' she teased, plonking herself next to him. 'You look like Marx.'

'Karl or Groucho?'

'Karl of course.' She pulled a face.

'What's wrong with that?'

'He was a communist – like you.'

'He was a Marxist.'

'Come on. That's like saying I'm a Kettermannist.'

'There's more to Marxism than just communism. Communism is only part of the Marxist picture. In fact, it's the last part – the final stage.'

She threw him a look that said *I can feel a lecture coming on*. 'Communists did awful things.'

'People did awful things.'

'In the name of communism,' she countered cheerfully.

'Is it Christ's fault how Christians behave? When Islamists behave badly it's not Mohammed's fault.'

'Anyway, communism failed and now it's a capitalist world, Dad.' She twisted a strand of shiny auburn hair around her finger.

'Marx believed in capitalism. He believed it would build up the wealth to pay for communism – to each according to his needs. There's still hope.'

'It's had long enough,' she stated abruptly, as though already bored with the subject. 'Who needs a theory no one wants and that doesn't work in practice? Have you joined the SA communist party?'

'Why would I? I'm only here for another few weeks.'

'And then?'

'Back to Lisbon.'

'Just a mo.' She disappeared into the kitchen, returned

with mugs of tea, and perched next to him on the arm of the sofa. 'Do you like Cape Town, Dad?' she asked. She seemed to hold her breath for a moment as if something else had occurred to her and she wanted to keep him talking while she thought about it.

'It's wonderful for the likes of us.' His reply held a vague note of defensiveness. 'It's beautiful for the prosperous middle classes, most of whom are a whiter shade of pale. And the rest? They can rot. Am I comfortable with this? No. But what can I do? Am I supposed to be egalitarian and live where I might get robbed, stabbed, shot or all three? I've got to sit this one out. I hate suburban existence. You know me. It's never right. Or if it is, it's not right for long.'

She was just staring at him, lips slightly parted. 'There's no need to be defensive,' she said, searching his face with a puzzled look. 'What possessed you to come here?'

He brushed a hair off the shiny, brogue shoe on his left foot, built up to ease his limp, and lifted his leg to cross it over the right one again. 'As you know, after the divorce, it took a while to start life again. A fresh beginning meant ending the previous life. That's partly why I moved to Lisbon.'

'Why Lisbon? I've forgotten.'

'There was a university job for an English speaker. I still had the Portuguese I picked up from volunteer work in Mozambique. Then I was offered this visiting scholarship here in Cape Town.'

'And friends?' She flicked back a stray curl of her hair.

'No, I didn't keep in touch with friends or do the same old things in the same old way. I wanted a new beginning.'

'Good job I didn't come with you, then.' She looked hurt, or pretended to.

'I'm sure I told you all this in London.'

'You were too busy shivering from the cold, and

whinging about how the English whinge about everything. Remember?'

She sprang to her feet, smoothed down her white jumper, and tripped lightly through the open door to the bathroom. He watched her and thought of all the frustration and irritation she had caused him during her teenage years, after his divorce. Long mornings spent in bed. At other times, her mind wouldn't keep still – always planning, wanting to discuss difficult issues, make decisions; usually during moments when Christian just wanted to relax.

She came back and forced a smile. Standing with her arms folded, she paused for a moment, and then remarked, 'You had a cousin over here, didn't you Dad?'

'No. Uganda. No one's heard from him in thirty years.'

'Weren't you curious?'

'Hardly knew him. Although he looked so much like me – then. We met when we were young, at weddings and funerals. We both liked Hermann Hesse. We decided he was Goldmund and I was Narcissus.'

'I don't know it.'

'It's about two friends in the Middle Ages whose wandering paths are completely divergent, but who unite towards the end of their lives, one as an artist, the other as a philosopher.'

'Sounds cool. Didn't anyone visit him?'

Christian removed his horn-rimmed glasses and polished them between finger and thumb with his linen handkerchief. 'No,' he replied, carefully slipping them back on. 'His parents were dead. His wife went out to join him. No idea what happened to either of them. They just disappeared into the jungle.'

It was late afternoon by the time Christian caught the

university shuttle bus from Upper Campus to Forest Hill. The scent of burning pine from the bush fires near Muizenberg mountain hung over Cape Town's southern suburbs. Saskya was in her pyjamas already, surrounded by empty coffee cups and cereal bar wrappers, evidently in need of a shower, bent over her laptop. Her sense of purpose was palpable.

'I've just completed a sixteen-page fully illustrated children's story I started weeks ago,' she told him, excitement rising in her voice. 'I feel very proud of myself. Let's just hope it's all worth it.'

'I'm sure it will be,' he replied absent-mindedly. He limped into the kitchen.

She followed and gave him a hug. 'You look tired, Dad. You okay?'

'I'll survive,' he replied in a mock-tragic voice. 'Did you get to the District Six Museum this morning?'

'Yep. I had a wander around the area first; the streets that used to be occupied by the black and coloured population.'

Christian nodded. 'I know. The District Six experience is like Soweto – enforced removal of people from areas the whites wanted for themselves. And the poverty in some of these places they were relocated to is appalling.'

'It's not just here, Dad.' She shook her head. 'The British government's complacency is just as bad. They should feel ashamed that they govern a rich country where people die from the cold, and kids go hungry. How many people could they fit into Buckingham Palace or Windsor Castle?'

Her expression reflected a dissonant blend of moral indignation and regret. She had always been concerned with the underdog. Most of her friends had been like stray cats – problem children, social cripples, people who needed a strong protector to shield them from bullying and from the high price of being different. They were all projects. Of all the virtues, the most important to her was probably loyalty. At the same time, she extended that loyalty to herself. Although she didn't necessarily like herself, she did feel she was worth being loyal to, and this often ignited fierce battles to defend her judgements and points of view. If she were ever asked to define love it would probably be to do with being needed by whomever she loved, and the feeling of being safe with them.

3

Almost a fortnight had passed. The day was pleasantly warm, with a clear blue sky except for a blanket of cloud resting on Table Mountain – the 'tablecloth' as locals call it.

A warm breeze rolled off the ocean. But the mood had changed. Christian had forgotten to switch on the anti-mosquito burners, and both suffered broken sleep plagued by the relentless whine of the insects gorged with their blood and probably that of others. After eventually dropping off, he awoke drenched in sweat, heart palpitating, frantically anxious, but without a clue as to why. And Saskya had forgotten to draw her curtains so that she woke up several times to the full blast of the sharp early morning light. Remarkably though, she seemed a lot brighter.

They had breakfast and chatted about nothing in particular as he drove her to the school she was working in on the edge of a small, shanty township near the Indian Ocean coast. Young, beautiful, pale and foreign, she might as well have worn a t-shirt saying 'kidnap me!'

Instead, she wore a t-shirt carrying the name of the manufacturer whose Asian sweat shops had produced it at a tiny fraction of the cost that she'd paid for it. She wore it outside her clinging blue jeans.

'Have you got cash with you?' he asked. 'And your phone?'

'Yes, Father.'

He reminded her for the umpteenth time to leave her purse behind and to keep the cash in her bra. 'Don't forget. If a mugger wants your phone, give it to him. Remember. Don't get lippy. It's a transaction. Your phone or your life.'

She rolled her eyes. 'How many times have you told me? Bye, Dad.'

Her auburn hair, with curls lengthened into waves by the hot, damp air, bobbed on her shoulders as she strode past the wooden security hut, waved at the guard and walked through the razor-wired entrance to the school.

He left work soon after lunch after several meetings. He wanted to be home when Saskya got back from the school.

He was already slightly apprehensive about hearing how her day had been.

He'd finished washing and ironing his shirts and trousers and turned his attention to meticulously cleaning his tooled leather shoes. The smell of shoe polish never failed to conjure up images of the school he hated as a child. He was shining his shoes to a mirror finish when he heard the key in the latch. He was expecting her. He'd already phoned the colleague who had offered to bring her home, just to make sure. He lumbered to the hallway to greet her. She pushed past him. He could see from her face that it had been another 'one of those days'.

She looked him up and down and giggled. 'You look so neat, Dad. Why don't you wear your shirt loose instead of tucking it in? It looks anal.'

He looked away and then looked at her face. Whatever was bothering her would emerge sooner or later.

'Need I ask?'

'Headache, tummy ache, threats of death to anyone who dares enter my hugely expanded personal space,' she warned him as though she'd rehearsed it. 'Unless it's to give me a massage. It's very likely that when I speak to you it will be to criticise you irrationally. And I strongly recommend you do *not* argue unless you want to play *catch the crockery*.'

18

She curled her top lip to expose her fangs.

He shook his head and smiled with his eyes. 'Let me put the kettle on,' he suggested gently.

As he moved through the hall he breathed in the scent of laundry detergent. It took him back over a decade to contented days at home with his wife when life was full of certitude, and before the rot set in. His moment of introspection was all too brief.

'One girl's been raped,' Saskya shouted through to the kitchen. 'One boy has attempted suicide and the grandmother of one of the girls came in to complain that the main carer had been selling the girl and her siblings for sex. It's been a normal day.'

He joined her, one hand on his stick, the other precariously holding the handles of two steaming mugs.

'You coping?' He squeezed her hand.

'Just about. I reckon in life the more shit, the better the roses, eh, Dad?'

He winced and resolved for the umpteenth time to do something about his anachronistic attitude to profanity and blasphemy. He thought that perhaps meditating on mantras of 'shit', 'fuck', 'Jesus' and all the other, for him, forbidden words might help. He'd only just got used to her using 'bloody'. A little chuckle to himself came out as a grunt, but she didn't seem to notice.

'I don't know how you keep going,' he muttered.

'I'm not. I'm out of here soon.' She took the mug in both hands and blew on it. 'The teachers are fabulous. They do their best in horrendous circumstances. The classes are jam-packed. It's a babble of languages. You can't hear yourself think. Most of the teachers are Muslim or Christian. It must be sheer faith that keeps them going. But if things go wrong and kids disappear they just fall through the cracks. No one sees them again. They could be dead.'

Christian reached forward and squeezed her hand.

'And I hate myself for being so judgemental. Who the hell am I to come over here like some missionary telling people how to behave? Yet, in anybody's terms, some things are just plain wrong, aren't they, Dad?'

Christian looked at her in admiration. Although she was upset, her resilience had strengthened. No longer 'his little girl', she was growing in character at a rate that would be difficult to keep up with. In response to her frustration with boyfriends, he remembered telling her that her greatest burden in life was that she was beautiful, not just because everything came so easily to her, but because her beauty distracted from her other qualities. In the eyes of most men, her looks were her main feature. She was Saskya, the gorgeous, long-legged object of desire. Not that loyal, friendly, helpful, charitable, wonderful person. He felt her personality easily made her even more beautiful, lending another dimension to her character that made her a force to be reckoned with but not always easy company.

'In a way it's understandable. As the recession hits schooling, you get overcrowding and – '

'Dad, you're theorising again. And for God's sake untuck your shirt, or at least undo another button!'

She strode into the lounge and put her bag on the floor at her feet.

He turned away and felt her scornful gaze scorching his back. There was a time when he would tell her off for speaking to him like that. But what could he do now apart from looking hurt or angry? He shrugged and loosened his shirt slightly, still leaving it tucked into his neatly pressed trousers.

'You're getting irritable. Are you hungry?'

20

She glared at him. 'Yes. As a matter of fact, I am.'

He hobbled to the kitchen and returned with two plates of her favourite pasta dish he'd made earlier – tagliatelle in an oyster mushroom sauce.

She cocked her head to one side and pursed her lips.

'Thank you,' she said, patting his knee.

After one bite, she pushed the plate aside. Her hand trembling slightly, she clawed inside her bag and unfolded a grubby sheet of lined writing paper.

'On top of all the other shit today, look at this letter to one of the girls in grade nine. It's from her cousin in KwaZulu Natal. I got a teacher to translate it from Zulu.'

She read aloud, her voice slightly hoarse: *I don't want to go to school. I must walk. It's five kilometres. There are men on the road who rob us, and my friend was raped. We've no food so I'm hungry when I get to school.*

'I checked online. A quarter of all school kids in KZN go to school on an empty stomach,' she said. 'Many have no flush toilets or electricity. Girls stay at home when they have a period.'

My teacher offers me food, but he wants me to give him sex in return.

'Can you imagine?' She brushed her hair from her eyes. 'About a third of child abuse cases are by men teachers, and many of them are HIV positive. Teenage pregnancy's a huge problem. '

There is so much work to do at home, I often get to school late, but then I turn around and come home again, otherwise, my teacher beats me. I'm scared to go. Would you go?

'And the government wonders why so many stay away.'

She shifted slightly on her chair, as though unable to find a comfortable position. To see her tortured and drained, more physically frail than he could remember ever seeing her, he desperately wanted to help and to hold her, but his typical reserve fed by his English upbringing held him back, as it nearly always did at moments when human warmth was required.

'The government's supposed to provide one free school meal a day for the neediest pupils, which is just over half of them,' she told him. 'This is maize pap, rice or potatoes, a fresh vegetable and a protein such as tinned pilchards. But because of corruption among the middlemen, the meals often don't arrive for weeks on end, or they're rotten. That's most of these kids' only meal. Some of them get sent home because they're too hungry to concentrate. Worse, when there is food, it's sometimes used as a punishment. Naughty ones go hungry which makes them even naughtier. Bloody brilliant!'

She tapped her teeth with a pen and looked away. There was a brief ruminative silence. He made no effort to intrude upon it.

She looked him in the eye and took a deep breath. 'It gets worse. It's the punishments,' she continued, shaking her head. 'One kid at the school stole another kid's pencil case. He owned up yesterday and gave it back. The teacher phones his uncle, and the kid comes back today with his hand bandaged. The teacher got him to painfully unwrap it. His hand had been skinned – flayed with a whip. It looked like a fresh slab of beef. The teacher made him hold it up and got the whole class to laugh at him. It renders me speechless. It's barbaric!'

His eyes widened in genuine astonishment.

She shook her head, her eyes swimming. 'It's sickening!' She pointed a finger at him, almost threateningly, and stabbed it down on the table. 'I tell you, the day you torture, molest or otherwise abuse a child, the world would be a better place if you bloody shot yourself!'

Her voice trailed off. Her helpless torrent of outrage had

suddenly become all too much, and quietly tears welled, overflowed, and slid down her cheeks, her shoulders heaving as she struggled to control herself. She searched her pocket for a tissue and wiped them away. Christian reached across and touched her hand for a moment. She gripped his wrist, then loosened it, and rested her hand gently on his arm. The warmth of her touch reached deep inside him, releasing an overwhelming need to protect her. He put his other hand on hers, but she pushed it away. She shook her head imperceptibly and lowered her eyes. She parted her dry lips and seemed to be searching for the right words.

'It was one of those moments when I desperately wanted to be the kind of person who would simply stand up and say, *Listen, no matter how you look at it, or how usual it is, or who does it, or why they do it, it's bloody disgusting.* Tears choked her voice. Her shoulders drooped, and she covered her face with her hands.

'They say that with fifty kids to a class, it's the only way to maintain discipline. And it works 'cos it's like that at home.'

Christian nodded. 'The problem is it's – '

'You know what my course leader said?' she struggled on. 'That it's a cultural issue. Culture my arse! It's absolute bollocks! In anyone's terms, it's bloody inhuman. It should be stopped. But I'm not that kind of person – not yet. I might have been a tub-thumping activist among sophisticated friends at dinner parties back in cosy London. But this isn't London. It isn't cosy. The stakes are too high.' She shrugged, her lips trembling. 'Moral courage had to wait for another day.'

She rubbed the tears from her face, but her nose was running. She pushed her plate away and filled her wine glass.

'You know even I used to smack you,' said Christian as though bound by a robotic duty to respond with the

23

alternative point of view. 'It was usual then. Not now. It's still usual here. It's – '

'Dad, please! This is brutality, plain and simple.'

He struggled to his feet, fetched some kitchen roll for her to blow into, poured her a glass of water, and waited until she'd stopped sniffing. He tucked his pale-blue shirt tightly into his slacks and put on music downloaded from the twenty-year-old *Live Aid* concert in the hope of cheering her up. He sat down again, his hands clasped in front of him, resting on his walking stick.

'For Christ's sake!' she hissed with abrupt anger, her face blotched and puffy. 'Bloody *Band Aid* hypocritical patronising bullshit!'

He turned it off. Her voice, usually a pleasantly resonant alto when relaxed, rose several semitones when upset. As a teenager, she had seemed full of anger, armed and ready at any time for heated verbal combat. But that was due to typical teenager emotional extremes. This was different. This anger was from the outside in. It had lit a flame under her deep sense of injustice. And it occurred to him that this was not going to go away.

She got to her feet, and headed for the kitchen, then stopped, turned and stood by the kitchen door, head back in a defiant posture. Her eyes met his.

'What do you do, Dad? Up there in your ivory tower teaching ethics to the pale-faced elite?' Her voice, sharp with irritability, was like a cold hand warding him off, as though the awful thoughts floating through the tributaries of her mind had suddenly flooded her sense of reason. 'Do you actually do anything?'

He studied her face for a second in the diffused light and felt his own doubts and her anger force a wedge between them.

'You don't, do you? You don't *do* anything!' she jabbed mercilessly. 'And for Christ's sake wear your shirt outside your trousers for a change. And go easy on the iron. You'll cut yourself on those creases.' She sniggered, and shot him a look of exasperation, although it gave way quickly to a forced smile before she turned her attention to the window and the view outside.

Her brief ceasefire of contemplative silence lasted only a few seconds. 'Call yourself a communist?' she said, as though talking to someone out on the balcony. 'I don't see you out there doing anything for equality; for – what did you call it? – giving to each according to their needs. I know you're not as mobile as the rest of us, but when did you last go on a march? Take power to the people to the streets? Face the water cannon? You're just an armchair communist up there on the hill with your armchair philosophers and your fat middle-class brain boxes.'

She turned towards him. Her eyes that had changed from deep green to a hostile grey held a rare flash of light that illuminated a whole new area of, even for him, uncharted territory.

She rubbed her smudged eyes, walked round the room and sat next to him again. She shrugged. Smiling weakly, he passed her the glass. She reached out, grabbed him by the wrist again, and dug in her fingernails so hard he thought they would draw blood. He winced.

'What can I do, Dad?' She held her breath for a moment as if listening to the music that drifted up from below. 'If this savagery is normal, I want no part of *normal*. Should I report it? Who to? It's a dilemma. You're the ethics oracle, the dilemma dude. Tell me what to do.'

Her voice was still smothered by tones of exasperation, her disenchantment palpable. He tried to keep his voice steady, sat back and tried to relax his shoulders. He removed his glasses to polish them and searched his jacket for a pen. It had fallen through the lining. He decided to make do without it.

'We need to look at the ethics of it,' he replied, massaging his head with his fingertips.

She nodded, but suddenly looked bored. 'I need someone down to earth, Dad. Not some archangel with his head in the clouds.'

'Sas, I'm trying to do my best. Let's go for a walk in the woods,' he suggested.

The fragrance of pine as they strolled along a path covered by a carpet of pine needles and cones reminded him strongly of holidays in Les Landes, north of Biarritz, and the long walks through the pine forests hand in hand with his diminutive Danish wife and carrying little Saskya in a backpack. He felt calmed by the swishing of the trees overhead, as he watched the bank of cloud spill over the edge of Table Mountain and thought about how much had changed since then – his wife remarried, and Saskya almost as tall as he was, and with a life of her own largely outside his influence and protection.

The setting sun cast a sharp light forming shadows far longer than ever found in Europe. Two squirrels shot to the top of a pine tree as they approached. He tensed slightly as they wandered back to Main Road and on to a bar in Rondebosch, an area popular among students from the university. There had been several reports of students being mugged, and he was aware of the need to be constantly vigilant. He took Saskya's arm in the hope that it would be taken as affection rather than protection.

4

'It's amazing what another day of sunshine can do for the soul,' she said before he could ask. Her smile broke into a giggle, her lovely face suffused with amusement and fleeting happiness. 'I feel like my toes are touching the ground again.'

They were back at the flat, a week later, on the balcony, sharing a chilled organic *Chenin Blanc* from Stellenbosch, their faces lit by a soft amber glow from the street lamps that blended with warm twilight from a clear sky. The apartment felt like a cool oasis.

So relieved to see the return of her old effervescent self he returned her smile and squeezed her shoulder.

'Not that it was all rosy,' she stated out of the blue. 'You wouldn't believe it. A dog messed on the soccer pitch, so the principal had it buried alive.'

'For Christ's sake!' He thought he sounded more outraged over a dog than he had the week before over the kid with the skinned hand.

'A parent saw it and went ballistic. Ordered the groundsmen to dig it up again. It was barely alive.'

'To us and lots of people here it's shocking, but – '

'There's no *but*. Don't start with this *culture* bollocks. It's shocking full stop.' She stared into the dregs of her coffee. 'If I hear the word *culture* again I'll bloody shoot somebody!' She suddenly looked up and giggled at herself.

'People think there's a moral vacuum,' Christian stated, running a hand through his hair. His mind drifted back to bleak Belgium and an ethics conference on the 'moral vacuum' he'd attended in rain-swept Charleroi – and the error of judgement that had planted the final kiss of death on his marriage. 'They think standards are declining,' he continued.

'Is this a lecture, Dad?' she asked. 'If so, I'll just grab a cushion in case it gets too much of a pain in the arse.'

He grimaced.

'What's wrong now? Is it *arse*? Too visceral for you? What do you want me to say – *posterior*?'

'It's coarse.' Christian kept his voice level in the placatory tone he used when dealing with haranguing students.

'Yeah, whatever. Pedantic prude.' She stared at her fingernails.

Christian forced a grin and reached for his glass. He paused and looked beyond the balcony wall to the mountain, now bathed in moonlight. He thought again about his ex-wife.

'How's your mum?' he asked.

'Not great. Her heart problems are worse. It's awful for someone who's been so active to be forbidden to get excited or worried. She takes it easy. Anyway, what are we doing tonight?'

'I've got my leaving drink with a few of the people who invited me here. Nothing official. I'm getting my hair cut first and having a shave.'

'Tired of Marx?'

She stared at him, her eyes full of the old mocking glint. *Smarty pants*, he thought and smiled a wry smile that turned down the corners of his mouth. If only he had more students like her, he thought, work would be so much more interesting. She wore her brilliance like a uniform. Not that she was arrogant or superior in any way but somehow the self-confident flow of her movements suggested that she could learn anything about anything without really trying. The sort of person who never did their homework, never seemed to be paying attention in class, but got distinctions in all subjects.

The entire world was her stage, and she charmed her audience with her elegance, her winning smile, and her quick wit. When she was passionate about something she could be full of rage and he would feel like teasing her with 'you're beautiful when you're angry'; but that would have triggered a nuclear meltdown. She could also be very severe in her judgements, sometimes so severe and so unfair that counter-argument was impossible because there seemed to be no common ground from which to launch one.

'You coming to the party?'

'Thanks, but no thanks.'

He wasn't surprised. She had long ago grown weary of witnessing his exhausting efforts to be sociable – the way he kept telling anecdotes, making jokes, and trying to make people laugh. It made him feel safe. The words were like a security fence between him and other people. But Saskya never seemed comfortable with it.

'The day after tomorrow we'll go to Jo'burg and fly back to London together. Back to normality. Sound good?'

Normality. She threw him a look resembling pity and reached to switch on a small spot lamp.

'Sure, Dad,' she muttered.

Once he would have countered with 'What's that look for? What do you mean by that?' Like he used to with his wife. Instead, he looked away and poured another glass of wine.

'Why now? she asked. 'I'm not expected back for another couple of weeks.'

'Me neither. But with the strikes, I think we should go in case things get worse.'

'Strikes?'

'Haven't you seen the billboards? Air traffic controllers are on strike. International flights are unaffected, but SA

Airways says it will ground flights between here and Jo'burg just before and during the strike.'

'When does it start?'

'Tomorrow. At eight in the evening.'

'How long for?'

'They said it's open-ended. We could miss the flight to London.'

'But my flight home is via Jo'burg.'

He reached into the inside pocket of his white linen jacket and produced two printed e-tickets. 'I've booked the train to Jo'burg.'

'Thanks for telling me.'

'We get to see the country. It's better than looking down at it from thirty thousand feet.'

'Is it safe? I don't want murder on the Jo'burg express.'

'Colleagues at work think it's safe enough.'

He managed to mask his concerns that he might be putting her in danger. 'There's an opportunity to get off at some stations and stretch your legs for a while.'

A colleague warned him that someone who had wandered off failed to return and that his body had been found in the woods some weeks later. But did Christian have a choice? The university might have hired him a car if he'd applied early enough. But his foot and his back ache had long ago put long-distance driving beyond him.

He thought back to her phone call a few weeks before, when she'd rung him to announce her volunteer work in South Africa, and whether she could stay with him. 'Please. Pretty please!' Even then the issue of protection had nagged him deeply, leaving him with the sense that he might be making a dreadful mistake. That sense of responsibility was now starting to choke him. He booked the tickets by phone in the hope that an irrevocable decision would help stop the nagging. He was wrong.

'And my air ticket to Jo'burg?'

'Keep it. We should get a refund.'

'I don't fancy being cooped up in a train. How much will it cost?'

'The economy class sleeper is six hundred each.'

'That's peanuts. It'll be packed to the gills. How long's it gonna take?'

'Twenty-eight hours. Come on. You won't regret it.'

They called Johannesburg 'Jo'burg' as though they were intimately familiar with it, like the nickname of an old friend. But neither of them really knew much about the city of gold – *Egoli* in isiZulu – apart from what they'd read in the guides, and from television documentaries, which they both believed exaggerated the danger. Little did they know of the reality of life in the old parts of the city around Park Station, from which the rich and white had long ago joined the mass exodus to the northern suburbs. On the other hand, they'd heard that statistics relating to murder, rape and kidnapping were skewed by the level of crime in the outlying shanty townships. Clearly, central Johannesburg was not for the unwary, but they could never have been expected to understand what should amount to an appropriate level of caution.

Only a few days later, those words – 'you won't regret it' – were spinning round his head with the mocking, vicious laughter of a court jester.

5

Cape Town's railway station echoed to the sound of singing and running feet as hundreds of protestors danced their way through the main concourse. *How can so many people sing in tune?* he asked himself. It was wonderful. It gave him goose pimples to think how beautifully Africans can sing, spontaneously and with a complete absence of self-consciousness. He and Saskya eventually turned their backs on the marchers and dragged their wheeled cases to the farthest platform that served the long-distance trains. Pale-blue shirt tucked into fawn trousers, he limped along behind her. She wore her white blouse and black flared trousers, her black leather coat slung across her shoulders. They passed through two sets of barriers guarded by ticket inspectors armed with truncheons.

The train was waiting beneath the arch of the station canopy, its dusty blue and purple coaches looking as if they hadn't seen water for months. The platform already thronged with the excitement and anxiety of departure – the coming and going of passengers and paperboys, and announcements in several languages. The platform was full of passengers who had twice their body weight in luggage piled on top of trolleys. Others with the mandatory one large case and one for hand luggage looked nervous and out of place. Blond-haired backpackers pushed their way past the fruit vendors. The place was like a street market.

'Welcome to the Sardine Express,' Saskya quipped.

She and Christian wrestled their way into one of the sleeper carriages and found their compartment that consisted of a single, bright purple, plastic-covered bench seat, a small table, and a similar fold-down bunk bed at eye level. Anyone suffering from cabin fever would have jumped off there and then. He shrugged resignedly as Saskya dumped their baggage on the seat, then stepped outside and smiled at the passengers already squashed into the corridor.

At exactly ten, the departure was announced in three languages including their own. Half the carriage windows were still open, with heads poking out, and bodies leaning in goodbye embraces. Down the platform, beyond the milling crowd, a guard blew a long shrill whistle, and a cheer went up, celebrating the start of hundreds of tales of parting and reunion, and for some perhaps the stories of sheer despair.

Doors closed along the length of the train, the whistle blew again, and the sixteen-coach train shook itself into life and picked up speed, the engine's melancholy whistle floating back down the long line of carriages.

As the express slipped free from the station, it started a one and a half thousand kilometre journey to Johannesburg via Kimberley – for the two of them, father and daughter, an epic path, physically and spiritually.

Saskya kicked off her shoes. Christian pulled down the window and leant outside to take one last lingering look at Cape Town, which he believed he would never see again, and gazed at the depressing sight of corrugated tin shacks, decorated with faded washing, coasting by. He thought that more than any other kind of travel available to him, a train gave him a sense of being part of the landscape, but that this landscape was one he would not want to be a part of. It struck him as a distinct counterpoint to the Cape's natural beauty, its sharp light, long shadows, breathtaking sunsets, kaleidoscope of paint-palette-coloured flowers and two oceans. He settled down and turned his mind to the twenty-eight-hour journey ahead.

After a bustling exchange of passengers at Belville and Huguenot stations, the train pulled out of the single platform at Wellington and cut its way through the yellow rapeseed fields and lush green vineyards with a seeming sense of steady determination to shake off the Western Cape.

Christian tried to read the newspaper he'd bought at the station kiosk. He couldn't concentrate. The sound of metal caressing metal made him feel pleasantly drowsy, his eyelids too heavy to support. Captured in the swaying train, the clippety-clop of the rails was such a regular background sound it became the equivalent of silence and the feeling of peace that goes with it. The two of them felt a sense of security completely at odds with the reality of the situation – that they were rolling across the African plains in a steel, wheeled box on rails a mere couple of inches thick, to one of the most dangerous cities on earth.

'I feel like a nap already,' he muttered.

'A railway sleeper, Dad?'

He managed a wan smile and removed his glasses before drifting off.

Resting her elbow on the window ledge, head in hand, she gazed at the landscape drifting by as though watching one of those over-long nature programmes on digital TV – miles of distant, flat farmland leading to the cloud-covered mountains; a truck driving parallel to the track as though racing to the next crossing; long-horned Nguni cattle drinking from a reservoir.

As they drew into Worcester station the express lurched across a set of points, throwing Christian's head hard against the window. He awoke with his mouth dry, his eyes burning. The plastic upholstered seat felt as hard as a park bench. Half a dozen passengers with rucksacks joined the train, and they were on their way again.

Christian and Saskya finished a snack of crisps and fruit juice as the sun reflected off the snow-capped mountains and lit up the fields of vines to the horizon on their approach to Africa's longest tunnel at Hex River Valley. After they had emerged from the tunnel, swaying drunkenly as the points broke the rhythm of the train's gentle rocking, he toddled to the toilet at the end of the carriage, using his stick and the handrail for support.

The carriages had no air conditioning, but it was pleasantly warm inside. Outside was the heat and dust of the vast African bushveld singed by wildfire against the backcloth of the vast panoramic sky. A bare tree with white bark stood alone in the vast expanse of scrub.

He returned, and the two of them walked unsteadily along the length of two carriages through hissing automatic doors to the restaurant car, treading carefully along the shaking corridor, grabbing the handrail for balance. They found a couple of seats and ordered mealy pap and vegetable stew. As if by unspoken agreement, they ate in silence, deep in thought.

The train laboured its way through nameless stations, as it slowly ate up the hills and plains, while night set in against a backcloth of a glorious sunset. It was soon dark and looking through the glass they could see only a ghostly reflection of their own features. Outside nothing was visible except for the occasional wink of station lights or distant street lamps. The train lurched across some points, an eerie green reflecting across the white concrete sleepers of the adjacent track.

Leaving the smell of cooking behind them, they headed back down the smoky corridor lit by dim, dirty lights in the roof, to their sleeping compartment at the other end. A cold draught blew up around the footboards joining the carriages. Some passengers, wedged on the floor between the walls of the corridor and the second-class compartments, were already sleeping soundly. The train shuddered and squealed over points, as it rolled to a standstill just as father and daughter entered the solitude of their tiny compartment.

Not long after dark, with formidable suddenness, a storm came up. The heavens were cracked into three jagged pieces by lightning so bright it turned night into day. Saskya turned off the night-light in their compartment as thunder crashed like heavy artillery fire, and rain fell in sheets. No amount of sensible adult in her could suppress her inner child's excitement about a storm. She prayed for an electricity cut so that the conductor would bring candles, and they'd have to huddle together in ethereal candlelight.

They pulled into the village of Hutchinson at around half past nine. A pleasant smell of wood smoke wafted in from the veld, signalling the recall of a distant memory of autumn garden fires at Christian's childhood home in rural England, and his frustration at not being able to help around the house and garden, leaving everything to his poor old mum and dad. His relationship with his parents had been simple – they gave; he took. And the fact that it wasn't his fault didn't seem to help.

Doors closed along the line of coaches and a whistle blew. The whistle blew again, and the train shook into movement as the clanking couplings took up the slack. The station lights slipped by, leaving them in darkness. Saskya leant her head against the window. The double glazing had the effect of flattening her face. She grabbed a book from her bag, and, her legs curled under her, tried to read, her face frowning in the poor light from the bare bulb above.

Two hours later approaching midnight they glided to a halt in De Aar. Christian and Saskya were still awake. He was reading; she was doing something with her phone. Thumping music from beyond the station buildings disturbed an otherwise peaceful night. A lone dog strolled along the dimly lit platform, and cocked its leg against a pillar, as a woman with a young body and elderly face, clutching a brown beer bottle, staggered out of the darkness towards the station exit.

'If you were South African, who'd you vote for?' Saskya asked, twisting and untwisting strands of her hair.

'If I thought only of myself in a prosperous, white suburb of Cape Town with property to protect, I'd vote for the conservative Democratic Alliance. If I widened my concerns to include all races in the whole of the Western Cape and beyond, I'd vote for the more socialist African National Congress. On purely political ideology, I'd put my cross next to the SA Communist Party. Not that it would make much difference. This country is an example of straight ahead, every-man-for-himself capitalism, where the middle classes – the bourgeoisie – the landowners and the new political elite exploit a huge and cheap labour pool – the proletariat – whose living conditions and rights are little different from those of mediaeval European peasantry.'

'Has anyone ever suggested you might be a sanctimonious moraliser?'

'No. At least, not to my face.'

She looked at him and saw a fleeting spark of humour in his eyes that reminded her of a father she thought she'd lost – a father who laughed a lot, who was relaxed, who was intellectual but light – her father before the divorce. Train travel seemed to unwind him. She turned away and stared at her reflection in the grubby window.

They didn't bother to lift the blinds for the diamond mining town of Kimberley. Both of them woke but drifted off once the train got moving. Having slept soundly for another couple of hours, lulled by the clackety-clack of the train's wheels, they awoke as they pulled into the one-horse diamond mining town of Christiana. He quietly pulled the curtains open and slid the blind up to find the sun just starting to share some light over the horizon. The big sky was wide and waiting for the day to begin.

Together, they watched the sun rise quietly and the landscape float by, and relaxed to the sound of the wheels, the hypnotic swoops of the telephone wires and the regular punctuation of the wooden poles.

But his mind refused to rest for long. It already raced ahead to the point where the train was taking them, and to what they would do when they got there. He was already starting to fret about how to get from Park Station to the airport on the eastern edge of the city. One thing Johannesburg had in common with several major cities throughout the world is that its main railway station was situated in one of its most dangerous districts and nowhere near the airport.

Swaying drunkenly as the points broke the rhythm of the train's gentle rocking, he left the compartment and headed down the corridor. The slanting morning sun flashed intermittently like a Morse lamp through the lines of trees. He returned minutes later with a small tray of instant coffee and went back to pick up a plate of toasted cheese and tomato sandwiches. Saskya, wrapped up in her sleeping bag, looked up and smiled. 'Just the job,' she said, rubbing her tired eyes. 'We'll soon be on that plane home, Dad,' she added wistfully. 'I'll miss this. Being together. It's made us more equal somehow. I don't seem to be your little girl any longer.'

Leaping at the chance to start another debate to distract his mind from his doubts and fears about what lay ahead, Christian settled himself into the corner of the compartment.

'You'll always be my little girl,' he said. 'Although, I don't reckon being young has got much going for it. There's so little freedom, no autonomy, no life choices – '

'Dad, please! It's a bit early for this.' She sipped her coffee took a bite of her toasty and looked at him with weary patience.

'They're forced to go to school,' he droned on. 'Which most of them hate, there's too much learning, too many tests, homework, not enough play. And in poorer countries, they also have to work long hours at home.'

'The third age doesn't look too great from where I'm sitting.'

Christian let it go. She had turned to face the window, and looked bored and tired, with dark smudges under her eyes.

'I don't know why, but you really get on my nerves at times,' she whispered hoarsely. 'I do love you, Dad, but when I was a kid at school you were a bit of an embarrassment. Why couldn't you speak normally? Every conversation had to be a bloody lecture.'

He looked away. It would have been easy to have smirked or smiled indulgently or given a knowing look that would say *I know you better than you know yourself.* But he managed, or thought he managed, to keep his expression as neutral as possible. He also knew that she had a point. He long ago recognised his weakness for lecturing and theorising. Whenever she'd come to him with a personal problem, he would listen keenly, and respond intelligently with advice in principle, when all she wanted was practical advice about what to do, and a hug to go with it. He knew the last thing she needed was analysis, and that even a stupid, irrational, passionate, off-the-wall reaction would have been better than what sounded like legal counselling. But he couldn't help himself. It was all done with loving kindness, but a vital element was missing – direct, emotional, corporeal involvement.

She got to her feet, slid open the door and walked off down the corridor towards the toilet or the bar or the restaurant car or maybe just for some space, he wasn't sure which.

She returned as they pulled into the old Potchefstroom station with its Cape Dutch façade.

The train came alive. The carriage was abruptly full of a babble of passengers, only one of them white, presumably on their way to work, talking not to each other, but to unseen colleagues, friends and loved ones on their cellphones. After a stop of only a few minutes, they were on their way again, passing derelict buildings with cracked windows like broken teeth, and watchtowers linked by fences of razor wire.

'Look at the sun, Dad. You can feel the warmth through the window. Sorry about earlier. I wasn't feeling too great.'

He threw her a nervous smile and squeezed her hand.

'If you want to worship something, it makes sense to worship the sun,' she whispered hoarsely. Her gaze seemed focused on the far-off horizon beyond the fields of dark-red earth. 'And unlike with gods, there are none of your silly intellectual arguments about whether it exists or not.'

She turned her attention to the big sky dipping and merging with the hoariness of the horizon. There was a lull in the conversation, which seemed to announce an agreement to drop the subject – or any subject. Christian wondered where her thoughts had strayed to. Had she too cast her mind ahead to Johannesburg, a mere three hours away?

6

They pulled into Park Station at just after one, only sixty minutes late. The train gradually dropped to a walking speed, then with a sigh of brakes, a jolt and a screech it swerved across some points and left the main track to slide alongside a platform.

'How do we get from here to the airport?' she asked, gathering up her things.

'By cab. I've got enough cash left, and I don't want to rush it. Let's give ourselves plenty of time for check-in. Then a drink and a bite to eat.' He was struggling to get the bedrolls to fit in the bags.

'So what time is the flight?'

'Nine-twenty-five.' He looked sheepish.

'And check in?'

'Seven-thirty.'

'That gives us more than six hours. Where *is* the airport, Dad – bloody Zimbabwe?'

'I just like to be sure.'

'You geriatrics don't leave much to chance.'

They grabbed their cases and stepped down from the carriage onto the crowded platform. There was something unexpectedly profound about the experience, the limits of one space feeling like the start of another. They walked as fast as Christian could manage, along the platform teeming with hurried passengers surging towards the exit as though all desperately late for something.

They found themselves in the covered area outside the station building and hailed a bright-red, elderly Toyota taxi. The driver's eyes were hidden by reflective sunglasses, but his smile had all the warmth of an African summer's morning.

'Where to?' he asked.

'Tambo airport.'

'Do we have to Dad?' Saskya interrupted, stepping back onto the pavement. 'We're so early.'

'You know what I'm like. We'll have a nice bite to eat there.' He nodded to the driver. 'Airport, please.'

The driver got out and heaved their cases into the boot, slamming the lid with such force the car shook. He squeezed himself into the driver's seat and kept them waiting a couple of minutes while he texted from his cellphone before pulling out into the dense traffic.

They had been driving for only a few minutes when Sas gripped Christian's arm. 'I've got cramps, Dad. It must be that bloody shit food on the train. Stop please!'

'Can't you wait till we get to the airport?'

'Dad, I'm desperate! I'm breaking out in a sweat. I'll do it in my pants!'

'Sas – '

'You want me to have to sit on it all the way to bloody London?'

The taxi driver, who had been spinning banal comment about the traffic into a full-length epic, assured her that there was a petrol station ahead. He smiled into the rear-view mirror and chuckled to himself.

She pushed her hands into her lap and shivered. Christian turned and felt her forehead. She was feverish. 'Food poisoning,' he said. 'Take it easy in the plane; drink plenty of fluids.'

'Thanks, Doc. Just get me to a bloody toilet.'

They pulled into the garage and drove under the main canopy past the pumps and shop, to the car park. She flung open the door. 'Where the bloody hell are they?'

The driver pointed to a sign to the outside toilet at the back of the shop.

'Have you got coins?' Christian asked, shoving his hand into the pocket of his slacks. She nodded and staggered off out of sight, holding her buttocks. Christian stayed in the taxi.

'Where you from, Boss?' the driver asked.

Christian told him, and he burst out laughing, putting his hand to his mouth to hide his crooked teeth. 'And you?' Christian asked, wondering what was so funny.

'Zimbabwe, Boss. I'm one of the three million that crossed the Beit Bridge or swum the Limpopo to get here.'

'Which did you take?'

'The bus. With my wife and kids.'

'How many have you got?'

'Only one wife.' He put his hand to his mouth again and gave out another burst of laughter. 'And four kids. We stayed at the Methodist Church downtown until we moved in with my cousin's family in Berea.'

'How old?'

'Nine, ten, eleven and fourteen.' He was still chuckling to himself. 'They go to a Catholic school in Observatory that takes Zimbabwean refugees for nothing. They are the kindest people on earth, Boss.'

'That's so generous.'

'Boss. Sorry. I can't help it. Your accent is killing me.' He laughed again. 'When I was a kid I was addicted to English comedies. Monty Python, Tony Hancock, all the Carry On films. Your accent takes me back. Sorry Boss.'

Christian nodded and smiled.

'It is taking too long, poor girl,' the driver said, suddenly serious.

Christian checked his watch. Fifteen minutes had slipped

by while he'd been chatting. He rang her number that was already on speed dial. No reply. Suddenly, he felt overcome by an urgent need to go to her. Could he leave all his belongings with the driver? No choice. He grabbed his stick and opened the door.

'I'm going to look for her,' he said. 'I won't be long. Keep an eye on my stuff.'

'You can rely on me, Boss.'

Christian believed him. Following the sign, he headed for the toilets, and asked an Indian woman coming out if there was a young white woman inside.

'No, I don't think so.'

Christian felt his insides go liquid, and the blood rush to his head and face, pushing at the roots of his hair.

'Could you go back and call out for Saskya,' he pleaded. His hands were clasped in front of him, pressing down on his walking stick.

She understood his panic and went back in. He heard her call. She came out again and shook her head. He felt the blood drain from his face. She stood stock still, her eyes peering through pebble-thick, horn-rimmed glasses as he turned to cross the forecourt and the main parking area in front of the shop. Nothing. Perhaps Saskya had gone back inside the shop. He lumbered back as fast as his disability would allow and searched all the aisles in case she was bending down.

Something was very wrong. Was this a joke? No. Sas had grown out of that kind of thing long ago. Christian fought down a panic that gripped his throat. He could hardly move. His lungs felt as though they were bursting. What would Saskya say now? *Well, Professor, we have a situation. What are you gonna do? Look it up in a book? Consult Aristotle or one of your disembodied colleagues? For Christ's sake do something!*

His head, muzzy with worry and despair, felt full of

44

noxious grey smog. He had no idea of how to deal with the situation, hopelessly alone in a crowd of people who were completely indifferent to his distress. He needed to overcome the numbness that slowed down his ability to think straight, and lay out a plan of action.

Desperately maintaining a grip on his nerves, he limped down the three aisles again, shoving against the backsides of several shoppers, and on past the rows of tinned food and toiletries. He felt the whole shop was now staring at him. He managed to keep his voice steady as he asked people if they'd seen his tall, auburn-haired daughter in black trousers and white top. They shook their heads. With panic rising he completely lost all self-consciousness and shouted 'Saskya!' Several people had gathered around him.

'You must call the police,' one of them told him.

He checked his jacket for his wallet and passport. They were zipped into an inside pocket. He felt sick to his bowels and gut-wrenchingly anxious. His back was killing him. What had become of her? What was the emergency number? 999? He rummaged around in his jacket to retrieve the simple cellphone he'd bought at Cape Town airport. Where was it? He could have sworn it was in his inside pocket. He felt a hole in the bottom of the pocket, ripped it open and retrieved the phone from the bottom of the lining.

What was the number? He asked someone. 10111. What a stupid number. Too long. Too easy to get wrong. He dialled it. No answer. No airtime credit. The people in the queue let him go to the front. He bought a one-hundred-and-ten-rand voucher. He stumbled outside to scan the area around the pumps. Nothing. He went back inside, dialled 100 and with shaky fingers typed in the voucher code. He redialled 10111. Someone answered so slowly they might have been paid by the second. He fought back a rising tide of nausea and forced himself to speak but his voice felt like it was coming from his stomach. He explained what had happened.

'Which petrol station?'

He didn't know. He asked the person next to him, who paused and just shook his head. Rather than push into the queue, he shouted out, 'Where are we?' Other customers that had just come in looked at him in amazement, one of them menacingly, as though wanting to knife him. The Indian woman appeared at his side, her face rigid with concern. She gave him the names of the two roads that intersected at the site of the petrol station.

He spoke them into his phone and was told to stay where he was and that an officer would be 'dispatched as soon as possible'. He wondered how long that would be. Fear sank into the pit of his stomach and crawled under the surface of his skin like an army of ants. He knew that in a minute he would hardly be able to move. God, he couldn't breathe!

He dragged himself back to the taxi, slumped in the front seat, and explained to the driver.

'Wait here. I look everywhere.' He took off at a pace that belied his excessive weight. Minutes later he returned and threw up his arms in despair. 'She's not here,' he said, eyes wide. 'I'll take you to the police station.'

'No. They're on their way.'

'Boss. Then I must dash. They may want to question me.'

'Why?'

'I've got no taxi licence.'

They got back in and drove the short distance to a parking bay in front of the shop. The driver unloaded the luggage.

He slapped Christian on the back. 'Good luck, Man. '

'What do I owe you?'

'Forget it. You got enough troubles. We'll meet again.'

Christian watched the red taxi drive away and felt a

sudden, acute sense of abandonment. Engulfed by despair, and with a sinking panic in his entrails, he stood, leaning on his stick, waiting in front of the shop for at least half an hour before a covered white and blue pickup truck slowly drove in, blue lights flashing, and parked in front of the shop. Its two occupants, both in an informal uniform of blue fatigues and Kevlar vests, pistols hanging low, strapped to their thighs like western gunfighters, slammed the doors nonchalantly behind them and sauntered towards the front entrance. Christian cut them off. 'I'm the father who called you,' he stated breathlessly. They each shook hands with him African style, and one muttered something like, 'We are sorry.' Then louder, 'You must wait in the car while we search for her and investigate. Put your baggage in the back.' He noticed Christian's stick and added. 'I do it for you.'

He heaved the cases into the back, and asked, 'What was your girl wearing?'

Christian told him. The colleague adjusted his holster. 'Hair colour?'

'Reddish brown.'

'Glasses?'

'No.'

'Wait here.'

Christian stood next to the passenger door until they returned some fifteen minutes later.

'You must come with us to make a statement.'

He was given the front passenger seat. The second policeman climbed in the rear cab. They drove so slowly, they were holding up the traffic behind them. Finally, they pulled up in front of the local police station for the city's notorious Hillbrow district.

7

The Afrikaner police officer was a hulk – arms as thick as Christian's legs, legs as thick as his torso, neck like a buffalo, his stomach boiling over the wide belt of his dark-blue fatigues tucked into laced army boots.

'Good day, Officer,' Christian said, anxious to be courteous. His voice cracked, and 'officer' came out in a squeak.

The man looked Christian up and down as though faced with a contagion. Christian had the feeling that the policeman probably looked at everyone like that. And that each new crime was a further endorsement of his jaded view of humanity.

'I'm Warrant Officer Cloete,' he announced, shaking Christian's hand in a bone-crushing grip. He turned to his constable. 'His daughter's been taken,' he said dryly, as though he said it every day.

Christian followed the two of them into a spartan office with a steel table, four chairs and a grey filing cabinet. A picture of the Jo'burg skyline hung on the blank wall. The room smelled of disinfectant. Cloete eased himself behind the grey table beneath a heavily barred window. Christian was given a hard, wooden chair in front of the desk. A spasm in his back made him wince as he sat down, clutching his laptop case, and wedged his stick between his legs. The uniformed man sat in the corner, pen and pad at the ready.

Cloete rested his elbows on the table and stared past Christian for several seconds as though studying something on the wall behind, before returning his attention to Christian. 'Let's get the facts first before we discuss your daughter,' he said without warning, his bloodshot eyes scanning Christian's face, his heavy jowls fixed in a sneer.

'May I see your passport?'

Christian handed it to him and watched him flick through the pages until he found the ninety-day entry permit. 'What are you doing in South Africa?'

Christian explained.

'Now, just a few details,' Cloete began abruptly. 'Your full name?' he asked, despite having the passport open in front of him.

Christian spelled it out. He also gave his address in Lisbon, his staff accommodation address in Cape Town, his arrival date in South Africa, his occupation, his marital status, his age. He then did the same for Saskya.

'And your daughter,' the officer continued. 'Tell me slowly, and in complete detail, what happened after you left Park Station.'

Christian told of how they'd taken an old Toyota taxi to Tambo airport.

'Colour?'

'Scarlet red.'

He explained that after ten or fifteen minutes the taxi had pulled into a petrol station because his daughter was desperate for the toilet. The uniformed man continued to scribble. Christian told him everything he could remember. Cloete regularly interrupted with 'Try to describe the driver', 'What time was that?' or 'What did you do next?'

'There was no sign of my daughter,' Christian told him. 'I looked everywhere – the shop, the toilets. So did the taxi driver. Everywhere. Then I rang you.'

'Has she a cellphone?'

'Yes.'

'The number? We'll try to track it.'

Christian told him. 'I rang but there was no reply,' he

49

added.

Cloete nodded to the uniformed man, who wrapped shut his notebook, stood up and marched smartly out of the room. The officer lazily brushed a fly from his face, briefly rubbed his tired-looking, puffed eyes, and linked his huge boxer hands in front of him.

'All we know so far is that your daughter's disappeared. If she's been abducted there can be many reasons,' said Cloete, leaning forward to emphasise his point, his face wooden. 'It's usually for ransom.'

Christian's jaw went slack. This was sweeping him out of his depth, and he was terrified.

'Don't worry,' the officer continued, in a patronising tone. 'Most kidnappings in this country are resolved without harm to the hostage. If it's a political kidnapping to further the political aims of a particular group, a ransom is demanded. Wealthy individuals are targeted for large ransoms of anything between a hundred thousand and several million rand. These involve local business people and foreigners. Smaller-scale kidnappings are more common, for lower ransom demands of between twenty and thirty thousand. They often go unreported. Parents prefer to pay up and get their kid back.'

'I haven't got that kind of money.'

'Don't let's jump the gun,' Cloete urged, hauling himself to his feet. 'Wait here for your statement.'

Christian waited. He rubbed his eyes with his left fist and pushed his shaky fingers through his curly hair. The blood thumped thickly in his ears and temples. His mouth was so dry he felt his throat closing.

About half an hour later Cloete returned and pushed two fresh A4 pages of double-spaced typing across the desk at him. In his slow, beefy voice he said, 'This is a statement based on the information you have just given. Read it carefully, and then if you agree with it, sign at the bottom.'

He handed Christian a pen. Christian read and signed it so shakily he hardly recognised his own signature. The officer wiped his forehead with the back of his sleeve and looked Christian up and down once with something like pity in his eyes.

'You can go now,' he said with flat finality, massaging his face as though he'd just woken up. 'We have your contact number. As soon as your daughter or kidnappers get in touch with you, you must ring this number.' He handed Christian a business card. 'This case will be passed to the Central Police Station. They handle kidnappings and hijackings. They'll SMS you a case number.'

The policeman stood up, towering over Christian. His eyes reflected a hard glitter. 'Don't try any heroics,' he warned. 'They'll tell you they'll kill her if you involve us. I know it's tempting to do what they say. But you must leave it to us.'

Christian got up stiffly and limped slowly to the door. He was desperate for a moment's peace to try and sort out his thoughts and feelings.

'Have you anywhere to stay?' Cloete asked.

'No. Our cases were in the police car.'

'Come with me.'

He escorted Christian to reception. 'Find a hotel room for this man,' he ordered a woman constable. 'Try the Chapman. When you've got somewhere, get Constable Dhlamini to drive him.'

He gave Christian's hand a vice-like grip, turned on his heel and strode back to his office, the clatter of his army boots on the tiled floor echoing down the corridor like a stern warning to subordinates.

The Chapman Hotel's receptionist, a tall, stick-thin Indian, took Christian by the hand in a greeting more suited to a long-lost brother and took the cases from Constable Dhlamini. A look of bewilderment briefly crossed the receptionist's face before he beckoned Christian to follow.

The darkly varnished wood-panelled interior was like a hothouse of pot plants. Faded postcards and banknotes of various nationalities lined the wall behind the tiny counter next to a tall, lush palm plant. Looking delighted with himself, the receptionist asked for Christian's passport and handed him a registration form.

Christian closed the door of his room and drew back the dark blue curtains to reveal a heavily barred window overlooking the hotel's car park. He threw his jacket onto one of the beds and inspected the dark-red bathroom tiles and cracked bath for cockroaches. Carefully pulling back the sheet on one of the beds, he searched every corner for bugs but found none. Satisfied that he was now the only visible living being in the room, he lay on the bed and tried to relax.

His mind had gone so numb, he thought it would never feel anything again. He sat up with his head in his hands. His mouth was dry and there was a steady tugging at his heart, pressing into his chest, pushing at his ribcage. He tried to concentrate, but his thoughts drifted back to the seriousness and sadness of his Saskya, her softness, her silliness, and how achingly he loved her. Hot tears welled up, burning his eyes and streaming down his face and shirt front, his whole body convulsing as if chilled to the core.

'God help me!' he groaned over and over, beating his fists on his thighs. 'What have I done? What have I done?'

Was it too late? – too late to tell her everything that was still unsaid during their closeness in the train? He was now

suddenly haunted and tormented by a multitude of regrets –
not having spent even more time with her; not making more
of an effort to understand her feelings and emotions during
her difficult teenage years and the time of the divorce. Had he
been too strict with her? Had he expected too much? He
fretted that he might even have leant on her for emotional
support after his wife left, rather than giving the kind of
support she must have been crying out for. Had he loved her
too much as an emotional substitute for his wife? He
remembered her warmth at the time – a brief hug, a squeeze
of the hand – in surprising contrast to the iron-fist exterior
she'd constructed for herself. She'd had the chance in the train
to ask more about the divorce, but it either hadn't occurred to
her, or she'd avoided it. Now she might never know.

And right now, she might be thinking she'd never see him
again. And that so many of *her* questions would remain
unanswered and mysteries unsolved. She'd often expressed
an interest in Christian's relationship with his father, and his
own childhood memories, perhaps to help her understand
hers with her own father. Christian had always been evasive,
not just because he lacked the facts, but because expressing
feelings was, for him, relatively uncharted territory, even
though any thoughts about his father consistently brought a
lump to his throat. When she'd once questioned him about his
spiritual beliefs, he'd denied having any.

He wanted to tell her that he was basically just an
ordinary bloke struggling through life as a man, and formerly
as a son and as a husband, and that he'd always had his head
stuck in a book, not to ignore her, but because fiction offers
certainty because it's obliged to stick to logical possibilities,
whereas truth is uncertain, and that he could not cope with
uncertainty.

If she never returned, he would have to live with the fact

that neither of them would ever know the answers to questions that would have become increasingly urgent to both of them as the years passed by. If she never returned. He felt as though ice water were coursing through his veins. Despite the heat of the day, the room felt cold, and his body was abruptly racked by a violent tremor.

With a huge effort, he cast his mind back again to the train where they'd seemed so close – sharing laughter and fears, and a sense of togetherness enriching their souls in the cosy womb of their *wagon-lit*. They hadn't thought of any need to 'talk things through'. They had simply achieved a mutual understanding and feeling of comfort that transcended any need for detailed examination of past misunderstandings. And all that hope about the future. Where was it now? Where was *she* now?

He thumped himself hard in the chest and wiped away his tears with his linen handkerchief. Hope had descended into gut-gnawing guilt, together with a harrowing feeling of powerlessness. Why the hell did he have to go and change their route home? All alone in this alien city, how could he ever hope to put it right? He should have tried harder to continue to nurture that harmony between them in the train. He still needed to know her even better. So much more to know. Opportunity lost. Why? Why? Why?.

He sat bolt upright and massaged his already painful back and neck.

He must tell her mother. But what could she do? This sensible, centred woman for whom most problems were approached head-on as challenges, would drop everything, fly over and take charge. But then what? First, he needed to think about how to tell her. Then he would get the hotel to put a call through to Denmark. Or should he? Saskya said she was ill. Heart problems. But he was desperate for help.

He lay down again, closed his burning eyes and his thoughts constantly returned to the petrol station and the red taxi. Their immediate reality was impossible to ignore. He tried to elevate his spirits by dreaming of how it might have been if... Eventually, he drifted off, but not for long.

A sharp buzz from his cellphone woke him. He had no idea whether he'd slept minutes or hours. The dull, muzzy feeling in his head, the stabbing at the back of his eyes, and the thick, parched sensation in his mouth, suggested that however long it had been it wasn't enough. It was a text message from the police. He frowned as he studied the message. A wave of disappointment swept over him as he realised that it was a police warning via his university and wasn't for him personally. The coincidence was uncanny.

Women travelling alone are now the targets for gangs, it read. *Gang members have been instructed to bring a woman's body parts to their gatherings. Or gang initiation is to kidnap a woman and bring her back to the gang to be raped by all the members.*

The message outlined ways for women to protect themselves by avoiding situations where kidnapping could occur, and concluded: *If the predator has a gun, always run. The predator will only hit you, a running target, four in one hundred times; and even then, it most likely will not be a vital organ.*

A buzzing from the black telephone next to the Bible on the bedside cabinet shook him out of his dark thoughts. He lifted the receiver and managed a nervous choking sound. The receptionist said he had a visitor.

'What's the time?' Christian asked drowsily.

'Five-twenty-five in the afternoon, Sir.'

Smothered by a sense of unease, he felt the crushing weight of the power the kidnappers held over him – a power that threatened to push straightforward dread into unmanageable, frenzied panic.

'I'll be five minutes,' he stuttered.

He hung up, hobbled into the bathroom, threw cold water on his face, brushed his teeth and pushed his hair into place. He dressed as quickly as he could, grabbed his jacket, and locked the door behind him. Struggling to keep his balance, he headed downstairs.

A plump woman dressed in a tight-fitting midnight-blue dress was sitting under a tall pot plant in a wicker chair staring at a laptop computer. She stood up when she saw him, and beamed a wide, brilliant white smile that withered slightly as she noticed his stick.

'Mr Kettermann? I'm Blessing Molokwane from *The Tribune* newspaper.'

She stepped forward to shake his hand. She would have been pretty when younger, but the prettiness had faded.

He would normally have been cautious about getting an uninvited call from a journalist, but this time felt almost euphorically relieved at the possibility of having someone to talk to – *anyone* to talk to.

'Pleased to meet you,' he said, holding out his right hand. 'Call me Christian.' He was unable to summon a smile.

'A police contact gave me your hotel and phone number.' She shook his hand African style. 'I hope you don't mind. Have you got time to talk? I can help you.'

She led him into the bar. They sat on a sofa next to a coffee table.

'Can I get you a drink?' she asked huskily.

'A sparkling water, please.'

She gestured to a waiter and ordered a juice for herself. Looping a finger inside her shoulder strap as though to ease the weight of her bosom, she turned to face Christian.

'Your daughter has been kidnapped,' she stated with simple eloquence. 'The people who did it have contacted the paper and want us to act as a go-between. They want a ransom, and they want publicity for their cause. They will ring me again to see if I have your agreement. These are not run-of-the-mill abductors. They are political.'

She paused to make sure he was taking it all in. He felt his face redden as a wave of vertigo swept over him.

'What cause?'

'Food and medicines for their informal settlement.' She mechanically lifted the lid of her laptop as though flipping open a notepad. 'Tell me what happened,' she urged, her fingers already racing.

While Christian told his story, she tapped away, interrupting only with the occasional question or interpolation of phrases in her own preferred style.

'That about wraps it up,' she said, after about a quarter of an hour. 'Meanwhile, I don't want you speaking to anyone else, especially other journalists.' She wagged a finger at him playfully. 'One more thing. Don't smile.' She held up her smartphone and snapped his picture. She switched it off and nestled it carefully in her bag.

She drew in her breath sharply. 'I've got your cellphone number. I'll ring the moment I hear from them again.' She drained her glass. 'I'm so sorry this has happened to you. Please avoid the police for now.' She grinned at him, showing perfectly white, square teeth. 'We must tread carefully. We don't want to confuse things.'

She stood up, smoothed her dress, threw him a bright, warm smile, and was gone. He slumped forward on the sofa, head in hands, trembling from bone-weary fatigue. He thought she seemed kind, but he doubted that this was based on anything apart from pure self-interest. He had about as much reason to trust her as a zebra would a hyena.

Johannesburg

8

Around lunchtime the next day, Christian and his cousin, Guido van Rensburg, were speaking to each other by phone for the first time in thirty years. They arranged to meet later that afternoon, and Guido told him that a young lady called Precious would pick him up from a bar downtown. Guido mentioned that he no longer went by the name of Marco but was now known as Guido. Christian sounded doubtful but gave the impression that he'd go along with just about anything.

'Meanwhile, speak to nobody about this, and certainly not the police,' Guido warned.

'I already have. They've just texted me the case number and the name of the detective in charge.' His voice and educated accent struck Guido as oddly familiar.

'Okay, but don't contact them before we meet. If they ring, don't answer.'

'Why not?'

'I'll explain later. I'm looking forward to seeing you after all these years, Christian. I just wish it were under different circumstances.'

Guido pocketed his phone and called out for Innocent.

'I want the talk on the street, Inno. Take the Merc and find out what you can. Don't be more than a couple of hours.'

Innocent knew everyone – everyone who would remain unknown to people of Guido's colour. He even knew most of the 'bloody immigrants' who came from places like Zimbabwe, Mozambique and the Congo 'to take our jobs and our women'. Not that it was true. Many of these immigrants were so entrepreneurial they *created* jobs. And as for taking the women, most of them had wives and children back home and spent all their time in Johannesburg working and sleeping. They often took huge risks by swimming the crocodile-infested Limpopo River between Zimbabwe and South Africa. They'd arrive with no papers and no passport. Having reached the other side, they then faced the prides of lions that got so fat eating immigrants they were unfit to chase wildlife. Those 'bloody foreigners' that survived often got picked up by the police and were dumped back where they started after their long, harsh and brave journey. Innocent would never admit it, but Guido sensed in him a secret admiration for them.

Whatever he thought about them, he claimed to know them all. If there was anyone who would hear reports about a white girl abducted downtown, it was Innocent. He was Guido's eyes and ears.

Innocent was back but had heard nothing. 'They must be new to this,' was all he could offer. Guido asked him to fetch Precious.

'Yes, Boss.' He forced a smile across his wide-open features.

'Inno!' Guido wagged his finger. He had long ago told Innocent to stop calling him 'boss', that it's a translation of the Afrikaner word *baas*, and that he didn't like its connotations. *I'm not your boss,* Guido had told him. *As you would say, we are all equal in the eyes of the Lord.*

But some habits, especially those originally built on fear, can be difficult to shift. Innocent apologised with a grin.

Minutes later, Precious stood in front of Guido, one hand on hip, the other smoothing the front of her turquoise dress.

'I want you to meet someone for me,' he told her. 'Bring him back here – alone. He's staying at the Chapman. You'll meet him at Funky Jo's. Here's his picture. He looks like me, eh?'

There are two expressions that are often completely misinterpreted. One is a blank, expressionless look, which is interpreted as insolence; the other is a shy, deferential look, interpreted as dishonest and sly. Her look was of the first kind – blank. Her expression simply reflected a complete lack of comprehension, due partly to a newspaper photo of someone looking like an exact double of her lover and protector, and mainly to what Guido had just asked of her.

'Why can't I pick him up at his hotel?'

'Instinct. Severing connections.'

She looked blank again.

'I'll explain some other time.'

'And you, Mr Guido. Why don't you pick him up yourself?'

'Same reason, Precious.'

He felt a hollow feeling in his chest as his thoughts drifted ahead to Christian; what he would say to him, and how he would greet him. And how he was nothing like the same person Christian would be expecting to meet.

He thought of the moment he had adopted the name Guido van Rensburg as respectably South African when he illegally entered the country from Uganda. 'Guido' was similar to his previous name, Marco. He had shed his identity thirty years before – when he killed someone. It was in a jealous rage. It was an accident. That was when he changed his name for the first time – and lost the old one; the real him? His years in Uganda, where he learned the craft that made his fortune, were profitable until the death of his business partner, a survivor of one of the Nazi camps. His motto had been 'you must do whatever's necessary'.

Without his partner's army of protectors, Guido was no longer safe. He moved to Johannesburg for its wealthy customers who pay in gold, and for its lawlessness. He felt most comfortable where the size of his wallet put him above the law and gave him a leg up over hurdle after hurdle of corrupt bureaucracy.

And now the past had gate-crashed in a most unexpected way.

9

Christian put down the magazine he'd found in the hotel lounge. It was mid-afternoon. He dressed again in the same pale-blue shirt and fawn slacks he'd been wearing since Cape Town, threw on his white linen jacket – the one Saskya called his 'ice cream man coat' – closed the door behind him and descended the flight of steps to the hotel reception. Although feeling drained, Christian couldn't bring himself to take a taxi. He asked the receptionist for a guard from the hotel to walk with him the short distance to Funky Jo's.

He was much too early. Christian slipped the guard a fifty-rand note, bought himself a *vetkoek* from a stand, and made his way across the main square to watch a troop of fire eaters from Zanzibar. One of them managed to limbo dance under a burning pole, barely two foot off the ground.

Christian couldn't finish the *vetkoek*, which looked as if it had enough calories to fuel a marathon. He looked around for a bin. Within seconds a beggar was at his side offering to take it off his hands.

Funky Jo's had seen better days. Cigarette smoke and spilt beer had taken their toll on the curtains and carpets. Sitting on a flower-patterned sofa in front of the fireplace, a middle-aged black woman he took to be the proprietor – Funky Josephine? – looked up from her knitting and smiled. 'Hello dear. Haven't seen you here before.' She returned to her knitting before he could answer. Three men on stools at the bar argued loudly about the identity of the soloist on the jazz piece playing from the speakers. They completely ignored Christian who, on top of everything else, was feeling mild discomfort at being the only white person.

He took a seat at a table towards the back of the bar and waited patiently for the barman to acknowledge his presence. He ordered a cheese and tomato toasty and mango juice and tried not to stare too hard at a young black woman striding purposefully into the bar. A slit up the side of her tight-fitting glittery-red, full-length dress, exposed a smooth bare length of black calf and thigh. Her oily hair was pulled back so severely from her face that it stretched her eyes into a far-eastern look. Surely this can't be the woman he was waiting for? The eyes glanced across at Christian with studied disinterest as she wiggled her tightly swaddled bottom onto a bar stool and turned to talk to the barman. Two more girls entered, brightly-coloured shawls draped over their shoulders, an eddy of heavy scent preceding their arrival, as they sidled up to their colleague. Their stares at the male customers seemed to imply knowledge. The bar was starting to fill up.

Christian was half way through his toasty, when a tall, noble-looking woman entered and strode straight up to him. She was almost faultlessly lovely. Her smile uncovered a row of white, perfectly even teeth. High, prominent cheekbones beneath perfectly unblemished brown skin added fineness to the fullness of her mouth. Her slanted, deeply set eyes were laughing. She placed her handbag on the table, smoothed down her long, turquoise dress, and eased herself elegantly onto the seat. Her hair was hidden beneath a cotton turban matching the material of her dress. She was a big woman, Christian noted, but not fat. Her tallness put her large breasts and hips into perfect proportion.

'Mr Christian?' she purred with no hint of humour. *Mutiny on the Bounty* would be too far removed from her generation and culture. Her voice was deep and resonant, soft, yet not weak. Her brother had never told her that it was better to introduce herself to white people as 'My name is Precious' rather than 'I am Precious'. Guido had put her right, but she loved to tease him with a playful 'How do you do, Mr Guido. I am Precious', accompanied by a husky giggle, and a look that to Guido meant only one thing.

'My name is Precious,' she told Christian. 'I'm very pleased to meet you. I am so sorry to hear about your daughter. But Mr Guido will help you.'

She smiled at him again, her long black fingers probing inside her handbag.

'The two of you look so much like each other.' She shook her head in disbelief and let her deep brown eyes rest on him again as if to make sure she hadn't imagined it. 'Cigarette?' she offered.

In one quick glance, Christian took in her appearance again. Her long neck and back were straight and upright. She struck him as someone completely at ease with herself, perfectly comfortable within her own body. She lit her cigarette, breathed the smoke towards the yellow ceiling, and glanced back at him with amused eyes.

'Would you like something to drink?' he asked.

'No thank you.'

She studied his face, and smiled warmly, scratching the top of her arm, leaving whitish, powdery tracks on her ebony-coloured skin.

'Do you come from round here?' Christian asked as he finished the remains of his toasty. He wanted to talk about Saskya, but didn't know where to start, or even whether he should.

'I come from Polokwane.' She tapped her fingers lightly on the side of her glass. 'My father was Zulu, my mother Pedi. They both passed away.'

'And now you live here in Jo'burg?'

She studied the tip of her freshly-lit cigarette, and then without looking up replied, 'We have to go now. Mr Guido told me not to be too long.'

Christian drained his glass, and watched her stub out her cigarette, and get to her feet effortlessly and elegantly, as though in mockery of his own clumsy effort to stand. She hesitated as he looked as though he'd lost his balance. As she grabbed his arm he caught a whiff of her woody perfume. She had already satiated four of his senses; the last – *taste* – would be forever forbidden. With a mesmeric, flowing stride, she led him gently to a black Mercedes in the side street. She handed the guard a five-rand coin and joked with him in what Christian took to be Sepedi language.

She eased the car into the traffic, her long brown fingers languidly splayed across the steering wheel. Peering through the windscreen in a meditative pose of complete concentration, she didn't once take her eyes off the road. He tried to engage her in conversation, but she completely ignored him as if she needed all her powers to avoid other road users.

Half an hour later she stopped the car outside a large bungalow converted into a synagogue for many of Jo'burg's Yiddish-speaking German Jews. Guido had told her that on Friday and Saturday nights the bustling street reminded him of Amsterdam's diamond district – the men in black frock coats, wide-brimmed hats, ringlets in hair and beards; the women in sober smart cotton dresses, and plenty of jewellery. 'Jewry jewellery' he'd quipped.

She rang Innocent's cellphone.

Guido's part of Jo'burg was a backwater of Hindus, Jews, Muslims, Africans and a few Europeans – including a Dutchman, a Swiss, and others, all of whom stayed behind, or were left behind above the tideline during the white exodus, and who were now part of one of central Jo'burg's many colourful melting pots where someone as shy as Guido could simply blend into the background. They were perpetual foreigners, many pining for their homeland but meanwhile basking in the warm comradeship of émigrés. On the corner, a couple of women were cooking maize on a charcoal brazier, while a lone ibis, known locally as a *hadeda*, stood on a branch, waiting for a chance to swoop down and help itself.

Innocent gave the all-clear, and Precious made sure there were no cars or people nearby before using her remote to open the iron gate. Once through, she stopped to prevent anyone from following her and waited until the gate had slid completed shut behind her before parking in front of the *stoep*.

'At last,' Innocent greeted her. 'You drive like a tortoise, Sissie.' She stuck out her tongue at him and laughed a deep belly laugh.

He opened Christian's door, helped him out, and shook him by the hand.

'Welcome Mr Christian,' he said, avoiding Christian's eyes. 'My name is Innocent. I'm very sorry for you.'

10

It was already late afternoon. The lofty, cavernous house with two stories was unusual in Johannesburg where no lack of space usually enabled the well-off to live in spacious bungalows, the less well-off in flats, and the residue in sprawling shacks outside the city centre. The garden was a blaze of colour across the spectrum between bright red and deep purple from the bougainvillea and jacarandas. The far edge of the sun was crowned with thunderclouds and a grumbling storm that headed west and away from them.

Christian followed Precious apprehensively into a dimly lit hall. He glanced briefly at the peeling paint on the door frames. *Faded glory*, he thought. She piloted him into a large, wood-panelled lounge with floorboards of Oregon pine, covered with the occasional Persian rug. A cat, whose tortoiseshell colouring looked like camouflage, eyed him suspiciously from the corner of the room. Precious threw open the windows to allow the gentle breeze to move the warm air inside.

Christian swung round as Guido entered and stepped towards Christian with a natural, athletic gracefulness.

'Christian. I'm so sorry, Man,' he said, in a deep sonorous voice. 'This is so awful.'

With a restrained smile, he took his hand and attempted a hug, which faltered halfway. Throughout his decades in Africa, Guido's style of greeting had become a genuine, open-hearted hug, unlike many white men of English or Dutch extraction, for whom such warmth towards a member of the same gender might reflect sinister desires, and who prefer the simple firm handshake and penetrating eye contact to ward off any unwelcome attempt at intimacy. He stood back, hands on hips.

They stood facing each other with a sense of recognition founded on something far deeper than merely shared history or shared appearance. Each saw himself reflected in the other. An onlooker would have had to look twice to tell them apart, were it not for the totally different impression given by what they wore – Christian, bespectacled, formal in his neat blue shirt tucked into slacks with creases so sharp his thin legs looked like two blades; Guido, with his black silk shirt hanging loosely over black jeans, giving the impression of a world-weary jazzman. And their faces – similar lines and creases, but Christian's lightly etched; Guido's deeply ploughed.

Guido oozed the self-assuredness of a habitual outsider; the air of a man who knew life from end to end. Not jaded. The deep lines around his eyes and mouth looked to Christian as though they had been etched by an expanse of experiences, good, bad and indifferent, but seemed as though they had been mainly good. His curly hair was almost white, a counterpoint to his impression of tormented vigour. He was no taller than Christian, but his restless grey-blue eyes seemed to look down at him. He stared intensely outwards with cautious scepticism and then appeared to look dreamily inwards as if to process what he'd seen. Now his vision was outwards and directed at the man in front of him. His look was one of astonishment. The likeness was uncanny.

'Sit down,' Guido urged, waving him into a chair.

Christian hung his stick on the back of the chair next to him.

'What can I get you?' Precious asked, in a voice keen to please.

'Marco. It's so good to see you.' He turned to Precious: 'A

coffee would be fine.'

Precious hesitated, and then looked up and stared at Guido with an expression of embarrassed surprise, as though she'd just become aware of blundering into the wrong room. She nodded, smiled a strained smile, and left for the kitchen.

'The name's Guido now, Christian,' Guido whispered. 'Not Marco. Guido van Rensburg. Marco passed away thirty years ago.' He grinned and winked.

What is in a name? Guido or Marco, they sounded more or less the same. His surname this time was quite different. He had shed the previous one like an old skin. He had lost his identity once before and had been forced to start life with a new name and, like many things in life, the first time was the hardest. Whether he was Marco, Julius or Guido was of little concern to him. The only problem could have been one of acquiring passports. He had lived in Africa long enough to know that crossing borders was not a matter of having a passport, but of greasing enough palms. And whilst travel further afield was now impossible, fake documents of sufficient quality to pass most of the smaller Southern African inland border posts were freely available in Johannesburg, a city where whatever you wanted, someone would find it for you.

A milestone he shared with the rest of the world was in September 2001 when his wife gave up her struggle against an auto-immune disease triggered by a yellow fever vaccine, and when New York's World Trade Centre was destroyed in an alleged terrorist attack. In the aftermath, tightened security across the globe meant that international travel, always risky on forged documents, became impossible for the likes of Guido. He finally and achingly accepted that he would never see Europe again.

'Cigarette?' he offered mechanically. His public-school

politeness was as much a part of him as his smoky voice and distinguished-looking grey hair. Christian declined with a raised hand. Guido lit one from a gold-plated table lighter. 'I'd like to ask you what you've been doing all these years, but for now, we need to concentrate on the next few days.'

'Of course.'

'Look.' Guido lowered his eyes and took a deep breath. 'I want to put your mind at rest. Nearly all kidnappings end without harm to the victim. We don't know yet what kind it is, but, as I say – '

'It's a political kidnapping,' Christian stated.

He told Guido at length about his meeting with Blessing, *The Tribune* journalist.

'She told me to avoid the police. But we'll have to leave this to them,' Christian concluded in a matter-of-fact voice. 'There's no way I could lay my hands on ransom money. I don't own a house; not even a car. Nor does her mother.'

'The police?' Guido inhaled deeply on a French cigarette, and threw his head back, exhaling towards the ceiling. 'Most kidnappings go unreported because the families fear the police. We have to deal with it ourselves.'

'Guido. I have no money,' Christian said, leaning forward for emphasis. 'Not even a few thousand. '

'No. But I have.' Guido lifted his arm and shook his sleeve, like a magician producing a fluttering dove or frightened rabbit. 'We're family. I can spare as much as we need.'

'How can you lay your hands on that amount?'

'I'm an artist. I've just finished a painting worth much more than that.'

Christian didn't go through the motions of *Oh, I couldn't possibly*. He didn't do or say anything. There was stunned silence.

70

Guido paused to light another cigarette from the previous one. 'You really want to leave this to the cops? Look at this press report,' he said, shoving a newspaper clipping toward Christian. 'You've heard of blue-light robbery? This is blue-light kidnapping.'

Christian, still moved to silence, read: *A police officer was arrested on Monday for kidnapping and extortion, Gauteng police said. Police have launched a manhunt for five other suspects who were involved in the kidnapping.*

Christian's look of sorrow was abruptly so complete and distressing that Guido had to turn his eyes away. 'It's a topsy-turvy world,' he stated, fiddling with his gold lighter. 'They do things differently here. Cops and robbers are sometimes one and the same. You can't tell the difference. We're better off without them.'

Christian reflected for a while on what Guido had told him. 'What about a private detective?'

'A thousand bucks an hour with no control over what they do. Why write a blank cheque with no guarantees? We handle it ourselves.' Guido dragged hard, exhaling the smoke through his teeth in a low hiss.

'But I've absolutely no experience of this kind of thing.'

'You don't have to. Has it escaped your notice how much we look alike? Peas in a pod.'

Christian's face registered a dawning comprehension.

'I couldn't let you take the risk.'

'Whichever way we handle this, it's a risk. Your daughter's at risk. The difference is that if my guard and I do this, it's less risky than leaving it to the cops or some private dickhead. Leave the cops to get on with ripping off motorists, and the PI's with sniffing out the seedier side of divorce.'

'The police are already involved.'

'We'll throw them off the scent.'

'You mentioned blue-light robbery?'

'It's the latest fashion in police corruption. Off-duty cops impersonating on-duty cops. They use their uniforms, cars and guns at night to pull over unsuspecting drivers of expensive cars – and then hijack them. Nice bit of moonlighting.' He gave a snort of impatience and clasped his hands behind his neck. 'We sort this out ourselves. Finish and *klaar*.'

Christian just stared in disbelief.

'Another thing. I see you've got a laptop. Don't mention this on social media or to anyone. Spectacular news like that can go viral. The kidnappers might pick it up.'

'I don't use social media.'

'My gut feeling is to batten down the hatches. It's not as if anyone else can help. The more people that find out about it, the more danger she's in. Where's her mother?'

'Denmark. I must tell her. Can I use your phone? Mine eats up credit.'

Guido shook his head. 'No way. Can you imagine? She'd want to tell everyone who might help her and then fly straight over here. Bad idea.'

'I can't just not tell her. It's not right. It's unethical. She'd never forgive me.'

Guido nodded. 'Okay. Save your credit. Let me try to put a call through on the internet upstairs. Give me her number.'

Christian pulled up the contact page and handed him his phone.

'I'll shout if I get through.'

Guido returned a few minutes later. 'No reply. A voice message says she's away for a couple of weeks and can't be contacted,' Guido lied. 'Don't worry. I'll vouch for the fact that you did your best.'

Christian frowned. 'I could leave a text message for when

72

she's got a signal again.'

'Are you kidding? You can't tell her in writing. You'll have to speak to her. Not now. It's best she doesn't know. She can't help. And it complicates matters. Agreed?'

Christian nodded reluctantly and reflected on what Saskya had told him about her mother's heart problems. He managed to convince himself that this was adequate ethical justification for failing to get in touch.

'There's another possible complication,' Guido continued. 'Stockholm syndrome, where the victim is so grateful not to be harmed that they sympathise with their kidnappers to the point that they want to join them. From what this journalist told you, these people are not your run-of-the-mill abductors for gang initiation or money. You said they're political. Idealists. She's young. Young people are idealistic. She might not want to be saved.'

'Saskya's not like that. I still think the police – '

'No. I've told you. The police would either be wheeler-dealing for a slice of the action or go in with guns blazing, killing anything that moves.'

'You sound as though you do this sort of thing every day.'

'I'm trying to impress upon you that this country's police are a lost cause.'

'I don't agree. You might be right for now. But in the longer term, with the right approach, police corruption could be a thing of the past.'

'Good God! There's something endearing about you, Christian. Come on, let's eat.'

'This isn't right.' Christian shook his head slowly, his face like stone. The whole situation had become absurd to the point of lunacy. Then he shrugged and raised his hand in agreement, and the two men fell silent for a moment, interrupted by a burst of laughter from the street as though in mockery of Christian's grim face. The sudden nightfall had reduced all other sounds to a whisper. Then, within a matter of seconds, the spell was broken by the rowdy chirruping of cicadas.

Guido guided him into the dining room. As Christian limped through the doorway, Guido noticed his built-up left shoe. Christian stopped to read a poster on the wall next to the dining table. Handwritten in a font designed to resemble Sanskrit, it seemed to serve as a form of grace.

> **Listen to the salutation to the dawn**
> *Look to this day*
> *For it is life, the very life of life;*
> *In its brief course*
> *Lie all the verities and realities of your existence:*
> *The bliss of growth,*
> *The glory of action,*
> *The splendour of beauty;*
> *For yesterday is but a dream,*
> *And tomorrow only a vision;*
> *But today well spent makes every*
> *yesterday a dream of happiness;*
> *And every tomorrow a vision of hope;*
> *Look well, therefore, to this day;*
> *Such is the salutation to the dawn.*

The two of them sat opposite each other, Christian reflecting in silence on the significance and implications of Guido's offer.

Guido thought for a moment and then remarked, 'It's already getting late. You'd better move in here. We don't want you disappearing as well.'

'My luggage is at the hotel. And I've got to check out.'

'Innocent will take you in the morning. You can borrow some of my stuff for tonight. It's not as if we're different sizes.'

Guido let his gaze fix on a potted dragon plant that was clearly desperate for water. 'Excuse me,' he said and left for the kitchen.

'Your cousin didn't know your name,' Precious whispered, her saucy lips touching his earlobe. 'He called you Marco. Is he stupid?'

'He's an intellectual.'

'Are you an intellectual?' She placed her hand on the base of his spine and squeezed.

'I'm a survivor.'

'I like survivors.' Her tongue brushed the inside of his ear. 'Would you like a pipe to help you survive?' Her hand ran down his back, her fingers tracing the skeletal path of his spine before edging down to the top of his thigh. 'Or would you like me first?'

'I would like dinner first, my Precious. Then a pipe.'

Guido returned to Christian in the dining room. 'How long's it been – thirty years, right?'

Christian nodded. 'I remember we both liked Hermann Hesse. We decided you were Goldmund and I was Narcissus.'

'Hah! I remember.'

'And our dads were locked into an argument. My dad refused to talk about it afterwards.'

'From what I heard, your father was rather an unforgiving type.'

'What?"

'That he couldn't bring himself to listen to his brother Heinrich's story about spending the war in a concentration camp – how the poor soul had had his testicles snipped off as soon as he arrived at Hotel Dachau reception. Apparently, the anaesthetic was a sound kick in the balls before he said goodbye to them for good.'

'I can't imagine my dad being like that.'

Guido explained that his own father and his two brothers – Christian's father and their younger brother, Heinrich – were orphaned in their teens. Their father – Guido and Christian's grandfather – had been living in London when the First World War broke out. Upon his repatriation to post-war chaos in Hannover at the end of the war, after surviving years in the notorious Stobs internment camp in Scotland, he died of tuberculosis. Their mother, unable to bear any longer the exhaustion and worry of coping with grinding poverty in 1920s Germany, finally gassed herself.

'I heard all that,' Christian told him with a faint tone of impatience to return the subject to Saskya.

'It was little Heinrich who found her with her head resting on a cushion carefully placed inside the oven. Peace in her time.'

In the early 1930s, all three brothers were involved in youth work but were already under pressure to join the *Hitlerjugend*. Christian's and Guido's fathers were able to get out in time and make a home for themselves abroad – Christian's father in London; Guido's in Amsterdam, and later in Britain. Heinrich stayed behind and continued with his youth work, defying Gestapo threats. Gestapo patience, rarely in abundance, was swiftly exhausted. Heinrich was arrested at four o'clock one chilly morning, and via various sleepless nights in prisons and interrogation centres, finally ended up in a cramped cattle wagon on a three-day journey south to Dachau concentration camp for political prisoners. He was a long way from home in every sense.

After the war, Heinrich joined Guido's father who had

returned to Amsterdam, and who was living off the meagre proceeds from his art shop and who believed Heinrich dead. Guido's father, surprised and delighted, immediately relayed the news by letter to Christian's father in London. Heinrich himself, after staying a few days in Amsterdam, set off for London.

'If you could uphold your values in Dachau you could uphold them anywhere,' Guido continued. 'Many, perhaps most, could not. Your father apparently believed that young Heinrich belonged to those who could not. He bluntly refused to welcome him into his home but did agree to meet him in the tea room at London's Paddington Station, where Heinrich gave him a silver clockwork model of a Buick automobile for you as a baby, Christian.'

'How do you know all this?'

'Heinrich wrote to my dad after he went back home to Germany. He was gutted by your dad's attitude.'

'I can't think why he treated him like that.'

'We'll never know how Heinrich managed to survive in a hellhole from which most never returned. He was a chef. Perhaps he was put to work in the kitchens, which would have saved him from starvation. Our fathers didn't have much time to find out. Because of his castration, Heinrich had become an overweight eunuch, a heart-attack waiting to happen. And happen it did, fatally, soon after he returned to Hannover. Any secrets died with him.'

'I'm surprised at my dad,' Christian commented. 'He wasn't like that. He'd be the first to say you should never judge people until you yourself have been in similar circumstances or have a thorough understanding of them.'

Guido shrugged. 'I don't know,' he muttered. 'So many secrets. We'll never know what really happened or why. Pointless speculating.'

'Marco – sorry, Guido – to get back to Saskya, I don't know how to – '

'Thank me?' Guido cut in. 'Thank me when we've got her back, sitting next to us, eating the best meal she's had in days. Meanwhile, try to get some sleep.'

11

The next day the fresh garden was bathed in a clear morning light and waves of floral scents. Birds were chattering again. Guido and Christian were drinking coffee on the *stoep*, discussing their being awoken at around two in the morning by the sound of semi-automatic gun fire, interspersed with single shots. It was almost certainly an armed response team responding to someone's alarm. Guido assured him that they were safe behind their razor wire and electric fences with enough voltage to fell a bull.

Guido shielded his eyes from the sun and stared up at two eagles wheeling in the clear cold sky, gliding in an overture to courtship, widely circling as if bound to an invisible wheel, keeping a respectful distance as though testing each other's suitability as future lovers.

Christian felt simultaneously buoyed up and depressed by the beautiful yet melancholic sound of the music floating on the summer morning into the garden. He had never been particularly keen on music of any kind – serious or popular – yet these meditative tones filled him with a glimmer of hope overlaid with a feeling of an irretrievable void and gut-aching regret. Almost every thought in his head concerned Saskya. Everything else was on the periphery of his mental vision, foggy and out of focus.

Having started out a flawless blue, the Highveld summer sky began to cloud over, and a faint breeze briefly disturbed the leaves. They listened to the sound of thunder in the distance, unusual for that time of day, and sensed the electric tension that comes when the wind suddenly drops, and everything is still. They collected their cups and coffee pot.

Guido rushed inside followed by Christian who struggled to keep up. The grey storm clouds swept overhead, heralded by a huge flash of lightning that split the big sky into three. A hawk spiralled awkwardly against the gusts of wind. The rain started with a few heavy drops the size of five-rand pieces shaking the leaves on the nearby trees. They shivered as a wave of coolness preceded the heavier rain, which, when it came, was so hard it was like sitting next to a waterfall. The guttering immediately overflowed, and they could hardly hear themselves speak. They waited inside in silence for the storm to pass quickly and the emerging sun to heat up the newly cleaned air with fresh intensity.

Christian's tinny ringtone startled him. It was Blessing. 'They rang,' she told him, her voice betraying professional excitement. 'Your daughter's fine. Come down and see me as soon as you can. They let me speak to her. They will ring back at lunchtime.'

Christian didn't even attempt to hide his tears of relief. He just sat and sobbed. In anyone else, he would have expected it to be a huge release to let the tears come, but in his case, it felt more like an experience of being stripped bare, of having the diary of his innermost thoughts thrown open in public and thrust in his face.

Guido went to look for Innocent. He quickly returned and rested his hand on Christian's shoulder.

'Innocent will take you, and you can pick up your luggage,' he said. 'Innocent will drop you before the hotel. You will ask the hotel guard to carry your luggage to the foyer of Market Theatre. Innocent will pick you up there.'

'Why can't he just – '

'Severing connections. Another thing. You must tell this reporter that you can't drive because of your – your disability. Tell her you need to have a driver.'

'Why?'

'Strategic planning.'

'I'm a very bad liar.'

'That sounds to me like a pretty good lie.' He slapped Christian on the back. 'Just do what you can.'

Christian dried his eyes with one of his immaculately ironed handkerchiefs.

Innocent drove him in the Merc. They obediently picked up the luggage in strict accordance with Guido's instructions. By the time they reached the newspaper's offices, the sun had already dried out the streets, leaving the air warm and moist. The walk from the car to reception caused a stream of perspiration that soaked the back of Christian's shirt. A dainty, high-heeled secretary led him into an editor's office.

She knocked and opened the door for him. A small man behind a large desk, dressed in light slacks and safari shirt, looked up from a single sheet in front of him. His tanned face was blotched with large, fawn freckles, his full head of silver-grey hair neatly combed. He got to his feet, his stiff bearing giving him a military impression that belied his smallness. He gazed at Christian over the tops of his reading glasses, stepped forward and held out his right hand.

'Good to see you,' he said rather formally. 'I'm George.' Christian accepted the man's hand and shook it. It was an honest, hard-gripping handshake.

George gestured to a chair in front of the desk and sank into a leather swivel chair purposefully linking his hands in front of him.

'We have good news. The kidnappers have been in touch with one of my reporters, Blessing.'

'We've met.'

'Quite so. She'll join us in a minute. And your daughter's safe. Blessing spoke to her.'

'I know. Thank God!' For the second time that day, Christian desperately tried to fight down the choking feeling in his throat. George handed him a tissue to wipe away a tear that had reached the corner of his mouth before he even realised he was crying.'

'Tell me how it happened,' George asked, kindly.

Christian repeated his story from beginning to end.

'She's being held at Honingsloot,' George told him. 'It's the last township to receive government help. Ghastly place. There's hardly been any development there – electricity, but no proper sanitation, flying toilets.'

'Flying toilets?'

'Yes. One does it in a plastic bag, knots it, and throws it as high and far as possible. Where it lands is no longer one's concern.'

'Disgusting!' Christian shuddered as he felt a chill run through him, putting his teeth on edge.

'Desperate. Many of the inhabitants of Honingsloot have been moved on from more developed townships like Alexandra which have become overcrowded. And many are foreigners, under constant threat of xenophobic violence. They feel abandoned, and with good reason. People are not going to accept that kind of squalor for much longer. The resentment, hatred and aggression in these townships are building up like a pressure cooker.'

He looked at his watch. 'Blessing won't be long. She's excellent. Considering her circumstances, one should tip one's hat to her achievements.'

'What should be my next move? Wait for the police to get in touch?' Christian asked, feeling uneasy about exploring the possibility of reneging on his agreement with Guido.

George linked his hands and leaned forward earnestly.

'We wouldn't normally recommend your leaving this to

the police.' He spread his hands upwards and lifted his shoulders in a gesture of hopelessness. 'In this case, you know nobody here, and you can't handle this alone, so perhaps you have no choice.'

Christian nodded.

'Unless you hire a detective,' George suggested, leaning forward and pressing his hands downward on the polished desktop. 'Here, take this number.' He scribbled a note and handed it to Christian. 'He's not cheap, but he might help if you decide to take that route.'

George's pale-blue, penetrating eyes searched Christian's face.

'She's how old, your daughter?'

'Twenty-six.'

'Don't ever let her out of your sight again.' A deeply sincere look came into the old man's watery eyes. 'These are dangerous times.' He chuckled at the cloud of fear that passed over Christian's face. 'Don't worry. Such events might be more common, but they're still rare. You've been awfully unlucky. But they nearly always end well.'

George's calm self-possession reminded Christian strongly of his own father, who had died over twenty years before. He seemed to possess a similar humility born of a philosophical understanding of the futility of self-importance and busyness. Even his skin reminded him of his own father – its susceptibility to bruising in purple patches that in his own dad's case, eventually became permanent, as though embodying his mental bruises of disillusionment.

'I'm breaking out this weekend – off to Pilanesberg,' George said. 'Do a spot of big game hunting.'

He smiled at Christian's raised eyebrows. 'With my camera. Want to come along?'

'Er...'

'We'll be passing through the Magaliesberg mountains. Magnificent. I used to camp there as a child. The perfect getaway. I always derive a thrill from being there. If you see any vultures near northern Jo'burg, that's where they come from. They like to nest high. And it's over eight thousand metres above sea level up there.'

'I'm sorry, but – '

'But you couldn't possibly,' he responded, a note of disappointment in his voice. 'No, you couldn't. Not with all this hanging over you.'

There was a knock at the door. 'Ah, there she is. Come in Blessing. You two have met.'

Blessing gave Christian a bear hug. 'I'm so happy for you,' she told him. 'They let her speak to me. She says no one hurt her. She even joked about the food. I believe her, Christian. They will ring again soon.'

'There's more between heaven and earth,' George quoted as though he'd thought of it himself. 'I'll leave you to it,' he said, shaking Christian by the hand and heading for the door. 'You two can stay here. It's too noisy out there. If there's anything more I can do…'

Blessing slumped into a chair next to Christian.

'Good story for us,' she said, although with a solemn look. 'But for you, as a parent, the ultimate nightmare.'

She reached across, held his hand, and stared at him, her dark brown eyes melting into his, until he felt uncomfortable and had to look away.

'I've got a good feeling about this,' she smiled. 'I think it will turn out okay. I'll let you know when I hear from them again.'

'How much – '

'They say the ransom is to pay for food and medicines for the Honingsloot community.'

'Yes, but how much – '

'One moment.' She disappeared and returned with two glasses of water. 'They'll let us know when and where the cash is to be delivered. She says she's being treated very well. She sounded quite cheerful and even supportive of the whole idea. But she's obviously scared of what will happen if you can't raise the money.'

'How much is the ransom?'

'A total of five hundred thousand.'

Christian winced, as though caught by sudden cramp. 'Half a million rand. How long have I got?'

'They said you have a maximum of seven days. They know you're not going to walk away from it, and they know that most Europeans have cars and savings worth much more than that. They've been sensible. They did add that if you deal with the police, that it will be the last you'll see of her.'

'And Saskya?'

'You get Saskya when you hand over the money. You must go alone. They said if you want your daughter alive no tricks, no marked money and no police.'

He felt a tightness of the stomach. 'I can't drive,' he blurted, surprised at his own assertiveness. 'I'll need a driver.'

She snorted loudly, her expression wide-eyed as if he had suggested something utterly preposterous. The smile had quickly faded from her face, to make room for a look of frustration. She stared into her glass, twirling it between her fingers, and then looked up. 'Why do you need a driver?' she asked belligerently.

'I suffer from concentration problems. I black out. I just can't do it. And there's my disability.' He wondered whether he was overdoing it.

Her dark eyes fixed on his stick and built-up shoe and roamed over him as if noticing him for the first time. 'But they want the registration number and the make and colour of the car.'

'I'll ring you as soon as I've hired a chauffeur-driven car.'

'Where do you stay?'

'In a hotel.'

'Where?' Her voice was straying towards irritability.

'Eastside.

'Have the police contacted you again?'

'Yes. They texted me the case number.'

She got to her feet and left the room with 'I'll be right back'.

He sat and stared through the slats of the venetian blind at a wisp of cirrus in an otherwise cloudless sky.

She returned some minutes later, sat down, rested her mammoth bosom on the desk, and took a deep breath.

'You know this could go badly wrong, Christian. Using a chauffeur. You're taking a huge risk with your life and with your daughter's life. Why don't you use a detective to drive you? An ex-policeman. I know someone. Family. He's tough. He knows everyone. I just spoke to him.'

Everyone knows a detective who knows everyone, he thought. He felt a wave of distrust and then dismissed it as paranoia. Innocent was tough and knew everyone. He'd gone too far down that path to turn back now.

He shook his head. 'Some things cannot be left to others,' he said, embarrassed at the melodramatic overtones and at his own deceit.

Her expression briefly hardened into carved ebony, then softened again as she struggled to retrieve an air of amiability. She shrugged and threw up despairing hands. 'If that's the way you want it.' She looked at him, and a curious weariness came into her face. She struggled to her feet.

'Goodbye, Christian,' she said softly. 'I'll be in touch when they ring me.'

As they shook hands, her expression resembled one of relief to be rid of a failed job applicant. He suddenly felt bewildered as if realising he'd lost his way. A minute later he was on the street ringing Innocent for a lift back.

Guido was standing in the garden on one leg, arms stretched out like the angular branches of a small tree. The exercise had a Chinese name meaning 'standing pole', which formed the basis of an unarmed martial art seldom found outside Asia, which a Chinese doctor taught Guido in Uganda. It was his only exercise. 'Standing pole' was a perfect description for his tall and gangly frame. Innocent was used to his master's eccentric habits and had learned to ignore them, or perhaps humour him.

Guido never forgot the crushing sense of impotence he'd felt when he was attacked on the street thirty years previously in Nairobi. He then vowed that if it happened again any humiliation would not be on his part. He preferred it to his other weapons, a sword and a walking stick. Guns he left to Innocent. He once told Innocent he preferred a sword to a gun, and that it is less likely to kill provided you slash rather than thrust, but that the effect should be just as memorable. He had told his bemused gardener that if the stakes are not so high he preferred a walking stick, which can be effective without causing so much damage and you can't be arrested for carrying one. Innocent had nodded, his jaw muscles straining to keep a straight face.

Innocent himself learned many of his own survival skills on the streets when he ended up homeless. He was working as a young guard and gardener for an Afrikaner family in Northern Limpopo, who gave him accommodation the size of a potting shed, a modest wage and five hundred rand a month for food.

Innocent had been asked to work at the top of a ladder to clean the guttering. The ladder slipped, and he fell to the ground, breaking his ankle. From that height, he was lucky to be alive. He dragged himself to his *baas* who gave him a couple of aspirins and told him to get on with it. Innocent had a half-brother whom he'd met by chance after moving to Johannesburg. He was from a different mother. He rang the brother, who dropped everything, drove all the way from his place of work in northern Johannesburg and whisked Innocent to the nearest clinic, where he received immediate attention at the brother's expense. When he returned, his employer asked him why he did these things to himself. Was it just to get out of work?

'Many people treat black workers as beneath them,' he'd explained. 'Apartheid was not long ago; people are set in their ways.'

The next incident leading up to a tragic finale was when he'd used a cup to test whether a basin that he'd been repairing still leaked. Afterwards, the boss's wife told him to keep the cup. Innocent was delighted. Later, the husband saw him with it and angrily accused him of stealing it. Innocent told him that the missus had given it to him as a present and how happy he was. The *baas* fetched his wife who said it wasn't a present, but that because he'd touched it, she couldn't use it again.

Innocent looked them in the eye and let the cup fall out of his hand, smashing it into several pieces on the concrete.

'They treated their dogs better than me,' Innocent told Guido, shaking his head. 'And they could not laugh – not a proper laugh. We are all ridiculous in the sight of God. But they could not laugh at themselves.'

But there was worse to come. It all started to go badly

wrong when they didn't want to give him his food allowance but just passed on their leftovers. There was no room for a fridge in his tiny room, so he had to cross to the main house, knock on the door and ask to get the food from his employer's fridge. Each time he did so he was met with a long face or a snarl. One night, when he knocked on the back door, he heard his employer say to his wife, 'Shit, it's that fuckin' kaffir again.' Perhaps if he'd been called a 'black bastard' or something similar, what happened next could have been avoided. Innocent would probably have shrugged it off. But it wasn't 'black bastard'; it was the 'k' word, the worst insult you can give a black South African.

Anyone knowing Innocent would have expected a bloodbath, and for the house to be burned to the ground. Instead, he tiptoed away, gathered his things and walked out into the night leaving the security gate wide open behind him. Whether he left it open on purpose no one knows. Even he doesn't know. He might have been too stunned by what he'd heard, how he'd been treated, or just blinded by humiliation. He said in a police statement that it was like falling asleep and waking up sitting under a tree some hours later. His employer and his wife were found the next day, their upright tortured bodies tied to chairs, their mouths gagged, their throats slit. The safe was open, and the savings and jewellery gone together with most of their other valuables. The thieves were caught in a police check next to a township but managed to escape into the maze of shacks and shanties where they could disappear forever.

Innocent rarely talked about it, but he mentioned it to Guido when he first started working for him. He was not directly responsible for their deaths, yet he carried the burden of guilt – a kind of burden that both men sensed they had in common.

12

It was late afternoon. Tsotsi rocketed at full pelt across the lawn chasing an ibis that left it to the last split second before rising into the air by a couple of metres and fluttering back to land on the same spot as though teasing him. The dog just managed to avoid the fat trunk of a giant palm tree before skidding to a halt in front of the electrified fence. Innocent, who was sweeping the *stoep*, looked up.

'Where's Precious?' Guido asked him, handing him a litre pack of *Inkomazi* soured milk. Innocent polished it off in a swift series of long gulps and explained that his sister was in tears because she'd heard that the priest at the church in their township had had his throat slit. For some cash and a cellphone.

'We loved him. He was like a father.'

Apparently, he was wearing casual clothes, and it was late at night in a rough area. Innocent said that the police will never find the killer, who will just melt into the background in one of the townships.

'But my sister says God will find him. She says it will take two or three years, but then he will die.'

'Perhaps she's right.'

'My sister is screwed up, Mr Guido,' he said, the corners of his mouth twisted down, his voice taking on a tragic tone that was close to comic. 'She sees things – always – things that scare her, things we can't see. She's always been screwed up.'

He shook his head in despair, and then suddenly slapped his thighs, and burst out in one of his deep, infectious laughs.

Guido gestured for him to sit next to him.

'Listen carefully,' he said, leaning forward. 'About the girl.

The ransom is for food and drugs for people in Honingsloot. Fortunately, they don't want these things in kind. We must pay cash.'

'Why is that fortunate, Mr Guido?'

'That way we have direct contact with them. Otherwise, we might have had to pay the food and drug suppliers direct, but never see the girl.'

'When they give us the girl, we kill them, right?'

'No. We give them the money; they give us the girl.'

'What if they don't, Mr Guido? What do we do?'

'We do whatever's necessary. Except for one of them. We'll persuade him to tell us where she is.'

'I need money for ammo, Mr Guido.'

Guido handed him a couple of notes. 'Get fifty rounds of soft points.'

At that moment, Christian appeared behind them. 'This is getting out of hand,' he cut in, his voice a parody of the affronted Englishman. 'I can't bring myself to be a part of this. It's quite wrong. You can't go around shooting people.'

'We probably won't have to,' Guido snapped. 'But this isn't cuddly Cape Town. In the rest of Africa, you adapt or become extinct. We have to prepare for the worst.'

Christian paused for a moment to think, his face anguished. 'And what is the worst?' he asked.

'That we all get killed.' Guido leaned back and let out a burst of laughter. 'Don't forget. We're amateurs. We're a couple of guys doing our best. But we must get this in perspective and understand the risks. These people are likely to be even more amateurish than we are. What makes them different, and therefore unpredictable, is that they're politically motivated rather than just out for money. But don't worry. The odds are in our favour. However, if they've had military training, we'll be a joke.'

'I've had military training, Mr Guido.' Innocent's eyes had changed from remoteness to black iciness. There was no twinkle of amusement left in them now. He jabbed the air with a finger as though in his mind's eye he was attacking with his switch-blade. 'If anyone thinks I'm a joke, they would not laugh for long.' He mouthed the words and spat them out like chunks of putrid meat.

Innocent could be menacing, not in the same way as some of history's tyrants; not the fatal blend of pure evil and disarming charm embodied in the likes of Shakespeare's Richard III, or Stalin, but he was a serious force to reckon with. Guido felt that if there were any limits to his violence, they would be few and tentative and would make him a very dangerous enemy.

On the other hand, sometimes he really was innocent. But if his innocence was abused, he would stop at nothing to avenge it. A month previously, he told Guido about how he had fallen for an old trick. He'd decided to save the bus fare and hitchhike from Limpopo to Johannesburg. He soon got a lift. The driver called in at a petrol station. When they tried to pull away the driver said there was something wrong with the engine. He asked Innocent to get out and push. As he did so, the car started and left without him. It left with his suitcase, papers, clothes, virtually everything Innocent possessed.

As he was telling Guido his story he had the calm composure of a man who was thinking to himself it could have been a lot worse, and who was convinced he could put it right. The next Friday he took the night bus back to the village where he'd been robbed. Sunday evening, he took a bus back and arrived just in time for work on Monday morning. When he turned up he had all his possessions with him.

'I found him. I dealt with him,' he told Guido. He never spoke of it again.

Darkness was already descending. Christian hadn't got the energy to continue the conversation. He just said 'goodnight' to the two of them and headed towards his room. He sat on the edge of the bed, rested his head in his hands, and tried to concentrate on the practicalities of saving Saskya. He understood he lacked the necessary experience to do it on his own. His decision to let Guido take his place, and particularly his motives for doing so, as well as his lying to Blessing about his inability to drive, worried him deeply on several levels. More importantly, he sensed a worrying sea change in his own attitude.

He hardly knew Guido, although he already regarded him as the antithesis of what he viewed as a morally good person. Yet he was becoming inexorably drawn into his world and his ways of dealing with things. At first, he had felt frightened but innocent. It was not his fault. But gradually he was feeling a nagging sense of responsibility for the direction he was taking. Step by tiny step the means to the end were leading him down a path he felt increasingly uncomfortable with.

But what choice did he have? He had been profoundly scared on several occasions since entering Africa, but this was different. This was a deep, gnawing fear that sent up waves of panic. How dangerous Saskya's situation was depended entirely on how dangerous Guido and Innocent could be. He tried desperately to smother his fear, but he knew his self-control was starting to slip. He plugged the electric mosquito repellent into the wall next to his bed and settled down to a troubled night.

Guido sat up with Innocent and continued discussing the

practicalities of meeting the kidnappers, until it was time for Innocent to do his rounds of the house and garden, checking that all was locked and safe for the night. Guido lingered on the *stoep* for a while, brooding over the events ahead. He knew the coming days would be the most difficult he'd encountered in a long time. He knew he should perhaps have thrashed out a fine-detailed plan of action that would get the job done and be acceptable to his cousin's craving for certainty and his ethical sensibilities. At the same time, he knew he shouldn't bother to think about it too much but do what he always did – outline a rough framework in his mind and leave the rest to chance. That way was always easier to adapt to any nasty surprises.

He went to his room and took a pad of paper, the black felt-tipped pen, his three gold coins and his copy of the *I-Ching*. He tossed all three coins six times until he had completed a hexagram on the pad. He looked it up in the book. Not for the first time, it confirmed the need to strictly persevere for a favourable outcome. Now his mind was made up. The rough outline of a plan was set. The die was cast. It was as simple and unequivocal as that. He found it difficult to suppress a self-effacing giggle.

13

Christian was woken by the sound of Shostakovich's Fifth Symphony. Dawn had already lightened the black sky with a streak of pale yellow. The sound of school kids playing on the street and the slap of a football hitting the fence pierced through the music's sombre tones and sent Tsotsi galloping to the gate barking his deep, wolfish bark.

Memories of Saskya hounded Christian with a vivid presence. Should he ever have moved to Lisbon, leaving her to fend for herself in London? After the divorce, he should have been more supportive, like his former wife, who would fly in from Denmark at the drop of a hat and stay for days on end if necessary. For the first time since the divorce, the melancholia that gripped him was close to making him feel physically ill. It felt like bereavement and he cursed himself for harbouring an emotion so inappropriate – one that was inextricably linked to the type of event that must not be allowed to happen. It almost smacked of acceptance of the worst.

He splashed water on his face and dried himself with a towel that gave off a pleasantly mnemonic smell of freshly air-dried washing sweeping him back to the safe, ordered existence of his marriage.

He found Guido downstairs sipping coffee on the sofa next to the music cabinet. The heroic music with its mixed undercurrents of optimism and mourning seemed to set the mood for the day they were preparing for – the day Saskya's kidnappers were ready to sell her back. The symphony offered two outcomes – grandeur and bombast reflecting success; or a meditative requiem reflecting a day that could end about as badly as it gets.

Christian tried to pass the morning by reading in the garden, but his mind was distracted by a chaotic jumble of thoughts jostling their way into the forefront of his consciousness. It was his father's birthday – or would have been had the poor soul not died a couple of decades previously. He cast his mind back to the fall that seemed to herald his dad's rapid decline into a prolonged, humiliating and agonising death.

It wasn't that his father's trousers were too small; it was that he hauled them up too high above his hips, leaving the bottoms at half-mast flapping above his ankles. One day, when he returned from shopping it was a flapping right trouser leg that caught Christian's eye – torn at the knee and caked with blood. The poor man had tripped over and sprawled flat out on his knees and face, taking a bite out of his lip that left him disfigured for the remaining two hellish years of his life.

Whenever Christian thought about his parents it depressed him. They were like two tiny, anxious caged sparrows at the end of their lives – helpless and trapped. His father died of cancer and his mother soon after following a bad fall. He felt guilty then; he felt guilty still. He had got caught in the crossfire between his mother and his mother-in-law that put him in a state of complete inertia and absence of comprehension.

His long-suffering wife was left on the touchline, powerless to intervene, frustrated and hurt. His attempt to achieve the 'morally right thing' – via the Aristotelian golden mean – by moderating his response, failed to adequately support any of them. It wasn't that he was disengaged – he was *too* engaged with them all and failed to see where his loyalties should have lain. It was an object lesson in how you cannot please all of the people all of the time. By that time his father was so ill, he wanted to die. This man who had survived two world wars and had lived in a Germany sentenced to extreme poverty by the Treaty of Versailles, a man who at the age of fourteen had to work to support his mother and sister who were so hungry they could barely walk. A man who, when he had time to himself, mixed with kids on Hannover's streets, who were so famished they were reduced to picking out the undigested oats from horse muck on the road. He survived and lived decently, only to be brought down by an agonising affliction in a country with unmerciful laws against mercy killing.

Christian often brooded on the thought that our relationship with the dead is very one-sided; that we can no longer affect them, yet they can ruin our lives.

His mind darted back to Saskya. He tried to tell himself that things tend to turn out all right in the end, but he wasn't convinced. He stared across the garden at an acacia tree used as a landing stage for a flock of bright-green parakeets. At first, he thought they were escaped pets, perhaps budgies. But there were too many of them and their long tails gave them away as a type of parrot found only in southern Africa. Their resplendent colour was such a fluorescent shade that pictures or photos of them could easily be mistaken for computer generated images.

It hadn't taken him long to feel strangely at home in the tranquillity of Guido's idyllic hideaway – safe, protected, as in a chrysalis – despite its proximity to one of the city's most dangerous districts. When Guido joined him Christian resolved to try to hide his sense of internal isolation.

'Sleep all right?' Guido asked, raising his eyebrows.

Christian shrugged. 'Not bad in the circumstances.'

He asked Guido if he could look around Honingsloot, just

to get a feel for the place. He said he needed to do something, and anything was better than just sitting around waiting. Guido called Innocent, and minutes later Christian was in the front seat of the Merc with Innocent behind the wheel, heading northeast.

Only a mile or so down the main road they were pulled over by the police at a roadblock. Innocent jumped out, called the policeman 'inspector' and started babbling away to him, pointing at Christian. All Christian could pick up was 'doctor' '*ingelisi*' and 'ulcer'. The inspector gave Christian a kindly look, and the next minute they were on their way again.

'When it is you, Mr Christian, what gets stopped by the police, reverse a little bit to show respect,' Innocent explained. 'At night you must stay in the car but open your window and ask if you can get out. In the day you must get out and start to open your wallet. You must smile and be polite and say *how are you, officer?* You must not make sudden movements in your jacket, or you will frighten them, and they will shoot you. If you have committed a small offence, you must say *here is my licence. I know I have done something wrong, so please let me buy you a cool drink*. You must say this very quietly. Then give him your passport with a note in it, or you must put the note in your hand, and shake his hand to say goodbye.'

'I'm sorry, Innocent,' Christian replied, puffing out his chest. 'I don't really approve of that kind of thing.'

'Otherwise, you pay a big fine.'

'I'd rather pay the fine.'

'But you must spend the night in a holding cell for everyone until you pay the fine the next day. The other prisoners will beat you and rape you in the night, Mr Christian.'

'I see,' Christian murmured to himself in a tone of disbelief. He bowed his head, deep in thought, and let the matter drop.

Honingsloot township was made up of rows of low, rickety squats, each one entirely individual in the way it had made use of resources available from a nearby waste tip – corrugated iron, oil drums, torn strips of sacking. Wide-open doors revealed that sheets from old editions of *The Tribune* served as excellent wallpaper. The sun was already blazing from a cloudless sky. The suffocating smell was of something rotting, or of everything rotting.

Potbellied kids, some naked, rushed up to the car as it picked its way down the narrow track between the shacks. Some had the stamina to keep up, but most fell back to return to their play among the bald, filthy goats and chickens, and bird-picked remains of rats next to an open sewer. The stench worsened as they pressed on deeper into the settlement.

They were soon lost among the nameless tracks. Christian was struck by the friendliness of the people they asked for directions – until they drifted into a more prosperous area at the edge of the township. The brightly-coloured brick bungalows with rooftop satellite discs for those that had managed to better themselves were hemmed in by razor wire, electric fencing and twenty-four-hour armed security.

Not for the first time he felt the need to re-evaluate the way he himself lived and the role of property in alienating people from each other. Not that he believed for one minute that his reflections would ever change anything he did. Not only because what he called his immediate 'stakeholders' would have a problem with it, but because he would never have the courage to do things differently. Such thoughts served only to make him restless.

As if his thoughts weren't restless enough. Where in this filthy warren of human joy, laughter, thumping music, violence and misery was Saskya? Was she duct-taped to a chair in a shack with a sack over her head, or watching satellite television in a bungalow? Was she scared or bored? Was she reading, or discussing Che Guevara with her revolutionary captors? Was she really here?

He'd seen enough and needed to put as much distance as possible between himself and Honingsloot and his dread of what might be happening to her. At the same time, he wanted to linger, and search every one of the thousands of homes until he found her, then gather her up and wrap her in her old woollen blanket from over two decades ago that still had her milky baby smell, so that he could nurture and protect and save her from the vileness that life can bring.

Innocent had stopped the car and was staring silently in front of him. He got out, banging his head on the roof as he uncoiled his long body. He stretched himself, walked around the car twice, and squeezed himself back behind the wheel.

'We must go, Mr Christian,' he stated gently, staring ahead again.

Christian nodded. 'Take me home.' It struck him as surprising at how quickly he'd come to use *home* to describe his temporary refuge.

14

Guido nurtured a reluctant admiration for Innocent, his integrity, his toughness and his command of six languages, although their conversations sometimes produced insane misunderstandings, after which they would usually collapse with laughter. But this time, the tension in the air dampened any chance of that.

Innocent announced that he'd like to go to his church in Soweto the next morning to pray for Saskya. In the circumstances, Guido didn't want him away for any longer than necessary.

'Why don't you attend the congregation in Melville Koppies instead? It's just down the road.'

'I can't. My angel wouldn't know where I am. He knows I am in Soweto. I must trumpet for him in Soweto. All people are welcome to our church. You must come with me. We love all people. They would make you feel at home. I say to them, this is my director. They will be very proud. You can pray.'

'Take the Merc, just this once,' Guido ordered. 'Get back as soon as you can.'

Innocent bowed, bringing his head on level with Guido's, and gave him one of his widest, brightest smiles. Guido chuckled, and thought to himself that Innocent's fortitude could never be acquired from books and gurus. It came from felt, deep-down experience and acceptance of his limitations and fallibilities, and especially of those around him. No so-called self-development classes could have given him that.

'Christian wants to use the iron, Precious.'
'What for?'

'His shirt. You washed it?'

'It's on the line. I'll iron it *now-now*.'

'He wants to do it himself.'

'What?'

'He wants – '

'Why?'

'He doesn't think it's right that women should be expected to do it.'

'Eh?' She looked blank, frozen by incomprehension.

'He hasn't got a wife.'

'I'm not surprised! Is he sick?'

'No. Just different.'

'I don't like different.' She shook her head, stood back, and straightened her striped apron. 'You are not different.' She looked him up and down. 'You are hungry again, Mr Guido? You are a child. You are old. An old man becomes a child again. He gets hungry like a child. *Ne*?' She patted his stomach, giggled and turned back to the stove. 'I make you something nice.'

Guido heard Christian in the dining room and wandered through to join him. He sat down heavily at the far side of the table and waved Christian into a chair opposite him. Precious stayed in the kitchen preparing a supper of mealie meal, a Dutch-Indonesian pickle called *achaar* and beef stew. Guido had already warned her in the nicest possible way that more vegetables would be welcome, to which she replied 'For sure. Soon,' the same as she did the previous times he'd asked her. Completely absorbed in her task, her husky voice softly sang a gospel song in Sepedi with an English chorus – *Life is beautiful, he died on Calvary*.

'A glass of wine?'

Christian thanked him, and let his eyes roam the huge room.

'Lovely place you've got here,' he commented.

Guido let out a deep chuckle. 'It'll do for now.'

Christian noticed a smell of *crème de menthe* on Guido's breath.

Precious sauntered in carrying two plates of steaming beef stew.

'I forgot to tell you, Precious. Christian doesn't eat meat.'

'What?' She had that blank look again, that usually heralded the onset of a fit of giggles. This time it was clouded with genuine incomprehension.

'Shall I make chicken?' she asked, still holding the plates.

'Chicken *is* meat.'

'Chicken is bird!'

'Make him an omelette from a couple of bird eggs. I'll show you how. Excuse me, Christian.'

She gave him a look, put one plate down and headed back to the kitchen with the other. Guido followed her.

She turned to him, hands on hips. 'Some white men are not real men, *ne*, Mr Guido?' she whispered. 'You eat nice meat, you are nice in bed, *ne*?'

She turned toward the cupboard and wiggled her bum at him. Glancing back with her wide, naughty smile, she subsided into a deep belly laugh. *My Precious*, he thought to himself, and then thought of Gollum in Tolkien's *Lord of the Rings* – Gollum, pitiable, loveable, deceitful, vile; a deeply divided creature of the night banished from his homeland, who loved and hated his precious ring in the same way that Guido loved and hated himself and how he was torn between his lust and love for his 'Precious', his special love for his deceased wife, and his desire to be free of attachment to everything and everyone.

By the time Christian went to his room, he was confused,

stunned, and exhausted. Another day without Saskya. He rang Blessing's number, but there was no answer. He threw his jacket on the bed and stared sadly through the window at the thin crescent moon and the evening star. He felt completely depleted of emotion, as though it had been drained from him like a blood donation.

He kicked off his shoes and lay down. Lying on his back, head on his hands, he tried carefully to analyse the situation against the background of his visit to Honingsloot and Guido's plan of action. He could hear his own indignant voice, a parody of the English stiff upper lip – *This isn't right!* No, it wasn't. But what was the alternative? Even if he'd had the mental strength to try to think of alternatives, his mind wouldn't let him. He was drawn irresistibly towards thinking only of Saskya – silly Saskya, frustrating Saskya, bright, warm, generous-natured Saskya, midfield defender in the local under-9s football team, saviour of the underdog.

At his wife's insistence, they had returned to her mother's house in a village outside Copenhagen for Saskya's birth. When the labour pains became more frequent and regular, Christian had run her a relaxing warm bath and cooked a full English breakfast. When the time came later that day, her mother called the midwife, and by late evening Saskya Eleonora was born in the bath to the sound of Pink Floyd's *Is there anybody out there?*

Then there were the holidays in France's Les Landes, singing as they walked among the pines along the sandy tracks leading to the lakes. Afternoons at the sea, body surfing in the Atlantic rollers. Her delight each morning when she awoke to find that he'd returned from the village with crusty baguettes, fresh croissants and proper apricot jam stuffed with *whole* apricots.

Back in Britain, she decided to study in Edinburgh on the

basis that it was the most prestigious university that was an acceptable distance from her parents in the South East. *Really* leaving home. In her first week, her bike was stolen. In the second week, she announced that she'd hooked up with a 'really nice bloke with a car' who happened to be a vital cog in the local branch of the ultra-right-wing British National Party. In a letter home, she enclosed a polaroid photo of the two of them at the Student Union bar – she with her hair dyed a bright red and spiked up, and him with no hair, tattoos across his forehead and a swastika earring. Christian was in a state of extreme alarm. His wife wasn't in the least bit concerned.

'They're young,' she told him, soothingly.

'Not too young to kick the living daylights out of any immigrant unfortunate enough to stumble under one of his *bovver* boots,' he reminded her.

But she would just shake her head as if he himself were the oddity.

To Christian's immense relief, the *bovver* boots soon marched the young skinhead into the arms of an older punk with a ring through her nose. Heartbroken, Saskya was suddenly history and without a cause. She quickly mended her heart, punched the air, re-dyed her hair auburn, took to wearing dresses, and joined the Spiritualist Church. She also dropped all three of her subjects, took up another three in a different faculty, and two years later passed all of them *cum laude*. Saskya was brilliant.

Saskya was gone.

He felt muzzy with tiredness, making it difficult to marshal his thoughts. They returned to his poor old father, his memory preserved only in fading black and white photos. In group photos, he would always be somewhere at the back or to one side so that if you pencilled in a circle around the group he would be on the edge or just outside it. His suffering had served as a stark judgement that there is no god, only a cold, indifferent universe.

What made it even more tragic was that if he'd been lucky enough to have settled in the Netherlands before the war, rather than a few hundred miles away in England – a tiny distance in world terms – he could have been put out of his agony under Dutch euthanasia laws. If he'd been a dog, he'd have been put down. After he had suffered weeks of agony, his nurse reserved a little bit of the poor man's morphine dose each day and hid it in his house. At huge personal risk, she finally injected the lot. And off he floated, in Christian's arms, reduced to a shell weighing little more than a young child.

After his father's death, his mother was admitted to hospital following a fall, after which he moved her to an old folks' home. Some weeks later she had another fall – this time fatal. He felt he had done his best by arranging a home, but that his best was not good enough. His mother's last words were 'I'll never forgive you for this'. And he never forgave himself. He regularly recalled the moment her blue bespectacled eyes had caught his own and then darted away. If they had rested on him a second longer he could have read what they were telling him. It was their swiftness and their refusal to return that left him suspended on one side of a bridge that she was about to cross, never to return. Whatever offence his good intentions had caused would remain forever beyond atonement. One week later she was dead. Poisonous, wrenching, corrosive guilt had nowhere to go apart from deep inside.

It took years for the pain to subside, and even then, it never completely went away. There were always little reminders. After his dad died, Christian got rid of most of his belongings except the pipe in which his father had smoked his honey-fragrant Golden Virginia tobacco. Years passed before he could bring himself to take that last relic into the garden and bury it.

Finally, his eyes heavy with worry and regret, Christian rolled over onto his side and drifted into a troubled sleep.

Guido too was restless. He switched on the ceiling fan, not because of the heat, but to blow away the mosquitoes, and then lay listening to Precious' rhythmic breathing, and the sounds of the night – the occasional gunshot and then the chain reaction of barking dogs started first by the one next door, followed by all the others up and down the street like a vocal version of a Mexican wave.

He knew he had no choice but to help his cousin, however irritating the man could be. And he could be extremely irritating. On the other hand, Guido realised long ago that competition and conflict with others is self-defeating and pointless. This wasn't because he was a naturally nice, sociable guy. It was at a philosophical level. Influenced by his previous business partner, he came to the realisation that all people basically are imperfect creatures in the same boat and that conflict derives from the illusion that individuals are exactly that – individual. Helping save Saskya wasn't a decision; it was just the way it was. But he knew there would be a price to pay that would be far higher than mere money. Meanwhile, he would shut his mind to the possible details. He rolled his shoulders back and resolved simply to get on with thinking about the planning this would entail. Perhaps a pipe would help.

'Precious.'

'I know, Mr Guido. I make it for you *now-now*.'

Guido pulled out the bottom drawer of the dressing table and gazed intently down at it, his eyes already in a misty state of contemplation. It was empty except for a photograph of his wife. She had been a beautiful soul taken too soon, leaving a huge, gaping space that could never be filled. He stared at it for a moment and allowed its presence to fill him, and the memories it evoked to scratch at old, still tender scars. The drawer also used to safeguard a scarf imbued with her perfume. He burned it when the perfume was exhausted, and the scarf smelled only of age.

He dragged his gaze away from the drawer, trying not to make it obvious for fear of – not offending Precious – but of making her anxious. He momentarily returned his eyes to let them rest on the photograph for a few seconds longer, imprinting the image onto the forefront of his mind, then quietly closed the drawer, lit the lamp, and switched off the lights.

He imagined his wife gently touching his face as she always used to before the yellow fever vaccine took hold of her and her own immune system began to feed on her like a rampant parasite. He let her hair run through his fingers, but she kept fading out of view to make way for other, less welcome ghosts.

It had taken him sixty-five years to get this far. Forty years previously he wouldn't have needed a pipe to view the world around him as he wished to view it now – in all its natural beauty absorbed by all his senses, and the impression of brotherhood with his fellow beings. But in the meantime, he had seen too much to contradict many of those feelings, which were now available only through dim visions to relieve him of his anxieties, and even obsessions, particularly regarding his own mortality which had been whispering more often and more loudly during the past year or so. He was now struggling to maintain a grip on the one entity that had not been formed by his senses – his basic *self* – and on the one recurring fear that the walls protecting this too could be breached by dementia or madness.

The pipe gave him a delicious sense of solitude within which he felt he would be safely preserved, even during and beyond his own death. As he drifted into a vague state of benign detachment, his lovely Precious was there at his side, but he was not available to her. He had entered an indifferent, infinite universe governed by the wisdom of the fool and the foolishness of the sage, where there was no truth or falsehood, no right or wrong, devoid of all the imaginary binary opposites that usually tormented him. There was just a delicious sense of the synthesis of all things.

Then, as his mind drifted down to his own world among the sound of chirping birds, the smell of pines and freshly baked bread, the touch of soft sand and the taste of salty lips, he was available to no one except his wife, whose smiling face, framed by her luxuriant waist-length chestnut hair, floated above him, full of care and forgiveness.

15

Christian had hardly slept before he woke up feeling drained by a nightmare about missing a flight. He'd been trying to pack his suitcase but couldn't shut it. He couldn't bear to leave anything behind, so had tried frantically again and again to close the zip. Finally, he had to search for a larger case. By the time he reached the airport it was too late.

He rolled away from the sweat-soaked half of the bed, stared into the darkness and tried to focus his mind on the consequences of missing his flight to London, then tried to drift off again but felt hunger pangs. He had a sudden craving for a glass of warm milk. He dressed and took the wide stairs to the ground floor 'one step at a time' as Saskya would have teased him, trying desperately not to make a sound with his stick. At the bottom of the stairs, he felt a sudden lump in his throat, and leant against the doorframe in a dizzy surge of nausea.

He entered the dining room. He stood stock still. Precious was sitting at the table. Her arms were curved around a cognac glass next to a bottle of Rémy Martin and an ashtray. She looked up and exhaled cigarette smoke.

'Can't sleep?' she enquired. 'Me neither. Come and sit with me. Drink?'

Christian shook his head and whispered, 'Thank you. I'd just like a glass of milk.'

She stubbed out her cigarette, pushed down on the table and stood up in one seductively fluid movement that caused Christian to look away. She returned with a glass of milk and as she handed it to him, she gently squeezed his shoulder.

'This is so awful for you.' she purred, looking straight into his eyes.

Thinking back later, he couldn't tell whether it was her touch, her look or her words, that caused him to break down. She pulled her chair closer and stroked his back as tears gushed down his face and his body convulsed.

'I'm, I'm so sorry,' he managed.

'Hush. It's fine. Just let go.'

In the faint, flickering candlelight that illuminated only their faces like an artist's use of chiaroscuro, and dizzy from the scent of her body that mingled with her musky perfume, he did indeed let go. Uncharacteristically, he didn't pull his hand away as she covered it with hers. He just surrendered to her overwhelming aura. Once he had started talking in a whisper, he couldn't hold it back.

'The thought of never seeing Saskya again makes me feel sick to the stomach,' he muttered. 'I haven't even told her mother. I can't. I can't put it in words.'

He confessed to her that he couldn't bear the thought of never having the opportunity to tell her things that he had kept from her; that he needed the opportunity to explain about his sole, rash moment of unfaithfulness in Charleroi, and that he was afraid that her lack of understanding of his divorce might mean that she would bear a grudge against her mother for leaving him.

'What was Saskya like?' Precious asked in the past tense and quickly caught herself in time to follow with, 'I mean, what was she like as a little child?'

Christian told her about how proud he was when Saskya emerged from her mother in the bath at home; how she quickly grew up into a tomboy regularly bunking off school, only to veer between the black, masculine clothes of a Goth and the feminine outfits she wore to the Spiritualist Church.

'What does she do for a living?'

111

'She started off as a freelance journalist writing for animal-rights magazines but is now training to be a teacher.'

'Has she got a boyfriend?'

'Not now. She's had quite a few. None of them was good enough. She recently dumped the last one.'

'Don't worry, Mr Christian. You do not know Mr Guido. You only knew him when he was Marco. He and my brother will make everything right again.'

'But I must tell her mother. I feel awful.'

'Not now. Soon. Now we must move silently. Like a leopard. She'll understand.'

She got to her feet and smiled a smile that filled him with a warmth that seemed to coil down to his abdomen.

'Try to get some sleep,' she told him, squeezing his upper arm. 'Good night.'

Christian was finally woken by birdsong at first light. There were no other detectable sounds. He languished on his back in the warmth of the cotton sheet and tried to fight down a nagging sense of abandonment. There were now four days to the deadline. The thought of it caused a tense ache at the nape of his neck. The implications of what had happened and the possible solution to it were deeply registered in his mind. Yet it was incredible it had come to this.

Without warning the weather changed. Christian, propped on his elbow, listened to the sound of a steady downpour. He reached for his stick and hung it on the edge of the bedside table next to him before hauling himself out of bed. He put on his glasses, limped to the window, and gazed at a row of pied crows perched on an electricity cable, preening themselves in ecstasy, ruffling their wet feathers and cawing at each other with delight. The rich, sensuous scent of various flowers rose up from the damp garden.

A vivid image of the gap-toothed smile of the driver of the red Toyota taxi, like a broken piano keyboard flashing friendly warmth, kept entering the forefront of his mind. He recalled the moment when the overwhelming enormity of the situation had begun to dawn on him. Agitation and self-doubt came rolling back in waves, churning inside him in a mad turmoil. His head throbbed, and his heart kept missing a beat and pumping in an erratic, irregular rhythm that made him lose his sense of balance and tighten his grip on the crook of his stick.

He dressed for the second time that night, splashed water on his face and shuffled his way downstairs.

It was Sunday. Bach's *St Matthew Passion* playing in the lounge lent a solemn, meditative tone to the start of the day. Tsotsi was on guard duty at the gate, barking ferociously at a lone priest outside, dressed in a white robe roped at the waist, and carrying a staff, whispering into a brand new mobile phone as though calling up his angels.

Precious, dressed in a fluorescent green that clashed sickeningly with the pink of her apron, served him a breakfast of scrambled eggs and toast in the dining room.

'Did you get back to sleep?' she asked.

He nodded. 'Thank you so, so much.'

She just smiled, squeezed his shoulder and left for the kitchen. A wide-open window let in a light breeze imbued with the fresh scent of the garden's exotic plants and flowers.

The rain did not last long, and the sun soon came out again. The air was drenched with the heavy scent of flowers and the earthy aroma of a freshly ploughed field.

Guido showered and changed into a black shirt and jeans, and joined Christian, suggesting they sit outside at the table on the *stoep* overlooking the garden lawn bordered by tropical plants and guarded by huge palm trees. Christian was

113

gradually taking to Guido, despite their fundamental differences. He had gained an impression of Guido as a man who knew how to grow old well, and who welcomed the wisdom and comfort that comes with the passing of the years. He also seemed to be extremely fit for his age.

As a child, Christian had been ashamed of his own skinny legs and gangly arms, and ribs that stuck out like the wooden notes of an African marimba. Riddled with senseless guilt about his perceived uselessness, he tried to help his father in the garden or around the house, but felt even more useless in the presence of this short, stocky German with sinewy arms, who lifted heavy weights effortlessly, had been an athlete and a footballer, and who could work long hours tirelessly.

He felt the same guilt towards his mother, a toned, fit, buxom woman who had met his father at an athletics club in London, after his father's flight from Germany, and who loved nothing better than to thrash his father at tennis. Christian was the only child to emerge from that flat, muscled belly. Meanwhile, no matter what his father's expression, even when full of love and tenderness, he read in it disappointment and would return to the corner of the garden and his Puffin books.

He basked in the intensity of his parents' love and tender care that was focused only on him. To relieve his solitude, he invented a cousin Paul as company of his own age, who would share his imaginary games, and sit next to him at mealtimes, bowing his head during grace. His mother never quite understood his annoyance when she interrupted one of these games to ask who he was talking to. And sleep was usually a long time coming, and only after a lengthy series of *Our Fathers* and *Hail Marys* and tearful supplications for heavenly intervention to replace his foot with a normal one.

Christian never took for granted the stroke of amazing

good fortune that had blessed him with parents whose bottomless tolerance and blind faith enabled him to be whatever he wanted to be whenever he wanted it. He was not spoiled in material terms. Times were tough after a war that had bankrupted Europe. Allowed a degree of freedom rarely enjoyed by his contemporaries to choose his path in life, he recognised that their selflessness and capacity for self-sacrifice were scarce.

Marked by his difference, and alienated from his peers, his orthopaedic shoe for which he'd been mercilessly mocked as a young child, held him back like a ball and chain. His recollection of grammar school was mainly of its smell – a disturbing blend of civilised wax polish and the ever-present fear of bullying and punishment. Yet it wasn't as much of a trial as it could have been because his parents had been clever enough to send him to one that was co-educational, where he could sit in the library during sports lessons, and spend breaks with the girls, a few of whom taunted him, but most of whom mothered him.

'How did you become *Guido*?' Christian asked.

'There are a lot of people in Jo'burg who share my profession,' Guido replied. 'A new passport was merely a question of money, which was not in short supply, thanks to my own gift for imitating real life.'

Guido, baptised Marco, had British nationality granted to his German father after the war. In his next life, in Uganda, Marco was a German-Israeli Jew with the name Julius. And now he was a South African.

'What did you do in Uganda?' Christian asked.

'I helped my business partner.' Guido took a sip of coffee. His hand was perfectly steady. 'His company supplied medicines to African countries. Kenya mainly. We sourced them from China and Taiwan. In breach of patent, but good quality. We sold them at a fraction of the price of brand-name drugs.'

'That's surely illegal?'

'Sure. But is it immoral, Prof?' He smiled wryly. 'The big boys tried to shut us down. An American drugs producer succeeded in court action for patent breach, trademark infringement and so-called unfair competition. They also falsely accused us of supplying sub-standard products. That was a long time ago, when our business was based in Europe, not long after you and I met for the last time when I was still a journalist. The courts seized all our assets, and it looked as though my partner would be gaoled. It was then that we set up in Uganda near the Kenyan border. It was around that time that antiretrovirals for Aids patients became a big market. We were popular with small hospitals and clinics because ordinary people could afford our prices. It was then that I learned the craft of copycat. To protect the buyer against possible legal action and culpability, I forged accompanying documents such as certificates of origin and goods inspection certificates.'

'Yes, I do think it's immoral,' Christian cut in, his voice rising slightly. 'Look at the millions of dollars the drugs companies pump into research and development and providing an after sales service. They deserve a fair return on investment. Otherwise, why would they bother?'

'A fair return, sure. But twenty capsules of an antibiotic from an American or European multinational cost the average family here their weekly wage. These drugs are protected by patent. It's like a monopoly. They can charge what they like.'

'Patents don't last forever.'

'Most of them are for twenty years. But that's not the point. They charge too much.'

116

'But if prices were lower, the manufacturers couldn't afford to develop new drugs.'

'Okay. Drug development is high risk and costly,' Guido acknowledged, shaking his head. 'But why should poor countries pay for it? Profits on many drugs essential to Africans, like antibiotics, go to fund research into medicines for typically western diseases like heart disease, diabetes and arthritis. They shouldn't have to subsidise the rich who eat and drink themselves sick.'

Precious joined them but remained standing. She looked down at her fingers fiddling with the sleeve of her green dress. Guido tapped his cigarette patiently on a silver ashtray. Christian shifted on his chair and looked passed her.

'I need to go back,' she announced solemnly. 'For a burial.'

'Whose?' Guido could hardly look at her with the sun in his eyes.

She lifted her face and swept away a long strand of wiry, jet-black hair. 'The priest. Remember?'

'Sorry. Yes. Did they find the killers?'

She shook her head and helped herself to one of Guido's cigarettes. She lit it, took a deep drag, turned and blew the smoke away from them.

'They'll die anyway. They're cursed.'

She suggested that if he didn't mind she'd like to leave immediately to take the night bus.

Guido stared at her in silence, and then asked, 'How long will you be gone? I need you here.'

Precious looked at the smoke curling up from the cigarette smouldering between her fingers. 'Three days.' Her voice trailed off with a sigh.

'And Innocent? Doesn't he want to go?' Guido was starting to sound annoyed.

'No. I can represent him. They say he must not come

there. It's the community people. They say that when he goes and there is a birth, the mother or father dies. Two sisters and two brothers have died. Everyone is jealous of him. He is different. Even his height is held against him. They get the *Sangoma* to cast a bad spell on others and blame him.'

Guido agreed that she should go but found it difficult to disguise a note of disappointment.

'Can I give you anything to take with you?' he asked.

'Please don't ask me if I want a gift. If I want apples or food what must I say? Please just put something in a bag and give it to me. Have you any old shoes? We have many children who have no parents. All bad shoes and clothes can be made good again.'

Guido nodded and smiled. 'I'll see what I can do. Wait for Inno. He's at church. He'll take you to the bus.'

She took his wrist, pressed the cigarette into an ashtray, and held his hand in hers.

16

Guido left his studio and breathed in the warm air infused with the scent of lavender that always took him back to the smell of his mother's dresses. The waning day was full of red and gold light. One solitary cloud in an otherwise clear sky floated above the house, its fleecy underbelly a candyfloss pink. As it crossed the sun it produced a fleeting, sombre shadow that made him shiver.

Then darkness descended with frightening suddenness, as it always does in Johannesburg. Guido went inside the house to look for Christian, and suggested, 'a little *tête-à-tête*' in the garden. Christian followed him through the French windows and across the lawn to the edge of the pool, the underwater lighting providing a deep sapphire luminescence.

The air around the pool was laden with the aroma of a blend of sun oil and chlorine. The sound of rustling leaves and the occasional sharp crack of a dry twig betrayed the presence of Innocent patrolling the perimeter of the grounds. Guido pulled out two wooden deck chairs and moved them to the edge of the pool.

He poured them both a beer and noticed Christian's hand shaking as he brought the glass to his lips.

'What are your feelings about all this?' Guido asked gently. 'Now that you've had a chance to take it all in?'

'I'm beginning to understand your point of view, but I would rather have left it to the police.'

'A few days ago, you seemed doubtful about police corruption.'

'I was?' Christian asked with a note of indifference, as though ready to forfeit a golden opportunity to let rip on one of his lectures.

'Let me start you off,' Guido suggested, sitting back in his chair. 'Some of these cops earn big bucks tipping off vehicle recovery companies about accidents and accepting bribes from drunk drivers and even fabricated offences. Then there's the sale of fake driver's licences, soliciting protection money from informal traders, sex from sex workers, selling operations information to criminals, leasing firearms, to name just a few examples. And don't say they have to because they're not paid enough. It's greed, not need.'

Christian managed to raise some enthusiasm. 'The training in ethical decision-making I used to do in Portugal can stop all that.'

'How?'

'It teaches skills such as how to confront a colleague about unethical behaviour, how to refuse an unethical proposal, how to disclose something one has done that, in hindsight, might be considered unethical. I'll tell you all about it once I've got my Saskya back.'

'Has this ever been put into effect?'

'Sure. In the Netherlands.'

'Did it work?'

'One hundred percent.'

A chuckle of laughter suddenly welled up in him.

'What's so funny?' Christian asked, his voice betraying irritation.

'I dunno,' he replied, still grinning. 'You're so – so wonderfully virginal. Have you ever dealt with this country's police?'

'On occasion.'

'And?'

'A decent lot. When we needed – '

'That's Cape Town for you – a little lump of Europe stuck

to the sole of Africa's foot. I couldn't see it catching on here.'

Christian hunched his shoulders and looked Guido straight in the eye. 'Sorry to change the subject,' he said. 'I can't concentrate on anything apart from Sas. I still need to decide either to involve the police or make sure we handle this properly. We can't go around shooting people.'

'For fuck's sake, man, how can you sit there moralising about this when your daughter's life might be on the line?' His outburst came out of a clear blue sky. Christian thought his use of the f-word seemed strangely at odds with his aristocratic accent.

'It's how I cope. I have to think in ethical theories to guide how I act.'

'Bugger the theories. They're not going to save anybody.'

'I've just explained – '

'I know. It helps you cope.'

Guido leant back in his chair, hands clasped behind his head. 'This isn't Cape Town. Your smart intellectualising over your G&Ts simply won't cut it.'

Christian just stared down at his hands. *What a prat!* he thought to himself. *I should tell him to his face.* But he told himself that there was something unsettlingly mercurial about Guido, that this was hardly the right moment to upset him, and that anyway he would never want to risk confronting an 'upset' Guido. Moral courage would have to wait for another day. He threw him a look that suggested he was missing the point.

'The question is, do you try to control your environment, or adapt to it?' Guido was leaning forward slightly. 'I heard you talking about Marx. He called on people to change history. He said the philosophers have only interpreted the world; the point is to change it.'

'You don't have to be so patronising, Guido. It's my

subject. It's my daughter. Have you got a daughter?' A sharp pang of regret shot through his chest.

Gritting his molars, Guido replied, 'No. Nor have you at the moment. I might not be a prof, but I do know what I'm doing. Could you do this on your own? If it went wrong, what'd you do – grab your stick and run for it?'

'My God, you've changed. That's so below the belt,' Christian shouted, his face contorted like a clenched fist. His anger, too impotent to translate into action, stifled him. He struggled to get to his feet but felt weak and powerless. Where was his stick? He managed to stand without it, glowering, feet wide apart.

Guido answered by getting to his feet in one nimble movement, flicking his cigarette butt over Christian's shoulder, turning on his heel, and then stumbling over Christian's stick. 'For Christ's sake!' he spat, before heading for the kitchen.

He returned minutes later with two more beers, a bowl of mixed nuts and a more composed attitude.

'Sorry, Man. Really sorry,' he said, with a wry, apologetic grin. He beat his chest three times in imitation of the *mea culpa*. 'I'm a bit tense. Not used to working with others. Bit of a loner. Just ignore me.'

Christian nodded. 'I'd appreciate your taking me a bit more seriously.'

'How old are you, Christian?' he asked, prising open the bottles, and filling the glasses.

'Sixty-five.'

'Same as me. How did you ever get that far just on the back of ideas?'

'It's what I do. That's what makes me who I am. I'm a philosopher.'

'Grab this idea. I take you seriously, but you can't

philosophise your way out of this one, or you might never see her again. It's action time. I'll handle it my way. I'll pay for it my way. If not, you're on your own.'

Christian looked away. He opened his mouth to speak but suddenly felt foolish, as though anything he could possibly say would fill the room with spiteful laughter. A dog barked somewhere outside in the dark. Christian pushed away his beer bottle, and then looked out beyond the fence and the amber glow to the darkness beyond. The lawn was a weird, unnatural shade of green in the artificial light.

'This is all too much.' He shook his head as though to clear it.

Guido took a pull at his glass, lit a cigarette, got up and paced the tiled edge of the pool. He reminded himself that you can't instil courage. You can encourage with stirring words but it's pointless to shout at someone to pull themselves together. All you can do is lend some of your own courage, give them support and make them feel good about who they are and what they are, and that it's worth remembering that anyone can be brave if they're not afraid, and that really brave people are not fearless. They are those who manage to overcome their fears. He was convinced that Christian could eventually count himself among them. He sat down again, drained the glass, linked his hands and leaned towards Christian.

'My friend Charles was an army officer in charge of interrogating Japanese prisoners when the war ended,' he said while refilling their glasses. 'He and two sergeants escorted a couple of prisoners in a truck to the interrogation centre. On the way, the prisoners, unaware that Charles understood Japanese, were exchanging anecdotes in gory detail about how they'd sadistically tortured their British prisoners. Charles said he might possibly have been able to ignore them were it not for their insane squeaky giggling and their obvious lack of remorse. When they reached the centre, the two were led upstairs to a top-floor office. Outside the door, one looked at the other and giggled again. Charles nodded to his sergeants, who threw them both over the bannister to their death at the bottom of the stairwell.'

'Good God! Why are you telling me this?'

'According to most moral rules, what he did was absolutely wrong – man's worst crime. Yet, I believe I would have done the same. I might even have sliced them in the truck. Wouldn't you?'

'No, I don't believe I would.' He sounded indignant.

'Charles thought about that incident every day for the rest of his life. Other killings on the battlefield didn't bother him. It was his cold-blooded killing of those two sadists that ate away at his conscience all those years, and for which he was unable to forgive himself. What do you make of that?'

'The conscience is a peculiar entity and quite random in its…'

As Christian prattled on, a dizzy feeling came over Guido. His thoughts returned to that defining moment in Nairobi decades previously when he'd hurled himself at the husband of his ex-wife, and how the balcony rail had given way. Guido balanced on the balcony's edge, cautiously peering through the darkness to the broken body below, face down, prone as though deep asleep except for one arm that stuck out at an odd angle, the broken body of a man whom he later discovered had betrayed South African colleagues whose own bodies had been broken at the hands of Special Branch interrogators. Guido had managed to slip away unnoticed. The verdict? Death by misadventure. He'd got away with it. Or had he? It haunted him night and day. That was the day the chakras shut, opening only at his discretion, only for the right people at the right moments; only partly open, like windows with a safety catch.

What would Christian make of it? Guido shook his head and lit another cigarette, his hands trembling slightly. Christian was still talking. Guido hadn't heard a word and doubted whether he'd missed anything.

'… precious,' Christian concluded.

'What about her?'

'What about who?'

'Precious.'

'Eh? Your domestic?'

'She's not a domestic!' Guido's voice again strayed towards irritation. 'In the late seventies, I freelanced for Africa's more progressive media. My impression of whites was that they were incapable of making their own bed, washing up, cooking a meal, gardening, cleaning their car and every other stupid thing people with any kind of dignity do for themselves, or, if not, then at least pay a proper wage to have it done for them. The way I saw it from Europe was that whites in Africa exploited what was little better than slave labour to carry out these domestic chores while they fattened themselves with their *braais* and drunk themselves silly. Since SA's democracy in 1994, the middle classes are now of all races and colours, but the domestic and menial jobs are still carried out by the bowing, curtsying poor, who earn a pittance and live in shacks. Precious is *not* a domestic!'

'And Innocent?'

'I pay Precious and Innocent ten thousand between them and give them a home. I provide all the food they can eat, so long as they cook it themselves, and leave some for me. Does he bow? Does she curtsy?' He shook his head. 'You should pay your helpers enough to enable them to live decently, right? The middle classes are accessories to poverty. And that includes you academics and liberals who bang on about it. It's a blind spot.'

Christian held up his hands to protest, but Guido pressed on: 'If you can't afford to pay a decent wage, then you should roll up your sleeves, muck in and clean your own house and car yourself. It's basic. And don't forget, when people like us live in Africa, we're among the wealthiest people on the continent. We can afford to pay our way.'

'Where's Precious now?' Christian asked, keen to change the subject.

'On her way to the funeral in Polokwane. She'll also see her kids.'

'She's got kids? But I thought – '

'You thought we were an item?'

'Sort of.'

'While she's here we suit each other. That suits us both. She's got a man back home. She's officially married to him, but...' He shrugged. 'He's not the father of her kids. Those men disappeared long ago. Responsibility-shy.'

'Have you ever met them?'

Who?'

'The kids.'

'No. I've seen photos of them when they were toddlers. A couple of little sweeties. I don't know what they look like now. She never talks about them.'

'What about you? You got any kids?' Christian asked.

'It can take less than five minutes to do what it takes to become a father. It takes a lifetime to become a good one. I've done the first bit, but believing I'd have a very short life, I never followed through. And the woman involved never forgave me.'

'Why did you think you'd have a short life?'

'A motorbike accident when I was younger. The doctors

gave me only a few years,' Guido stated vaguely.

Convinced that he had acquired sufficient skills to make a living, and impatient with subjects that bored him and the slow pace of those that enthralled him, Guido quit school at the age of sixteen to pursue life astride a motorbike usually adorned with a lovely, long-legged pillion passenger looking for a chilly ride with someone cool.

If he'd kept his eyes on the road and his grip on the handlebars instead of on his passenger's silky thigh, he might have avoided the oncoming traffic, the long-term hospitalisation and a warning from the doctors that his days were numbered because of damage to his organs and especially his spleen. Faced with that prognosis, he chose to assume that life could terminate at any moment and decided to live it accordingly. This also helped distract him from dwelling on the fact that his passenger no longer looked so lovely; that beauty not only fades but can be smashed in one single life-wrecking instant. As the years rolled on by he proved the doctors wrong, but he never took his luck for granted. And he never forgot the girl.

'Have you got a wife hidden away somewhere?' Christian persisted.

'She died a long time ago. A neurological complaint. I've had a few women since, but only arrangements like Precious.'

'I don't know how you can do that,' Christian commented as though abruptly struck by residual Calvinism. 'Don't you get attached to any of them?'

Many women had passed through Guido's younger life. He wasn't particularly good-looking, but he had that indefinable 'something' that attracted women to him like beautiful, brightly-coloured moths to a candle. He felt good about that, but bad about the one or two that had been drawn in too close, had burned their wings, and would never fly

127

again.

He nearly got married at the age of eight, Native American style. The two of them agreed that after school they would slit each other's wrists and allow their blood to mingle. He would supply the razor blade. At the appointed hour and place – after school in the woods at the bottom of the playing fields – they met. He made the first cut; she screamed and ran off, leaving him bleeding profusely from the wrist and from the heart. Their relationship subsided into a simmering state of animosity leading to the point when she declared she would never marry a matchstick man with the ankles of an Ethiopian refugee.

Eventually, with no effort on his part – no sport, no weight lifting – his self-image took a complete about-turn with the coming of the mid-sixties, and the adoration of rock stars whose bodies bore a comforting resemblance to his own skeletal frame. He had been fortunate to be a teenager at the time when aesthetic types into debating, philosophy and religion were a hit with the girls. Not all girls. He still remembered many who had ridiculed his physique; who wanted to meet, marry, buy a house and have children with a dominating male – an athlete, boxer, rugby player or similar. Now, at the age of sixty-five, his slim, wiry body would have been the envy of those porkier contemporaries.

His first serious relationship was with a local girl whose mother was a college lecturer for whom life itself seemed as academic and theoretical as the subject she taught. She and her husband rarely spoke. Not that she deliberately ignored him; her mind was elsewhere. Finally, the invisible man walked out on her. He left on a Monday; it was Thursday before she noticed. Guido regarded this as an important lesson in the need for visibility in relationships. One day, convinced rightly or wrongly that the mother's daughter was showing a similar absent-mindedness, Guido himself failed to return.

It wasn't long before his life collided with another. His next companion, the secretary to the French ambassador's personal assistant, a Communist and philosopher born in Algiers, initiated him into the art of exotic love-making, as well as the French classics such as Zola and Flaubert, and the existentialists, Sartre and Camus. It was she who convinced him to pursue the part-time languages degree that led to his successful career as a journalist. This tiny, olive-skinned woman, slightly older than him, quickly became the fundamental source of his hatred of bourgeois attitudes and petty puritanical religious prejudices – cleanliness and godliness – attitudes he associated especially with the Protestant countries.

Inside one of the stacks of French books she bought him she inscribed 'Just passing, no matter for how long, as long as we learn from each other'. He learned far more from her than she did from him, and the 'just passing' occurred sooner rather than later. Having successfully indoctrinated him with prejudices he would carry with him for the rest of his life, she explained to him over Turkish coffee in the holy Persian city of Shiraz that, 'The art of belonging's over, and it's never coming back'. She also added that she was leaving him for a beautiful blond girl she'd fallen for in St Tropez. But her presence still flowed in his veins.

'I like women,' Guido said, candidly. 'I'm not a ladies' man. I'm not a man's man either. I just prefer the company of women. I like the way most of them think and do things. They're more selfless somehow. It's just a shame that so many feel under pressure to think and act like men. But even those, inside they're still women, and I feel drawn to that.'

Guido's ringtone was the Bach Fugue in D Minor. He

pressed the answer button. 'What a coincidence!'

It was Precious. 'Mr Guido, they are killing people!' She sounded scared.

'Who are?'

'Taxi drivers. A taxi is burning. I'm on the tar road.'

'Where?'

'I only got as far as Tembisa. They are killing Mozambican drivers. Trucks are across the road. The bus can't get through. I want to come home. It reminds me of – ' Whatever it reminded her of suddenly choked her. She gave a hoarse sob and a gulping sound. 'Please!'

'Get away from there,' Guido ordered. 'Run to the shops and wait inside. I'll send Inno. He'll ring you when he gets there.'

Guido watched the Mercedes' lights disappear down the drive. He left for the kitchen and joined Christian with more beers. He lit another cigarette. Christian backed away from the smoke. 'I'm very much attached to Precious,' Guido stated. 'In a way, you could call it love. Nothing like I felt for my wife or still feel for her. Love's not always a moonlight sonata; it gets complicated in ways I can no longer be bothered with. And Precious loves me in her own way – like you love a full stomach if you've ever known what an empty one feels like.'

Something reassuring about Guido's down to earth attitude silenced Christian for a few moments. He looked out into the night and tried with some care to weigh up his feelings about his cousin. Despite his 'standing pole' antics, his quick temper, his rudeness and his cynicism, there was a solid strength that caused Christian to experience a new wave of hope for Saskya. Perhaps he was right about the police. Were they really the right people to handle a situation this delicate?

Guido just sat, arms folded, staring dreamily into space, processing the day's events. He exhibited few mannerisms and trivial actions to betray his state of mind. He gave the impression of being either totally dominant in the situation, or completely detached from it.

He turned towards the light, and suggested gently, 'Let's go back inside.' They walked side by side, with Guido on Christian's left, opposite the stick. They entered the dimly-lit dining room and on into the darkness of the hall and wished each other 'goodnight'. Christian lumbered up to his room, leaving Guido to wait for Precious.

Christian's brief sense of hope didn't last long. Once he reached his room and was outside the immediate influence of Guido's infectious, pragmatic optimism, fear came creeping back into his stomach like a tapeworm, fed by bewilderment and helplessness. He lay listening to the wearying chirp of cicadas, their insistent shrilling grating on his nerves, and he tasted the bitter fear of his own possible failure.

About two hours later the Merc's lights lit up the drive as Innocent, behind the wheel, waited for the gate to slide shut behind him. The street was deserted. Precious leapt out of the car and rushed at Guido. 'Thank you, Mr Guido.' She flung her arms around him almost pushing him off his feet, smothering his face with wet kisses. 'You see me from so far. You know my mind. You know my face. You know my body.' He looked her up and down and smiled at the comic yet alluring effect of her flowered dress and black and white striped socks with shoes that looked more like bedroom slippers.

'Strikers?' Guido asked.

She nodded.

17

Christian woke at seven to the sound of birds chirping and chattering. He washed and shaved and dressed in clothes Guido had lent him while his own were in the wash. They fitted perfectly in size if not in style.

Guido was at his usual place on the *stoep* sipping coffee and dragging on a *Gitanes*, his ritual before starting work. And this morning, work was a distraction from apprehension about events to come. He had already sold enough paintings through art dealers to enable him to have few money worries. But he'd pledged a small fortune to Christian and gained comfort from the fact that the proceeds of this latest forgery might just about cover it. And this one – the one he would finish this morning – would probably be the last. That would bring down the final curtain on his present persona – as an artist and con artist. What would he be next? At his age, there was probably enough time for only one more act.

In a previous life, he had been a journalist. He had been proud of his writing skills, and his ability to translate jargon and complex issues into everyday language that ordinary people could understand. And he could do this in three languages, for which he had to thank his German father and his French mother. He devoted the same sort of extreme care to his natural aptitude for drawing. He was highly talented in art and had impressed his art teachers at school with his ability to turn out passable copies of classic masterpieces as well as his own original works.

Despite his love of all things French, and especially the French Impressionists, Guido also adored the 17th-century Dutch painters, and especially Johannes Vermeer. And he immensely admired a 20th-century Dutch artist who shared Guido's love of Vermeer, and who was convicted of forging paintings in Vermeer's style.

Guido's former business partner had done business with the Dutch art forger before the second world war, and he passed on to Guido the techniques of preparing paint and canvases in the way it was done in the 17th century, and how to 'age' a modern copy. His partner was the one who handled the preparation of the documents accompanying the forgeries, providing them with a convincing provenance. Guido soon learned all that was necessary to survive on his own. When he had to leave Uganda, he found an art expert in Johannesburg who for a cut of the huge profits was happy to verify the authenticity of just about anything.

Not that Guido copied paintings; he painted 'genuine fakes' in the style of well-known, long-deceased artists. Whether the dealers sold them as genuine or not was none of his business. They gave him a good price; his concern stopped there. The only real forgery in the true sense of the word was on the very rare occasions when he painted a copy of the signature of a famous artist and passed it off as an original. He preferred not to and did it only for what he called 'a good cause'. Saskya's cause would fall into that category. And his invented history of each real forgery – its provenance – was a work of art in itself. A painting by a famous artist could not suddenly appear from nowhere. A good provenance confirming that it is of the period it claims to date from, together with a certificate of authentication, meant the difference between having little value and being worth a fortune.

As human models, he used white beggars, who had fallen on bad times after the end of apartheid that had provided jobs for all – all whites. He would pick them up in downtown

Johannesburg with the promise of a decent meal, a dive in the crystal-clear pool and a few rand. Their faces usually had much to recommend them as models – pain, weariness and resignation. Women models were more difficult to arrange, until one day he came across a white woman beggar at a road junction. He made his usual offer, with Precious as a chaperone.

He maintained that if his work was considered art, even if under a famous artist's name, then it was indeed a work of art, and therefore worth the substantial amounts of money that the dealers paid him for it. The value, he would argue, is in the work of art itself, not the name of the painter. If that same work failed to sell under the name of Van Rensburg or one of his previous aliases but sold under the name of someone accepted by the art world, it didn't matter. It was not a forgery. It was not a copy. It was his own work of art sold under a different name.

Although he enjoyed the creativity of it, he was tiring of its secrecy. It had been a long, hard, lonely road requiring patience and tenacity that had stretched him to the limit. He was used to secrecy. Private by nature, he'd initially found little difficulty in hiding his crimes, the first of which was man's worst crime. But there were limits.

There was a time when he used to kid himself he was an extrovert. But gradually he had to accept that he was deeply introverted and that the extrovert was the public self, the one that acted out the character he himself could have written about back in his days as a journalist and fiction writer. He could make people laugh, say the right things at the right moment, nod attentively, and occasionally after enough glasses 'ham it up'. Away from the public eye, he would retreat into his hermit state where introspection and romantic melancholia were the bread and butter of his emotional makeup.

Introspection had become second nature, and he would nag himself about his actions and motives, but a childhood enveloped in religious doctrine and superstition had left him prone to irrational guilt. Yet, on the subject of his worst crime, it was an accident, and it rid the world of a man who himself had betrayed so many to their torture and death. Not that he'd known that at the time and not that a judge and jury would have seen it that way. But he saw it that way, and that was good enough. Guido van Rensburg's conscience never slept soundly, but it did sleep.

'Christian. Good morning. Hungry?'

'Not yet, thanks.'

'No hard feelings?'

'I just want Sas back, Guido.'

'I'm spending the morning in the studio. Join me?'

Christian nodded and noticed that Guido's hands were stained with paint – a deep ultramarine and vermillion.

'Are you working on the painting for the ransom?' he asked.

'Sort of. It was already finished. I just need to complete one finishing touch.'

Determined today to resist any temptation to make any disparaging remarks about his poor cousin, Guido led Christian out the back door and across the lawn to a brick outbuilding that had probably been built for domestic staff. Its corrugated tin roof was painted a deep green. Christian took in the blazing plants and flowers of all colours in the beds around the building, against a rich backcloth of purple and white rhododendron bushes and bushy, bright-red bougainvilleas in the shade of jacaranda trees – Mother Nature's work of art with a palette of natural colours. As they approached the entrance, a warm breeze wafted the sweet, treacherous fragrance of frangipani blossom.

Guido unlocked and opened the door. Christian experienced a momentary feeling of unease as though invading something private, like opening a personal diary, or someone else's post. At the same time, his pulse quickened with curiosity. Warm sunlight streamed through the windows into the centre of the room, illuminating a canvas about three by two metres mounted on a large easel. Brushes were laid out neatly in a row on a small square table next to the easel. A palette knife and one brush were resting on the easel's ledge.

A larger oblong table against the back wall held a jumbled assortment of tins of all colours, paint-stained cloths and a couple of used palettes. A redolent, mingled smell of linseed oil, turpentine and French cigarette smoke permeated the room. The painting's depth of colour was stunning, particularly the blue, which gave it a typically Dutch or Flemish appearance; a rich Delft blue in a world more perfect than any real one. A floor of black and white tiles in a chessboard pattern added to the atmosphere of the place and the time.

Christian laughed out loud. The woman in the picture was clearly an albino version of a buxom Precious, and her male partner bore a close resemblance to Guido himself, but with a Van Dyke beard. They were sitting at adjacent sides of a lush green, baize-covered card table. The only object on the table was an olive branch, snapped in the middle. Two cages hung above the table, one with a dove, the other a raven.

The light fell mainly on the woman's upturned face, smiling cheekily, and on her ample, bulging décolleté. The sumptuous blue of her laced bodice and of the man's crimson jacket gave such a solid impression that Christian wanted to touch them. Their multi-coloured feather hats reminded him of the headband Precious wore just after he arrived. The painting struck Christian as a masterpiece. The use of *chiaroscuro* gave it a dramatically three-dimensional effect, reminding Christian strongly of Italian artist Caravaggio. The ultramarine blues and ochre colours shone from the canvas with a depth that gave an immense impression of age.

'What's it called?'

'*The Temptation of the Philosopher,*' he replied. 'This painting will save Saskya.' His friendly smile sent crinkles down the edges of his wary eyes.

Christian squeezed Guido's upper arm. 'I can't tell you how grateful I am, Guido.'

'Thank me when she's back. We've a long way to go.'

'How did you manage it? It looks so authentic – not only the style of the Dutch Golden Age, but it looks three or four hundred years old.'

'If you've got the time and the patience, I'll tell you.' Guido grabbed two wooden folding chairs and opened them. 'It took thirty-odd years of practice to reach this point. Sit down.'

Guido explained that first he needed 17th-century canvases to paint on. That was easy in a country that was colonised by the Dutch in the mid-sixteen hundreds. There were plenty of minor works of the period by second-rate artists in Cape Town. Carefully following the instructions of his previous business partner, who in turn had learned them from the forger in Amsterdam, he created his own paints from raw materials, and ground his own colours by hand in accordance with old formulas to ensure that they were authentic, and used the same kind of badger-hair brushes that artists such as Johannes Vermeer were known to have used. The blue colours were ground from lapis lazuli, yellows were in clay, red was from cinnabar. They had to be hand ground rather than machine ground because even the simplest of tests would have revealed machine-ground paint made up of much finer particles than would have been possible in the 17th century.

Guido partially removed the surface of the original painting with a pumice stone, taking care to retain the old web of craquelure. He next applied a layer of paint to form the basis for his own painting which had to have a hard surface consistent with its supposed age. He explained that conventional oil paints, made with linseed oil, dry very slowly, and take decades to achieve complete hardness.

His solution to the problem, passed on by his partner, was to use a phenol formaldehyde resin dissolved in turpentine. When he had finished the painting, he baked it in a specially-constructed oven for about an hour at forty degrees Celsius. Next, he varnished it and spread ink over the picture to seep into the cracks and simulate the dirt of centuries. He then removed excess ink and varnish from the surface and re-varnished it.

'It might not be perfect,' Guido concluded. 'But if challenged I can point to the fact that many of these well-known artists used assistants for much of the background, which would explain any inconsistency of artistic quality. And you're bound to get some minor damage to a work of that age, which would have been patched up using techniques and materials available at the time. With this work, some of the damage is deliberate. Then there's the provenance – its certificate of origin, as it were – which is as important as the work itself. It's a bit of problem explaining where some picture three-hundred years old has been hiding all those years. I'll tell you about that later.'

'There's a signature. Whose is it?'

'Dutch 17th-century artist, Franciscus van der Linden.'

'You've forged a signature?'

'You look shocked.'

'It's fraud.'

'Indeed, it is. In good 17th-century Dutch tradition.' Guido was untroubled by Christian's indignation. He explained that even after Vermeer died, many of his paintings were left unsold.

'You know how his family got rid of them? By forging the signature of Rembrandt among others. For years one of Vermeer's most famous paintings, *The Art of Painting*, bore the forged signature of a more famous contemporary, Pieter de Hooch. And the Old Town House art museum in Cape Town has a painting signed by De Hooch, *Interior of a Dutch House*. It looks like pure Vermeer.' Guido chuckled.

'You must know this is wrong,' said Christian, his voice rising a note. 'It doesn't matter who else did it, or how good your painting is, even if it's as good as the original that it pretends to be. The reason the original is worth so much is that it's by a famous artist, a long time ago, and was then original. Not by you, right now, and unoriginal.'

'If it's an object of beauty what does it matter? It's irrelevant from an aesthetic point of view. Why should the circumstances of its production make a difference to people's enjoyment of it? If this painting looks as good as a Van der Linden, why shouldn't it be valued just as highly?'

'Because scientific tests could reveal that it's not original and *not* by the artist it pretends to be.'

'But it's sensory inspection that counts – not scientific inspection. We use our eyes to decide whether something is beautiful or not, not some technical apparatus. Anything not visible in the painting itself is irrelevant to the aesthetic appreciation of it. Our own eyes might even convince us that the imitation is better than the original.'

'But aesthetic qualities can be dependent on their historical context – daringly innovative in the 17th century, but commonplace in the 21st,' Christian stated, his confidence steadily rising. 'The same goes for the painters, their lives, struggles and challenges.'

'It's irrelevant. Knowing all that stuff can't make the painting more beautiful. It might be interesting, but it doesn't affect the aesthetic qualities. And don't forget that copying a work and overcoming technical and other practical challenges involves far more effort than was ever faced by the originator.'

'Listen. The fact that a painting is by an artist whose works have stood the test of time makes it worthy of special attention. That's not true of imitations. Our experience of it is affected by the belief that the painting is the self-same object that Van der Linden had in his studio, on his easel over three hundred years ago and on which he worked out his original and creative ideas.'

Guido paused to light a cigarette. 'We're getting nowhere.' He shrugged and gave a wry smile. 'Let's agree to disagree on the basis that I'm talking about purely aesthetic appreciation, and you're referring to the possibility that other considerations such as historical context and originality are difficult to separate from it.'

Christian seemed to ponder the issue for a moment, running through the possible answers. 'Okay,' he replied at last. 'I suppose that's a reasonable compromise. But you're still guilty of deception.'

'Guilty? Art is all about deception,' he asserted, with more than a hint of satisfaction. 'Vermeer and his contemporaries earned much of their living by painting commissioned portraits. Artists nearly always deceived their subjects by making them appear more beautiful or handsome than they really were. They forged ugliness into beauty. They were paid to deceive.'

'That doesn't make you right. It makes them wrong. What's even worse is that people often don't buy paintings just for their aesthetic value, but as an investment. It's not too much of a stretch to imagine how they'd feel about spending all their savings on something that, later in life when they need the money most, turns out to be worthless? How can you justify it?'

Guido, who all his life had laboured under the handicap of an extremely low boredom threshold when it came to interacting with his fellow human beings, just shrugged. But there was no stopping Christian, especially not the sort of bored shrug of the shoulders that he was used to from his students.

'Basically, ethics boils down to the golden rule,' Christian continued unabated. 'And you yourself wouldn't appreciate being sold one thing, when you believed it to be something else – especially when it turns out to be worth a fraction of what you paid for it, perhaps at an age when you need the money to survive.'

Guido nodded as though to thank him for his advice, while mentally telling him to shove it. 'Cousin, I think you need a glass or two,' he suggested, exhaling smoke through his teeth in a low hiss. 'I admit that when you put it like that, I've little defence. My life has been extremely interesting, but you could hardly call it moral. I wish it had been different, but it is what it is. I can argue a perfectly rational case for doing what I'm doing, but I admit that the moral issue is confusing.' He lowered his voice a fraction. 'Just remember, this painting that I was going to sell for a lot less as *in the style of*, can save Saskya just by forging a signature and some supporting documents. Let's draw our own conclusions about the rightness or wrongness and agree to differ for now. Unless you prefer to plant your flag on top of the moral high ground and lose your daughter?'

'There was no need for that.'

'No, there wasn't,' Guido replied, with a hint of regret in his voice. His face looked weary and sombre, but he managed to summon a lopsided grin. 'Sorry, Man. Let's have that drink now.'

'I prefer to eat something.'

Christian's excruciating anxiety, eating up all his energy, caused him to feel permanently hungry. 'What's the plan for tomorrow?'

Guido paused for a moment to think, his face slightly anguished. 'More preparation,' he said. 'And taking it easy. My throat's getting worse.'

'Try cutting down on those cigarettes of yours,' Christian advised, rather didactically. 'They're pure camel dung.'

'What! They're an essential ingredient of my beautiful life.'

Christian thought later that if he were asked his opinion of Guido he would be thoroughly disapproving. Yet he seemed reluctantly drawn towards him by a fascination for everything about him that was different – his outlaw status, his independence, his worldliness. But would he, or even could he, save Saskya?

In only a couple of days, he would find out. There was no turning back.

18

Precious sauntered in. She had changed into a full-length black dress tailored to hug her perfect figure. A short, crocheted cardigan just reached the bottom of her rib cage like a 17th-century bodice. From behind, were it not for her cropped, tightly-curled black hair, she could have been Dutch, and the perfect model for a painter like Vermeer or one of his contemporaries – as perfect as she had been for the so-called Franciscus van der Linden. It was late afternoon. She was looking as fresh and sunny as ever and showed no ill effects from her experience of the xenophobic attacks in Tembisa.

'Precious, get the clippers. I need a haircut.'

Guido grabbed an old plastic chair and dragged it to the edge of the *stoep*. 'Nice and short. Just like this photo.' He handed her the front page of *The Tribune* featuring a clean-shaven Christian with short, close-cropped hair.

Precious covered his clothes with a towel and tucked it into his collar. She clipped and cut for the next quarter of an hour, then she fetched a feather duster, brushed the hairs from his face and the front of his shirt, before sweeping the mountain of grey hair from the floor. She disappeared, and returned with a small looking-glass, and held it in front of him. He looked ten years younger.

'You look even more handsome now, *ne*?' She said, punching him playfully on the shoulder.

At first, he hardly recognised himself. The sides were almost bald. The top was perhaps a centimetre long at most, but without the curls. The hair stood up straight like a field of corn stubble. He just had to shake his head and laugh, which set her off, and they giggled and hugged and giggled some more before he managed, 'These hairs are itchy, Precious. They make me feel nervous.'

'Perhaps you should have a nice relaxing bath, Mr Guido.'

'Perhaps you should have one too, Miss Precious.'

As they headed back inside, arm in arm, the sky had deepened to a mauve tint heralding the end of one of those summer days Guido wished could last forever but knew would die suddenly at six o'clock sharp, winter or summer, like they all do.

He smiled at the woman whose closeness caused him so much comfort, and such inner warmth. She cast a sideways glance at him, while slowly biting into a succulent ripe peach with an air of dreamy lasciviousness that seemed to serve as a counterpoint to the haunting melancholia of the finale of Tchaikovsky's *Pathétique* symphony, playing downstairs. She knew how he loved the finale. Even though she had little acquaintance with Europe's serious music, she had to stop and listen each time, as though it stirred a vague, distant memory connected with something dark and disturbing.

'Shall I make a pipe?' she half whispered to him.

She needed a shower. Her skin gave off a musky, earthy aroma that was almost as addictive as his smoking habit. She giggled as she lit the match.

He lay back on the bed and closed his eyes. The flame cast strange shadows across her face and the black and white photo on the small table next to her side of the bed. It showed an introspective boy of about ten years old who, with the help of hindsight, seemed destined for tragedy. He thought that his vision was distorted already before he'd even taken his first puff. He handed back the pipe and dozed. All tension had drained from him, and he felt unable to move, as though hypnotised. He listened hard in the gloom and heard the light brush of her bare feet against the bare boards.

He closed his eyes again, pretending to sleep. He never worried about the effect of a pipe on his quality as a lover. She would forgive anything and everything. He was her protector, and his presence was more important than his performance. He heard her tiptoe to the edge of his bed. He opened one eye and saw her gazing at him, her face dimly lit by the candle light. She smiled nervously and then slowly removed her clothes like unwrapping a present.

She knelt naked by the narrow bed. Bending her head, her lips brushed against his mouth, and then pressed more urgently. He felt his body take over, a wave of remote sensuality that almost felt as if it wasn't his. Dragging the sheet from his naked body, she drew herself towards him. He very gently eased her away. She slowly curled onto her back and rested her head under his arm. Sleepily she murmured, 'It's okay, Mr Guido.'

She hid her disappointment, not just for missing the pleasure of sharing their bodies, but also the opportunity to escape from her mind. She would be the last sort of person to be seduced by the fashionable, new-age commandment to be mindful – to live life in the 'here and now'. But unconsciously she made every effort to fully concentrate on what she was doing, to avoid letting her mind idle for fear it would trespass into barren, forbidden territory.

Love-making was an escape from her mind's waywardness. Over the years her mind had become her enemy, relentlessly thrusting at her with memories that opened deep wounds again and again and casting unwelcome light into her deepest secrets and into one secret in particular. The passion of orgasmic abandonment not only smothered the bewildering mystery of the human condition, but also defeated death – the death that was omnipresent in her early years and was at the core of her biggest secret.

He rolled over to face the wall. In the quiet of the candle-lit night, he lay listening to her slow, rhythmic breathing. She was a friend.

Their relationship was so different from how it had been with his wife. Unlike any other woman he had ever shared bits of his life with, his wife had no role to play. She was irritatingly direct and boringly honest as though life had failed to rob her of her basic innocence and her belief in universal truths.

Her fundamental goodness made him feel safe, yet at the same time made him feel inferior. It was this that meant he would always love her. This he knew. He also knew he had finally travelled to where the long shadows of those who loved him or judged him could never reach – to a place deep within the inky darkness of himself. And Precious didn't judge or love or possess. He felt at ease with her. He liked her simplicity and straightforward honesty. She was a lovely human being who had already suffered too much simply for being part of a certain culture. Precious simply *was*.

And love? Guido reserved that for his wife. She had died in Uganda many years before, following several hellish months of a creeping paralysis caused by a yellow fever vaccination. Did he love Precious? What did it mean? His lack of formal commitment to her seemed to make space for something much more natural, more spontaneous that lasted as long as they needed each other and would evaporate the moment they didn't. There was a kind of relaxation in the relationship between them that gave it a dimension that he had never experienced during his married life. He was reluctant to categorise his feelings but companionship and comrade in arms sprang to mind.

And here she was, lying beside him, 'under his wing' as she loved to say. So, whilst he reserved the word 'love' for his wife, he thought that the present alternative, particularly at his time of life, seemed more appropriate and satisfying. All he knew with certainty was that he needed Precious, wanted to be with her, touch her, draw on her energy, feel her warmth. He opened his eyes and gazed at her. She had stretched out on the bed naked, resting on one elbow, reading a paperback, and looking like a black version of Velázquez's *Venus at her Mirror*. He touched her bare arm and felt her warm satin skin against his palm. She shifted slightly away from him, turned her head and searched his eyes with an expressionless gaze.

19

That night Guido woke up from a nightmare feeling drained, crushed and consumed by self-doubt. He had been saying earlier that the house needed painting on the outside. In his nightmare, he came across a ladder leaning against the end of the house. At the top was Precious, on top of her shoulders, Christian, on top of his shoulders Innocent and on top of his shoulders Saskya. She had a brush in her hand and was trying to paint the top of the wall.

'Get down, it's dangerous!' Guido shouted.

Christian jumped off Precious' shoulders leaving Innocent and Saskya hanging in mid-air. Guido couldn't decide which one to catch as they dropped like a stone to earth so he decided to catch both in quick succession. But he was too slow. He not only failed to catch both, he failed to catch *either* of them. Both were dead on impact, their heads shattered on the concrete ground. Lying face down, prone, they could have been deep asleep were it not for their arms that stuck out at odd angles, like those of broken dolls.

'We must have a better car. When we pull this off we must get home quick.'

Guido looked up at Innocent. 'What's wrong with the Merc?'

'It can be traced.' He blew his nose with great violence into a tissue. 'We must have another car. A fast one. A BMW. With a manual gearbox.'

'Sit down,' Guido ordered. 'Explain.'

Innocent draped himself over the chair and animatedly told Guido that the kidnappers might take the money, and

148

then catch them up and kidnap her again, or that others from the township might follow them with the idea of kidnapping the kidnappers and Saskya. There was even the possibility that the journalist, Blessing, knowing how much was involved, might have tipped off underworld contacts. He knew that in his world anything was possible and that everything possible was necessary to prevent it. 'We must be faster than everybody.'

'Where are we going to get a BMW? I don't carry that kind of money around in my back pocket.'

'You won't need money, Mr Guido.'

'Forget it. They're unstealable.'

'I know somebody who has one for sale. I phone him tonight. I agree to meet him at a shopping mall. I ask to take it for a ride. While I take it for a ride I stop, and I deal with him. I subdue him and tie him up. I leave him to rest beneath a tree. Then I take the car.'

'What! And he's just going to take it lying down?'

'Yes, he must accept it.' He wagged a long, brown finger.

'Why?'

'I know about this man. If he has a BMW for sale he has stolen it himself. He will be angry, but he cannot tell the police. By the time he tries to do anything about it himself, this matter will be finished, and I'll return it to him.'

'And if it's got a tracker?'

'If it had a tracker, the owner would have tracked it.' He brushed his long fingers through his thatch of crinkly hair, then let them dance on the table in front of him.

Guido grinned, and lit one of his French cigarettes, lifting his head to blow the smoke skywards. With nicotine-stained fingers, he tapped his ash carefully into the ashtray, considered the suggestion for several seconds, and then nodded his head. 'Okay, Inno. But be careful.'

Innocent shook himself as though to stand, but then shifted his weight pushing down on his strong thighs. 'Can I borrow one of your smart suits?' he asked tentatively.

'Sure, help yourself. But don't pull the trousers up too high.' Guido let out a deep chuckle and slapped Innocent on the back. 'And get me a pair of horn-rimmed glasses from the chemist.'

'Horn-rimmed?'

'Just like Mr Christian's. Lowest magnification.'

'Magnification?'

'They're numbered zero to four. Get a pair with the lowest number.'

Guido handed him a two-hundred note.

Guido knew that when he got to the rendezvous with the kidnappers, he would probably be frisked for weapons, particularly a gun. He would carry his walking stick which he knew would be carefully examined because so many walking sticks are in fact sword sticks. He would also be checked for carrying a knife – they would examine his trousers, and particularly his socks. But he believed that what they would not examine would be the inside of his jacket sleeves. The next day he went downtown to a shop that stocked every possible knife under the sun and bought a double-edged sheath knife. The blade was about four inches long, the handle almost the same.

He called in at a tailor's a couple of streets away and asked him to stitch the leather sheath between the lining of his smart maroon jacket and the fabric of the jacket itself, leaving an opening at wrist level the width of the sheath. He returned home and split open the knife handle. Using an angle grinder, he filed down the handle end of the blade to a fine point. The result was a double-edged blade with a razor-sharp point at both ends. He returned after lunch to pick up his jacket, and paid thirty-five rand, no questions asked.

The next step was practice making perfect. He put on his jacket and slipped the blade up the sleeve into the sheath. The end of the blade was hidden by about an inch of sleeve and could not be felt by running a hand down the inside of the sleeve. He fetched an old piece of hardboard and nailed some plastic bottles to it as a target. He then stepped back, put his hand behind his head as though to squeeze the nape of his neck, and brought it down sharply. The blade shot out of the sheath, somersaulting through the air and embedded itself deeply in the plastic bottle and the board.

It all seemed too easy, but knowing he was rusty, he spent another hour practising until every time the blade pierced the target where he wanted it.

His other weapon, the walking stick, was used by the Chinese on the basis that few weapons look more disarming. The only difference between his walking stick and an ordinary one was that instead of a rubber tip, it had a metal tip, which was meant to hurt. He had practised a walking stick fighting form for many years under the tuition of his Chinese doctor in Uganda and was convinced that he would be able to use it to good effect against at least two assailants.

He stood up when he saw the front gate slide open. A bright-purple BMW with dark tinted windows entered with Innocent at the wheel, his vision partly obscured by a white plastic rosary and crucifix dangling from the rear-view mirror. Guido surveyed the lurid coloured car with a doubtful expression. He hardly recognised the driver. He was wearing what looked like a policeman's peaked cap, a black Kevlar bulletproof vest, mirrored sunglasses and black fatigues. Innocent extracted himself from the car and grabbed a pump-action shotgun. He had an extra magazine hanging from his belt. Also hanging from his belt was a holster carrying a police-issue semi-automatic pistol. The whole outfit including shiny black policeman's boots looked ridiculously small for him.

'Where on earth did you get all this?' Guido asked.

'It's fine,' Innocent beamed, a triumphant gleam in his eye. 'I borrowed it to help me subdue the BMW owner. My half-brother works for a security company guarding Jews in the north.'

'You'd better get changed before someone sees you.'

Innocent looked deflated. 'The vest is for you, under your jacket. The shotgun I fix under the car. The pistol I hide under the seat. Just in case.'

'In case of what? A war? And where's my suit?'

Innocent opened the rear door and handed it over.

'I must learn to drive much faster, Mr Guido. I must learn to escape quickly. Can I take the rest of the afternoon off to get to know this car?'

'Sure. But get changed first!'

Innocent returned just as Blessing from *The Tribune* rang Christian. 'They want to do it tomorrow morning, early,' she told him, excitement making her voice rise a couple of semitones. 'Have you got the money?'

'I – I'm not sure.'

'They'll ring again in an hour. Christian, you must let me know for certain. They are nervous. Ring me back.'

He turned to Guido. 'It's tomorrow morning,' he said, his voice rising. 'How the hell are you going to sell that painting and get the money?'

'Sit down, Man,' Guido suggested, waving him to a chair at the opposite side of the table. The tortoise-shell cat sauntered in from the garden, a mouse jammed between her jaws. Before sidling out of sight behind a chair she eyed Christian with suspicion as though fearing that he might want a share.

'The painting is already sold,' Guido said calmly. 'I have the money. There's nothing to worry about.'

'Thank God!' Christian let out a hiss of relief. 'Are you sure?'

Guido nodded. 'I'll show you. Come with me.'

Christian rose to his feet cautiously, as if testing the firmness of the floor, and grabbed his stick.

Guido led him to the studio. He unlocked and opened the door. *The Temptation of the Philosopher* had gone. The sharp light streaming through the windows lit the large easel, now vacant except for the palette knife and brush on its ledge. The assortment of tins and paint-stained cloths were still on the table. Guido locked the door behind him, pulled away a Persian rug in the far corner and lifted a length of the floorboard. He pulled up his sleeve, reached down and extracted a flight case, and placed it on the table. He flicked the catches and lifted the lid to reveal a stack of wads each of one hundred freshly minted two-hundred-rand notes bound by paper sleeves.

'Voilà!' he said, waving his hand like a magician.

Christian just stared, mesmerised, resting on his stick. Never having worked in a bank nor been involved in crime, he had never seen so much money in his life.

'Thank you,' he muttered. 'I'll tell Blessing.'

Guido carefully clipped the case shut, put it back beneath the board, and replaced the rug. They left the studio, and Guido carefully locked the door behind them.

'Blessing?'
'Yes.'

'I have the money,' he stated, tension mounting in his voice.

'How will you get to them?'

'A chauffeur-driven car.'

'They want the number plate, make and colour.'

Christian hesitated. 'One minute.' He limped to the front drive and read out the number of Innocent's newly acquired car.

'It's a purple BMW.'

She gave him the time and rendezvous coordinates.

'I want this story,' she ordered. 'Don't be naughty. Don't tell anyone else. And don't tell the cops. Have they rung?'

'No.'

'Typical.'

She wished him luck and hung up. Christian slipped the phone into his trouser pocket, irrationally worrying that cellphones might cause sterility. Guido told him to rest for the remainder of the afternoon, while he went downtown to 'a business meeting'.

'Make sure you come back,' Christian said nervously. Guido answered with a grin and raised his hand as though holding a glass.

Christian had long accepted that pleasurable moments in his own life would have to be earned by the drudgery and boredom of hard work, and he believed that such satisfactory moments were all the more satisfying simply because they had been earned. Their pleasantness depended on their contrast with the unpleasantness of the work with which they'd been achieved. He was starting to pine for his routine days that were a holy trinity of work, play and sleep, balanced in equal proportions, and when one of them wouldn't feel right without the others.

Guido could not have been more different. Perhaps because of the doctors' prognosis when he was young that terminal ill health was just around the corner, he seemed to make every moment satisfying, and the least sacrifice that went into it the better. Not that he wasn't capable of hard work, but the long hours he often devoted to it were for his own benefit and were satisfying in themselves. It wasn't work; it was a labour of love.

As for guilt, Christian's existence was founded on it. There was no god to wag a finger at him. He managed that all by himself. Guido, too, was haunted by extreme events of the past, but his life was too packed with the business of living to have time to morbidly dwell too long on the sins he wished he'd never committed. And he viewed regret as a lot healthier than guilt.

Guido was a lapsed Catholic. If it had taught him nothing else, his candle-lit religion with its ancient, mystical cathedrals scented with lighted frankincense and myrrh had impressed upon him the belief that, although humans were God's creations, they were far from perfect, and to regard them as possessing the potential for perfection was a viciously misleading form of wishful thinking that raised unrealistic expectations and the inevitable stresses of disappointment. For the past three hundred years the world's greatest minds, influenced by even greater minds over two thousand years previously, had claimed that by using reason, 'man' could not only avoid being misled by superstition but could and *should* also arrive at the perfect way of conducting himself.

Catholicism thought and taught otherwise. *Errare humanum est.* Most people are fearful, uncertain, fragile creatures craving love and recognition on their tortuous journey through life and cannot help but commit errors of judgement on the way. Recognising this allows for compassion and a level of forgiveness for others and oneself that is not possible when a mistake is regarded as a failure. Guido subscribed to this. And forgiving others made it so much easier to forgive himself.

The sun had sunk beneath the treetops, and a breeze came up, instantly chilling, bringing with it a strong scent of rosemary from the garden, as night fell in a brief moment. Dogs barked at wraithlike passers-by in the gloom of the sparsely amber-lit street, and at occasional voices, some loud and already fuelled with alcohol.

Guido returned later in the evening and parked the Merc on the drive, leaving the BMW out of sight in the garage. Christian had just finished a salty dinner of mealy pap and vegetable stew Precious had prepared for him. His eyes had almost lost the power to focus. In the depths of exhaustion, when all the senses are sharpened just prior to surrendering to sleep, he was at the mercy of the entire gamut of his emotions from fear to giggly optimism. For now, he experienced a sickening feeling of abject terror.

They both knew they were unlikely to sleep. Christian's riotous heartbeat was so wild and thrusting that it seemed to bang against his breastbone, shaking his brain with vertigo, and soaking him with the sweat of hope mingled with paralysing anxiety. His eyes focused beyond the window flung open to the night sky and the half-moon suspended like a child's drawing of a boat in an orange-black ocean. During the silence, his mind returned inexorably to the image of Saskya, her bobbing hair, her laughter, her anger, his anticipation of their imminent reunion. He felt weak with fear.

Eventually, with images playing in his mind, exhaustion

overtook him, and he managed to drift off in the early hours despite sharp pains in his stomach and a nagging backache.

As the evening wore on into night, and night into morning, Guido, on his bed alone, except for the cat that had snuggled in a dip of bedding next to him, lay wide awake, mentally rehearsing every possible scenario that might confront him, and how he would deal with it, whatever it might be. In a moment of doubt, he got up and opened the drawer next to the one with his wife's photo. He took out the pad, the black felt-tipped pen, the three gold coins and the *I-Ching*. He tossed the coins on the table top six times until he had completed a hexagram on the pad. It was the same as before – 'persevere'.

20

A silver line along the edge of the tree tops betrayed the start of a clear dawn, full of promise and dread. The early morning birds started their dawn chorus in the trees. Already the city was wide awake to the hooting and growl of traffic and shouts of passers-by in the street below. The moon was still suspended overhead.

Guido had briefly savoured the silent immobility as day broke. In that peculiar lucidity that often accompanies the dawn after a sleepless night, he carefully observed his thoughts and objectives. He was more tense than nervous and harboured an almost irrational feeling of confidence. His tall, thin body and gaunt face could give a weak impression, but his resoluteness testified to a strength wholly held together by sheer willpower.

It wasn't that he wasn't brave. It was just that he had a vivid imagination that helped his precision in trying to work out consequences. If it went wrong, it was meant to go wrong. He knew that all decisions taken so far were the right ones and that he, Innocent and Saskya were now in the capricious hands of fate. Only time would tell.

He dressed, slung on his jacket with the blade 'up his sleeve' as he'd joked to Innocent, but decided to leave the bulletproof vest in case he was frisked. Innocent had already installed the shotgun out of sight and put the pistol between the springs of the passenger seat.

After a shallow, troubled sleep, Christian got up to see them off. An even greater sense of anxiety had seemed to well up from deep inside and spread like flood waters into every part of him. What would the day bring? Would it bring back his lovely Saskya?

The street barber had put up a poster on the wall behind him, advertising a lotion for straightening curly hair. The Mozambican newspaper seller next to him had been at that road junction every morning and evening for all the years Guido had lived there. He was crouched down cutting through the sisal around a bundle of the latest edition of *The Tribune*. He looked up but didn't recognise the car whose occupants were concealed behind the tinted windows and whose deep exhaust note seemed to serve as an aggressive challenge to other road users.

They soon left behind the grey-blue monolithic tower blocks and headed north. The sky was already a deep sapphire blue, crisscrossed with a couple of vapour trails from planes circling above Tambo airport. Guido wiped the cold sweat from his upper lip.

Having left the city behind them, they sped north-west down a dusty dirt road with the burning gold of the rising sun reflecting in the rear-view mirror. This was the one appointment for which they could not afford to be late. Gusts of warm, heavy wind sent litter scurrying into the ditch. The paths and tracks either side of the road were coming alive with people. Innocent swerved to avoid a smartly dressed man in a suit standing in the middle of the road, swaying slightly while brushing his teeth.

Innocent glanced at the mirror and looked again. 'I think we're being followed,' he muttered. 'It could be police.'

Guido positioned his vanity mirror so that he could see the car following them. It was a bright-red Toyota saloon. He massaged his inflamed eyes with the backs of his hands and shuddered as he felt a chill run through him, putting his teeth on edge.

'I don't think so,' he said calmly. 'It could be anybody. What car has the owner of this BMW got?'

'He has many, Mr Guido. I'll shake them off.'

'Not yet. Wait until we're away from these shacks and out in the open.'

They were already leaving the tiny settlement behind, and the Toyota was still on their tail.

'Now!' he ordered, sliding his seat belt away from his collar bone.

Innocent's concentration was absolute. His eyes intensely staring at the dirt, stones, sand and gravel ahead, his reactions measurable in tiny fractions of a second. One minute he was clutching the wheel with claw-like hands, the muscles standing out on his strong, thin, sinewy arms. The next minute his long fingers were making fine adjustments to the steering, while his delicate balancing of accelerator and brake held the speeding vehicle on the dirt road.

It was sheer artistry. The arid, sun-scorched scrub stretched out in front of them. Behind was obliterated by a cloud of dust from the wheels. Guido momentarily wondered whose plaything this vehicle, built with such Teutonic thoroughness, had originally belonged to – or still belonged to.

'Stop,' Guido ordered. They abruptly came to a halt and waited for the dust cloud to clear. The Toyota was gone. Guido nodded, and the wheels spun as Innocent pulled away and wrestled the BMW at speed down the meandering track.

They reached the meeting point, by mid-morning. A clearing, a short distance from the road, was in the middle of nowhere, the kind of harsh, merciless country where death would be natural, and where nature would swiftly dispose of the remains. The sand track behind them was sparsely dotted with low scrubby bush, the view of the road ahead obscured by dense acacia.

Innocent made a tight U-turn to face the car in the direction from which they'd just come. Guido checked the satellite coordinates again and reached into the back for his walking stick. It looked exactly like Christian's, except for the steel tip. He put on the horn-rimmed glasses Innocent had bought at the chemist.

Guido's stomach muscles ached as he watched the minutes slowly tick by on the car's digital clock. He softly whistled a jazz tune. Innocent stared in silence at the rear-view mirror and the bushveld beyond. The capriciously changing wind shook the acacias and blew the dust into tiny tornadoes.

After a tense quarter of an hour or so, they picked up the clatter of a diesel engine and the grating of a gearbox. A rusty pickup truck was suddenly upon them in the clearing, skidding to a halt about a hundred and fifty feet away, the body rocking on its springs. It had three passengers. One of them was Saskya, still dressed in black and white.

A strong-looking young man in slacks and khaki t-shirt in the centre seat reached across her and opened the door. She jumped down. As she walked towards Innocent's car, Guido noticed she was tethered by a thick, bright-red, nylon rope around her neck. The driver, a tall, wiry youth in a similar t-shirt, stayed behind the wheel. He was leaning out of the window, holding a hunting rifle with telescopic sights. It was pointed at Saskya.

Guido's blood froze. He reached to open the door.

'Stay in the car!' the driver shouted. Keep your hands where I can see them.'

Innocent left his hands on the wheel. Guido held his at shoulder height. Saskya reached the passenger door. An aspirated squeak of air emerged from her throat. She coughed. 'Who are you?' she asked Guido in a whisper. 'I thought you were my father.' Her eyebrows were tensely drawn together, giving her a puzzled look.

'Guido, your father's cousin.' His voice sounded like sandpaper.

She began to babble a disconnected stream of words, before getting a grip on herself. 'So, I really am saved?' She laughed manically, her voice rising a note, and then hugged herself as if a chill wind had caught her. 'They want the money. Please!' The rope around her neck was clasped with a small closed-shackle padlock.

Guido handed her an attaché case. She turned and walked slowly back to the pickup, careful not to trip over the rope being reeled in through the window by the man next to the driver. He grabbed the case and left her standing for a few long seconds while he examined the contents. Innocent stared out of the rear window with a predatory look in his eyes more appropriate to a leopard about to strike. Guido closed his eyes and concentrated on breathing deep into his abdomen.

The seconds that ticked by felt like minutes. Just as Innocent started to slowly move his hand towards the pistol hidden under his seat, Saskya turned towards them, the coils of rope in her hand. The passenger handed her the padlock key. Their eyes met. With a crunch of gears, the pickup reversed in a semi-circle, its spinning wheels sending up clouds of sand, and bumped away in the direction from which it came, dust billowing behind it before it disappeared into the bush. Guido grabbed Saskya and bundled her into the back of the BMW.

'They're just boys, Mr Guido,' Innocent urged. 'We catch them and kill them. We keep your money.'

'No!' Saskya blurted.

'It's only money,' said Guido.

'It could feed my village for months.'

'It could feed *their* village for months,' Saskya cut in.

'We can't take any risks,' said Guido, his voice strained with impatience. 'Let's go home. Quick, before they change their minds, or before others come. I'm still curious about that Toyota. These are badlands.'

Innocent gripped the wheel and stared ahead. 'Mr Guido, we can pull a fast one.'

'Sometimes it's best to pull a fast one slowly, Inno.'

'But *they've* pulled a fast one.'

'No, they haven't. *We* have. I'll explain later. Just get us home.'

Innocent accelerated hard, his long brown fingers languidly splayed across the steering wheel, a dust cloud obscuring the rear window which burned fiercely with the reflected light of the sun. Guido took Saskya's key, turned to face her, and carefully unlocked the padlock. She shook herself free of the rope and looked him in the eyes for the first time. He broke the silence as coolly as he could, but his voice trembled slightly. 'They didn't hurt you?'

She answered with a quick, shy shake of the head. 'They were good guys,' she murmured, and then looked away declaring the subject closed.

There was no sight of the red Toyota. A couple of hours later, they were 'home'.

21

Relief. At last, Christian felt he could breathe.

'It's so, so good to see you,' he understated, hugging her hard, and then hugging her again, tears streaming down his cheeks. She seemed stiff and numb. Although slightly perturbed by her reaction, he felt as though he were floating. He had a strange sense of self-consciousness and wondered whether the others could see the tidal wave of relief that had broken over his face and washed down to his innards. It was a struggle to hold back more tears.

'I must sleep,' she told him, hugging herself tightly. He asked her if she'd caught a chill. 'Not that kind of chill, Dad.' She gave him a wan, ironic smile. 'Could you stay with me?'

He nodded and blew into his handkerchief. 'I'm done in too.'

Finally, for the first time since leaving Cape Town, he felt some of the tension start to drain from his neck and shoulders.

'Have a well-earned siesta,' Guido suggested, leading the way upstairs. They followed him, Christian leaning on her arm.

Christian sat beside her on the double bed and took her in his arms again, and they remained silent, father and daughter, until finally she raised her head and said in a voice so faint that he could hardly hear, 'I was so scared, Dad.' Her lips were trembling, and he gripped her even more tightly. The trembling became more violent until her body was shaking. She pulled away from him and looked him straight in the eyes. 'I felt so abandoned, like all that I cling to had been snatched away.'

She fell silent, and he too pulled away, as though to give her room to find the words to describe so much that lay deeper. She shrugged and turned down the corners of her mouth to say, 'It's hopeless'. He put his arm around her shoulder again in another effort to soothe her and kissed her on the forehead. She shook herself free in one impatient movement, got to her feet, gave him a wan, apologetic smile, and lay down on the other side of the bed.

She raised her ashen, tear-stained face and blew into a tissue. 'I'd like to – to just...' She tried to say something, but her voice had become incoherent. She looked at him, but whether she saw him he couldn't tell. Seconds later, she was deep asleep, her eyelids shut tightly as if held down by the weight of coins. He thought that knowing her, she would soon pull out of it, but also that she would never be completely the same again. That he knew for sure.

Frustrated by an irrationality born of exhaustion and worry, sleep for Christian was a longer time coming, nagged as he was by guilt and regret despite the day's success. Turning his head away from the sharp light that crept through the edges of the curtains, and ignoring the sweet fragrance of Precious' cooking below, he finally slipped into a few hours of fretful dozing.

By the time he awoke it was completely dark. He frantically scratched at his chest in the belief that it was crawling with insects, but it was just the itchiness of his shirt drenched in sweat. Saskya was gone. He listened for sounds in the house but could hear only the sound of his own breathing and his heart pounding in his ears. He dressed, half asleep, staggering as though tormented by a colossal hangover.

His phone rang. 'Christian?' It was Blessing. 'Have you got Saskya?'

'Yes. I'll ring you back in an hour.'

'We're going to press. Please ring as soon as you can.'

He found Saskya in the dining room and sat next to her at the table. Not once did she look at him. She sat with her head bowed as though in meditation, the only sign of life being the slight rise and fall of her breathing. After several minutes she raised her head. There was a glimmer of a smile. The smile widened. 'Dad, you're wearing jeans!' she teased suddenly. 'I hope you're not revolting? Or have you hit mid-life again? What will Mum say when she sees you?'

'They're Guido's. Mine are in the wash.'

'And that must be his shirt. It's not pale-blue, and it's not ironed. You really are breaking out.'

Her laughter suddenly subsided into tears, her shoulders heaving in rhythm with her sobbing. Christian put his arm around her as she struggled to smile her tears away.

'Love you, Sas.' He wiped away her tears with his linen handkerchief.

'You too, Dad.' She maintained an uncertain smile. 'At least you still managed to iron your handkerchief.' The smudges of fatigue beneath her eyes matched her carelessly applied eyeliner. 'Chin up and positive steps forward, eh? Is Mum here?'

'No, she – '

'You did tell her?'

'Yes. No. I tried. She's away for a week or so, and has no signal.'

'Did you leave a message?'

'The message didn't allow for leaving an answer,' he lied.

'Did you leave a text message?'

'No. I wanted to speak to her in person.'

'That's weird.' She paused for a few seconds.

He asked tentatively, 'Are you at all ready to talk about what happened?'

She clamped her eyes shut as though in enforced meditation, and then opened them once more to gaze upon some distant object or memory. 'Sure,' she stated, returning her attention. 'But let's take it easy. The last thing I need is an interrogation.'

'The journalist rang. What can I tell her?'

Guido appeared, and Precious joined them with rooibos tea with lemon, and a homemade jam cake made from cornmeal. Saskya leant over the teapot and breathed in the scented steam.

'What should I tell her, Uncle Guido? I feel numb,' she muttered. 'Switched off. I know it will have undermined my sense of trust. I'll never use a public toilet again, for starters. And it'll be a while before I feel safe again. And as for irritable, if you thought I was bad before, you'd better stay out of my way now or it's the catch the crockery game again!'

They all laughed, more out of relief than amusement.

'So, what happened at the petrol station?' Christian asked tentatively.

She took a deep breath and explained: 'When I was washing my hands, the woman at the basin next to me asked me to help her. She said the front doors of her car were stuck, and if I wouldn't mind crawling in one of the rear doors and try to open the driver's door she would tug at it from the outside. She looked lovely – taller than me, with a stunning full-length, yellow-patterned cotton dress and a matching turban. And she seemed so distraught. I didn't think twice. How daft can you get? Especially because her little red Toyota was parked on its own, out of sight in the far corner of the car park under some trees. She opens a rear door and in I go. At this moment, a guy appears out of nowhere and slides in next to me. He was skinny, wearing a baggy, blue hoodie, and quite nice looking, but ultra-tense.

'At that moment I know something's wrong. Scared witless, I grab the other door handle, but it must have been on child lock. He tries to force me down onto the floor. I knew if I'm on the floor, there's no chance of escape, so I beg him to let me sit up because I get panic attacks. I promised not to scream and to sit still. Thankfully, he agreed, and loosened his grip, telling me to behave and act normally.

'He tied my hands behind my back and searched my pockets for my mobile. At the first set of traffic lights, he removed the SIM card, slipped it into my pocket and gave the phone to a beggar.

'At one point a police van followed us. I looked back, but then it turned off. From that moment on, everything's a blur. At first, I was shaking with fear, and so afraid I was going to die. Then I became strangely calm, and completely focused on getting through it, and looking for ways to escape. It sounds like a cliché, but I also concentrated my thoughts on those people who really matter to me.

'Once we were on the outskirts of the city, he put a blindfold over my eyes – the fluffy type they give you on long-haul flights. I thought it was a good sign because if they intended to kill me, why worry about what I saw?

'When we arrived where I was held, they turned off the bumpy road onto a driveway. Three younger guys helped me out of the car and took me inside. Once the doors were closed, they took off the blindfold. My eyes adjusted to the light and I found we were in the lounge of a tiny bungalow.

'I sat on a sofa for what seemed like hours watching telly. I remember feeling exhausted from sheer terror, and isolated because I couldn't understand what they were saying.'

'Did they threaten to hurt you, or kill you?' Christian

asked cautiously.

'No. I told you. They were nervous but nice. My terror was partly distracted by the need to focus on total control of my sphincter. All three of them were young and black. About my height. They said they were Pedi from Limpopo. They told me it's Zulus that cause all the trouble, and that Pedi people are basically peaceful, so not to worry. I never saw the first guy and the woman again.'

'I felt awful for letting you go to the toilets alone,' said Christian, reaching for her hand. 'If I'd gone with you none of this would have happened. It makes me shudder to think what could have happened to you. I'll never forgive myself.'

'Don't worry, Dad,' she reassured him, pulling her hand away. 'They treated me with respect. And you couldn't have left the taxi with all our stuff in it.'

'Still...' He shook his head and looked away.

She twisted a strand of hair around her finger. 'I was constantly desperate for the loo,' she said. 'One of the guys fetched Imodium from a pharmacy. The cramps were regular like I was giving birth. I felt nauseous, head thumping, impossible to concentrate. The guys made me plain toast and boiled water. Then bananas. A couple of days later I was as fit as a butcher's dog. I carried on as normal – washed my hair, cleaned my teeth. They were a bit stingy with hot water, but that's all.

'One of them had been to a private school, and he said I reminded him of his favourite teacher. In some respects, I could identify with them and their efforts to help the poor and sick. We had a sort of community vibe. I was dependent on them for food; they needed me for computer games, and I eventually made them laugh – helped them relax. I guess it was also because of what we shared – fear; for them the fear of getting caught, and for me the fear that the police might try something, and I'd get caught in the crossfire. Believe it or not, I'm going to miss them. And I couldn't stop thinking about you, Dad, and how you must be feeling, and what you could possibly do on your own. Thank God for Uncle Guido.'

Christian looked away for a second and caught Guido's eye, and then focused even more intently on her eyes. 'What did you do all day?' he asked.

Her eyes again became clouded with a far-away look as though gazing through him and onto the horizon. 'Watched telly. Played computer games. With the guys.'

A look of annoyance fleetingly crossed Christian's face. Guido thought of Stockholm syndrome.

'The guys were really committed to their cause,' she continued. 'I didn't see anything of where they live, but they told me the conditions are appalling. My ransom money will go to buy medicines and food.'

Guido shook his head as if lost for words.

'According to them,' Christian cut in.

She cocked her head to one side and gave him *that* look.

'Now I feel like I've just completed an exam that went well and won a great prize in a competition, all in one day. I feel like doing very silly dances around the house.'

'Feel free,' said Guido. 'We should celebrate.'

'I'm exhausted, but I won't sleep anymore either. I was so bloody nervous. I don't know how I survived. On the other hand, my appetite's back. I want to spend a whole day just eating. Eating everything I didn't eat. Oh, what a good day that would be!'

'We'll eat out, and get back early,' Guido suggested.

'The pita place,' Precious cut in. 'Then you can have all those fresh vegetables you nag me about.'

'Is it safe?' Christian asked. 'Where's Innocent?'

'Taking the car back.' Precious said it as though it were

the perfectly normal act of returning a car to a hire company. She seemed completely oblivious to the possibility that he might be in danger or wonder how he'd get back. 'He'll call when it's done,' she added in response to Guido's look of concern.

'Leave a note,' he told her. 'Tell him to ring and that we'll bring food back for him.'

Christian remembered Blessing.

'What shall I tell the journalist?' The question was aimed at no one in particular.

'Keep it brief,' Guido warned. 'Give the basic details from what Saskya just told us, but that she was blindfolded and hadn't a clue where she was held. Tell her you met the kidnappers somewhere in the North West. They all listened while Christian rang back and did exactly as he was told. He covered the phone. 'She wants to come round in the next hour to take a photo, and – '

'No chance,' Guido whispered. 'Tell her she's traumatised and asleep and you haven't got a photo. Just get rid of her. Add a quote that it's thanks to *The Tribune* newspaper's sensitive reporting, investigative skills and careful mediation that Saskya was successfully saved. That should keep her happy.'

They put Tsotsi on guard in the front garden, set the alarm, and drove off with Guido at the wheel. He parked in the road outside the restaurant. Christian reached back for his stick, but it had got stuck awkwardly behind the front seats and Saskya had to climb back in and inelegantly retrieve it, her legs sticking out of the rear door. The car guard couldn't drag his eyes away.

It was Guido's favourite restaurant, in the Jewish quarter, run by identical twins, one of whom used to greet him like a long-lost brother and one of whom ignored him, so he was always slightly hesitant when entering, not knowing what kind of reception he'd get. This time he was ignored.

Christian and Saskya were already locked in heated argument, while a bemused Precious looked on. The waitresses hovered obsequiously.

'They shouldn't feel they need to be like that any longer,' Christian commented.

'When you say *they,* who do you mean?' Saskya seemed to be regaining her old self.

He was irritated at her obvious determination to spark an argument so soon after she'd returned, and just when he wanted to unwind. His backache was gnawing at his mood. His heart had started its clumsy, erratic thumping again. He cut in with a surprising firmness.

'You know exactly who I mean. Black South Africans.'

This served only to trigger an equally fierce comeback.

'There's something I don't like about the way you talk about them. It's like you're talking about children. They say this, they do that, it's so cute. There's something wrong about it. It's not racism exactly, but it's sort of superior, not patronising, just superior. It makes me squirm. Sorry.' She pulled a face.

'This white guilt of yours! You've hardly been here five minutes.'

'It's collective guilt. It includes you too.'

'Collective guilt? What's that? Guilty for what?'

'Because you were born somewhere that got rich by exploiting poor countries like this. Of course you're guilty.'

'You can't be guilty if you had no choice. I never chose where I was born. I haven't chosen to exploit anybody. The guilt isn't mine. It belongs to those who chose to take part in colonial exploitation and the apartheid system. The slavers,

172

the politicians, the torturers, the murderers. They're guilty – as *individuals*. Don't talk to me about collective guilt, it's meaningless.'

'This is pointless, Dad. You don't understand.' She sounded troubled and upset again.

No. For once he didn't understand. She couldn't do the simplest thing without turning it into a crusade. Always on a mission. It was admirable, but sometimes just plain annoying. Nonetheless, he was so, so glad to have her back. And what did he expect? That her awful experience would make her milder? He shook his head, and turned his attention to his halloumi wrap, while Guido and Precious were huddled in conversation about a recent housebreaking where the police had shot and killed the owners, mistaking them for the intruders.

It was late by the time they got home. Innocent was back.

'You promised to call me,' Precious shouted at him.

'Sorry, Sissie.' He gave her a cheeky smile.

She poked out her tongue at him. 'Did you eat? Sorry – I forgot about you.'

'Lend me a fifty. I'll get a burger.'

Innocent was permanently short of cash. He was going through the lengthy process of securing a bride, and consequently the security of the bride's extended family. By marrying, he would hugely enlarge his family - a vitally important support network in a country where there are few social benefits. 'We all help each other,' he explained to Guido. 'The more of us there are, the more there are to help.'

The bride price, a *lobola*, was the cost of two Nguni cows, a jacket, a hat and walking stick for the bride's father. He had already met the parents and had agreed to split the *lobola* into staged payments, the final one being due in a year's time.

After that, they could hold their wedding ceremony. Guido helped Innocent whenever he could, to prevent him falling into the clutches of 'micro-lenders', whose rates of interest were extortionate and whose collection methods were brutal. More baseball bats were sold to micro-lenders than to baseball players.

At the same time, Guido was careful to avoid an obvious increase in Innocent's dependency on him. Innocent never mentioned the money, and Guido was never quite sure whether it was a gift or a loan. He presumed it would depend on whether he ever paid it back. Meanwhile, Innocent was a relieved man as though he believed one of his angels had sent down a Samaritan. He didn't behave as if he was indebted. He seemed to think that his god or his angel had lent it, using Guido as a go-between.

Tiredness descended on Christian suddenly like thick smog. His feelings towards the day's developments were oddly ambivalent – overwhelmingly relieved at getting Saskya back while terrified of the eventual effect on her. He couldn't be certain. Nothing was certain anymore. He said goodnight to everyone, hugged Saskya so hard she winced, dragged himself upstairs, and flung himself into bed without bothering to wash.

Saskya stood staring at the dining room wall. She looked drawn and tired, her mood funereal. Guido moved towards her to keep her company. 'Drink Saskya?' He was reluctant to call her Sas in case it was too familiar or personal to her dad. It was as if she hadn't heard. With a deep despondent look in her eyes, she gazed vacantly at the Hindu prayer on the wall, as though mesmerised by the hope and inspiration of the uplifting words of worship.

With a blank look on her troubled face, she moved

towards the French doors, paused for a moment, then wandered onto the *stoep* and took a deep lungful of the cool, fragrant evening air. She now seemed mired in the most profound gloom, reminding Guido that her lovely soul was ill-equipped for the stresses she'd been through since alighting on African soil. He left her alone but decided not to turn in until he was sure she was safely tucked up in bed. She came back in, bringing with her a wave of the warm night air, and stood still at the bottom of the stairs, her back to him, one hand on the stair rail. Her shoulders drooped. She stood impassively rooted to the spot.

She brushed her hair from her eyes and covered her face with her hands. She let her face drop so far it was buried out of sight. She let out a single hoarse sob. 'I felt, felt – so invaded at first,' she muttered, lifting her head and turning towards him, her lips trembling. She suddenly seemed childlike and dependent, sunken within herself. Tears welled, overflowed and slid down her cheeks. She wiped them away with the back of her wrist, and said, 'I can't help feeling so bloody vulnerable.' The tears choked her voice.

Guido stood beside her and touched her lightly on the arm. She looked up, threw him a quizzical look, and nodded pensively before climbing the stairs laboriously as though moving knee-deep through thick mud.

'Goodnight, Saskya,' he called. Nothing else seemed appropriate. He clumsily tapped a cigarette from a soft pack, lit it, and exhaled smoke at the ceiling. The cat sat on the window-sill, silhouetted against the sky outside, its back to him. All at once he too felt physically drained, like after a long walk in the snow.

22

The police kept track of developments by reading the morning edition of *The Tribune*. A front page boxed text headed *Tribune helps free kidnapped English girl* pointed to a short feature article on page three with the photo of Christian. His quote about the paper's mediation skills was emboldened. There was no mention about the size of the ransom.

A detective from Central Police Station phoned Christian to arrange to meet him and Saskya at the hotel.

'What do I say?' Christian asked Guido.

Guido snatched the phone from his hand. 'Sorry, we're leaving now.'

The young-sounding detective explained that his task was to draw up a detailed plan of the house in which Saskya had been kept prisoner, in the hope that it could be traced.

'Sorry, we can't possibly.'

'Would your daughter recognise any of them?' he asked Guido.

'Not a chance. She was blindfolded at all times. Sorry.'

'How much did you pay them?' The voice was starting to sound exasperated. 'A hundred thousand,' Guido lied. He claimed to have used a twenty-thousand-rand emergency money and to have drawn cash at three different cash machines each day using UK credit and debit cards.

He told him he took a private taxi to meet the kidnappers somewhere in the wilds of the North West, but to have been so distraught he could remember next to nothing.

'Which taxi company did you use?'

'I don't know. At a taxi rank near here.'

'Can you describe the kidnappers?'

'They were young and black.'

'What was the make of their car?'

'A pickup truck. Sorry. I'm not good with cars.'

'I see.' The detective paused. 'Where are you staying?'

'Sorry, not sure. We really have to leave. We'll miss our flights. Thanks for your help.' Guido didn't wait for a reply before hanging up.

'Guido, there's an airport strike!'

'Shit!' Guido's face reddened. 'Our first mistake. Don't worry. He sounded no older than sixteen. Probably doesn't know his arse from his elbow.'

Christian looked down as though in critical analysis of his beautiful shoes and went outside.

After the call, Saskya drank a cup of tea with Guido in the dining room and came out with it as though just in passing. 'Uncle Guido, maybe I should also mention that part of the ransom money was to pay off the local Honingsloot police. They knew all along who the kidnappers were.'

Guido's expression froze. 'What?' Not a real question, but a word to gain time, to let the mind catch up. For seconds neither spoke. He stood up sharply and turned to face the garden, his hands behind his back, playing the sentence back to himself to make sure he'd understood correctly. What now?

Saskya looked dumbfounded as though repeating to herself what she had just said, in the hope that it could shed some light on Uncle Guido's sudden display of extreme anxiety.

He sat down again. His fingers tapped out a nervous rhythm on the table top as he tried to concentrate his mind on the problem in hand. He got up, poured a drink, and sat down again.

'What's the matter, Uncle Guido?' She sounded scared.

'When are you leaving for Europe?' he asked, in a flat, controlled voice.

'I haven't discussed it with Dad,' she replied, taking the chair next to him. 'No offence, but if I could leave this minute, I would. I want to feel safe again – cold, wet and miserable, but safe. But we haven't got the money for new flights, and now the airports' strike has extended to truck and taxi drivers. Trucks have blocked the road to the airport. We're trapped. Could we stay till it's over? Uncle Guido, what's wrong?'

'You're most welcome.' Guido lit a *Gaulloises* and blew a lungful of smoke towards the ceiling. 'But what you've told me changes things somewhat. Go and fetch your father.'

Guido let his gaze momentarily drift towards the garden beyond the French windows. He watched the trees move in the gentle breeze – some in short jerky movements; the taller ones in more dignified waves.

'Christian, join us. Sit down.' Guido's expression was tense and solemn. 'I've a confession to make which might affect your travel plans. I'm afraid it's not over yet. In fact, it might only be just beginning.'

His eyes reflected a brief flicker of unease. He placed both hands face downwards on the table, pushing back slightly in his chair. Christian and Saskya sat opposite him.

'What do you mean?' asked Christian.

'Saskya has just told me that part of the ransom money was to pay off the local police, who knew all along who the kidnappers were. They probably guessed that rich foreigner Christian Kettermann would pay up, and that there'd be plenty for everyone, and no need to waste the courts' time.'

Christian returned his gaze, wordlessly watching. The

web in the corner of the ceiling was still there; the oddly shaped spider was gone. Seconds ticked past before he found his voice.

'How could they possibly have known?'

'Not sure. The journalist?'

'Why didn't you tell me this before, Sas?'

'I haven't had a chance. I didn't think – '

'It's okay, Saskya.' Guido's voice grated slightly as it strained through a sore throat already parched by too many cigarettes and now a sudden feeling of immense agitation. 'There are two pieces of information you have a right to know. The first is that apart from the top layer, most of the ransom money was counterfeit. I should know. I forged it.'

For a fraction of a second, she stared at him as if he'd slapped her face. She held her breath for a moment, then, leaping to her feet, screamed, 'Bloody hell! Uncle Guido! How could you? Do you realise what you've done? You've – you've – ' Her eyes blazed. Her expression reflected a dissonant blend of moral indignation and impotent rage. 'I thought my ordeal was for a good cause. Now I feel like a cheat and a fraud. I want to scrub myself raw!'

'When did you forge it?' Christian cut in. 'You haven't had time. You told me the picture – '

'Months ago.' Guido shifted slightly on his seat and avoided their gaze. 'Just in case. A nest egg. We didn't make a particularly good job of it. It's passable, but it wouldn't take much of an expert to reveal it for what it is – wads of worthless scraps of paper.'

'Jesus!'

Saskya looked at her father in amazement. He'd always made a point of never blaspheming.

'Who's *we*?'

'I helped design the plates. A print shop in Hillbrow.

179

Nigerian. They did the rest. And kept a wad for themselves.'

'Was that the money you showed me?'

'Yes.'

Leaning forward on his elbows, Guido continued, 'The second piece of information is that what was going to be the source of the genuine money was a painting that wasn't one of my usual works in the style of a famous painter, but was a genuine forgery, as you know, Christian.' He leaned back. 'That's why it sold so quickly at that price. I sold it to an Israeli dealer in Sandton as a genuine Franciscus van der Linden, with the artist's forged signature on it, and a completely fictitious provenance claiming that the painting was brought by a family to Cape Town around the middle of the 18th century for the VOC.'

'The what?'

'The *Vereenigde Oost-Indische Compagnie*. The Dutch East India Company. Works of art were needed for government buildings and the houses of wealthy traders. It's accompanied by a forged statement from the family. The dealer couldn't believe his luck. The problem is that my previous dealings with him have been on the basis that he knew they were forgeries. In this case, I convinced him that this was the genuine article.'

'And the significance?'

Guido looked down at his bony hands. His eyes felt prickly.

'At my meeting with him a couple of days ago he told me he's decided to boost his profit by selling it at auction in Amsterdam as a Dutch national art treasure.'

'So?'

'They'll have the expertise in Amsterdam to discover it's a fake.'

Christian's silence betrayed his bafflement. 'I see,' he

managed to say. He looked depressed. 'You told me about the fake signature. You might have mentioned the dangers. You told me you'd use the money from the picture to pay the ransom. Why didn't you? Why use counterfeit notes?'

'Two reasons. First, I had to offload them quickly because this country's about to issue new banknotes with a different design. With the big five animals. Almost impossible to copy.'

'And the second?'

'My health,' Guido told them with a weary smile. 'I don't improve with age.'

'What's that got to do with it?'

'This isn't cosy England with free health care.' Guido heard his own voice sharpening. 'A short stay in hospital costs a fortune. If that happened I'd need all the money I can lay my hands on to look after those who depend on me.'

'Come off it. What about your medical insurance?'

'I haven't got any. I'm here illegally.'

Christian felt the back of his skull tighten. His mind spun madly between anger and fear. '*We* depended on you. You took a risk with my daughter's life!' His voice sounded more petulant than angry.

'You got her back, didn't you?' Guido pressed down on his knees. 'And we had it covered. In the unlikely event that they'd realised that the money was fake, we'd have saved her anyway. Just a bit rougher.'

'I don't believe you.' The muscles around Christian's mouth were drawn tight. 'Listen to you. You sound like some small-town gangster, yet – '

'Believe what you like. You got your girl. It cost you nothing. It was at no risk to you. It was something you couldn't have done yourself. You probably thought it amounted to one of your ethical choices. But I tell you, considering the circumstances, the people involved, the

181

country and the dreadful consequences of getting it wrong, there was only one option. And one option is not a choice unless you think that to do nothing is an option. I knew what was necessary, and I did it. So, I suggest you pack away your sanctimonious whining and try a little humility.'

'Wait,' said Saskya, gesturing for silence. 'Dad, be reasonable.' A frown puckered her forehead.

Christian looked as if he'd been slapped.

'This will have consequences,' Guido continued more calmly. 'First, assuming some of the forged two-hundred-rand notes have ended up with the police, they could go after the kidnappers, and then they might try to come after you, Christian, as the gang might if they know where to find you. Secondly, the art dealer, who also runs a nightclub near the airport, is a nasty bit of work with gang connections. No one knows why, but his lawyer was found in his car recently, burnt to a crisp and with most of his teeth missing. That's the kind of person we're dealing with.'

'*You're* dealing with…' Christian remained immobile and grim-faced.

'*I'm* dealing with,' Guido agreed, turning his head to exhale the smoke away from them. 'It's only a matter of time. I wasn't going to tell you because I thought you'd be long gone by then.'

Guido's hands met each other on the table as he hunched forward to press his point home. He paused to watch the effect of his words. Christian's gaze returned dumbfounded silence.

'You took that risk for us, Uncle Guido?' Saskya managed to ask, her eyes softening.

'Has the dealer got your address?' Christian interrupted.

Guido took a sharp intake of breath and cleared his throat. 'Not as far as I know.'

They both exhaled in relief.

'To find us, the police will start with Blessing.' Guido pressed a button on his cellphone and held it to his ear. 'No answer. I'll ring the paper. Hello. Give me Blessing please.' He put the phone on the table. 'She's not come in. She was expected but they don't know where she is. Christian, have you given her this address.'

'No. Only the hotel. She's got my mobile number. That's all.'

'Hang on.' Saskya sat bolt upright. 'How did she first contact you, Dad?'

'The police tipped her off.'

'There you have it!' She sat back and folded her arms.

'Turn your phone off, remove the battery and SIM card and don't use it again,' Guido ordered. 'Clear? Same with laptops. No internet. I'll do the same. I gave the journalist my number when I initially contacted her. Keep our heads down for a while.'

'What about Mum? We haven't told her yet.'

'That'll have to wait.'

'I'm staying till this is finished,' Saskya stated. 'After all you've done for us.'

'Me too,' said Christian, hesitantly. 'But don't expect me to kill anyone. We'll help all we can. Without compromising our values.'

'You compromised them when you let me rescue Saskya,' Guido reminded him. 'You're already on the slippery slope, dear cousin.'

'I never asked you to do it the way you did.'

'For God's sake. There you go again! Did you stop me? What I did was on your behalf – that's the same as doing it yourself. And the same applies to what we're facing now. Don't kid yourself. We'll do whatever is necessary and bugger the moralising.'

He flicked out another cigarette from the pack, lit it from the previous one, and allowed the smoke to screen him momentarily from Christian, who looked away into the garden.

'Give Innocent your passport, and we'll have a fake one made.'

'What for?'

'Strategic planning.' His tone was tired and exasperated.

'How? They're impossible to copy.'

'They use stolen ones. Perfectly adequate for this part of the world. Give him a passport photo. Have you got one?'

'Yes, but – '

'Innocent!' he called. Guido ran upstairs and returned with a brown envelope. He counted out fifty notes of two hundred rand each and handed them to Innocent.

'Sort it out *now-now*. And fix me up with another cellphone and SIM, a used one.' He nodded to Innocent, who grabbed Christian's passport and photo, turned on his heel, and headed for the car.

'One more thing.' Guido leapt to his feet and marched after him. 'Wait.' He extracted a passport photo from his wallet. 'Use this one, Inno. Understand?'

Innocent nodded.

Guido returned to the others. 'My guess is that the Honingsloot police will put the screws on the kidnappers,' he continued. 'It'll be child's play for them to lock those guys up, and *sjambok* them till they produce all the money. If they come for us, they'd have to trump up some charge, explain why they're operating outside their territory, get a warrant and risk revealing their involvement with the kidnappers. If they took that route, it would take them several days – at least a week. But what for? To punish us, get more money out of

184

us? Punishing us makes them no richer, and they wouldn't know whether we'd have any cash here. Most likely, the cops that were in on this, as well as the kidnappers, will assume that because the money was good enough to fool them, it will be good enough to fool others. They may simply spend it, but anonymously and a long way from here. My guess is that they're the least of our problems, but we've got to be ready for them. If we get any visitors, they're more likely to come from the dealer. In his world, vendetta counts. He'll want blood, teeth, fingernails and whatever else he can lay his filthy hands on.'

'How long have we got?' Christian asked, his voice heavy with concern. 'Assuming they find out where we are.'

'Like I said, at least one week for the unlikelihood of a police visit, and a lot longer for the dealer's men, depending on when the Amsterdam auctioneers carry out their tests.'

'Are you sure this will happen?'

'The police, the kidnappers, the dealer. When that many very angry people are involved, retribution is inevitable.' He got to his feet. 'In case it goes wrong, everyone must have access to the key to one of the safes.'

'Why?' Christian asked.

'What are you going to do when there's a gun at your head or knife at your throat and you're asked for the key?'

'Tell them I don't know where it is,' he replied weakly.

'And why should they believe you? You don't want me to tell you what will happen next, but by the time they've finished with you, you'll be wishing to God that you knew where the key was. You might even wish you were dead. Believe me. They will be acting for people who are extremely angry. Come with me.'

He led the two of them up the stairs to a door in the corner of his bedroom. Behind it a grey-enamelled gun safe stood about five foot high and two foot wide. 'Inside is a pistol and five thousand rand, which is enough to keep most robbers happy. I'll add another twenty thousand that'll hopefully achieve a bloodless conclusion,' he told them. 'The key is in the corner cupboard downstairs with the other keys.'

'Real or fake money?' Christian asked.

'Real.'

Guido closed the door behind him and led them back downstairs.

'Have you seen this?' Christian asked pointing to a newspaper headline about a Mozambican taxi driver dying after being dragged behind a police van. 'Innocent told me that beatings and rape of prisoners is quite usual. No wonder you're wary of the police.'

Guido took a sip of *rooibos* tea to wet his parched mouth and sore throat. He lit another cigarette, inhaling deeply, feeling a delicious dizziness overlay his nerves.

'I'm worried about their off-duty activities. But getting arrested doesn't worry me,' he smiled. 'In this country, money can buy you anything, including custodial comfort.' He shrugged in a way that dismissed the subject as a bore and turned his mind to speculate about the looming threat. He crushed the half-finished cigarette underfoot and headed for the studio.

23

It was just after lunch. The sweet smell of flowers blooming in the fresh hot summer air had brought Guido back into the garden to read. He looked up as a shadow fell across his book.

'I'm here, Mr Guido,' Precious whispered, running her long fingers through his hair. '*Sawubona*. I see you. Please grow your hair again.'

She looked gorgeous. Her stunning knee-length turquoise and white cotton skirt was the perfect dress for the perfect body. They hugged.

'It's very hot in the garden. Look at me. I'm completely black. I look like a Nigerian.'

Guido's chuckle subsided into a spasm. She had indeed turned from dark brown to ebony. She was in her prime – literally. Her fertile energy and her vitality were full of promise that he believed she'd promised to no other man in the way she had to him. How she had never fallen pregnant by him he could attribute only to his own physical decline – certainly not to hers.

'You sound sick, Mr Guido. My mother made me eat raw garlic to stop me being sick. I hated it. You must try it, or maybe peppermint root so I can breathe your breath.'

They hugged again, and she dug her strong fingers into his back. Her hug was no harder than usual, but it caused a deep pain in his throat and chest. *Love does hurt*, he thought to himself.

The pain worsened during the night. Guido thought he'd caught the flu and could feel his chest closing up. He went to bed early without a pipe or Precious but had to keep getting up and walk around just to get air. He tried hanging over a bowl of steaming water with a towel over his head. It had no effect.

He went back to bed, but it became more and more difficult to breathe. He could feel fluid bubbling up at the back of the throat that he couldn't clear. He felt like he was drowning. He got up again, gasping for air, and went to fetch Precious.

'Your voice is sounding sicker, Mr Guido,' said a worried Precious. 'You didn't take peppermint root. I am taking you to the clinic.'

'Inno, look after the place while we're gone,' she ordered.

'Okay, Sissie. I am here twenty-four hours. Don't worry. I cannot allow us to be robbed while I am still alive.'

'So, if you hear anything, I can rely on you to deal with it,' Guido croaked. 'Beware of unexpected visitors. Let no one in.'

'I was nearly a policeman. I have my weapons. I am stronger and I am faster. I know all ways in this place. I won't sleep. They wouldn't know I am here. Then, I will subdue them and deal with them.' He snapped his fingers in imitation of a flick knife and stabbed the air imitating the thrust of the blade, pulling his hand down as though piercing the neck of his assailant like a matador's sword entering a bull's neck. His wild look reflected that in his mind's eye he was completely living out the act of murdering somebody. He seemed to grow in stature as he spoke, and Guido had no hesitation in believing him.

They took the Merc as fast as Precious dared to drive, hoping that there would be no police checks on the way. They were immediately admitted to the trauma unit in a clinic that looked more like a hotel than a hospital. The woman doctor in charge made a quick diagnosis and put him on oxygen just in time before he passed out. Then, blood tests, x-ray and a scan.

'You've got a severe bacterial infection, but we've got to get to the underlying cause,' the young doctor warned. 'I believe there's something else as well.'

It was four in the morning when the scan results came back. She said that there was either an abscess or 'growth of some kind' as well as the swelling from the infection and that he must see a consultant immediately. The nearest consultant that she could find at that time of night was at a hospital in a suburb outside Johannesburg.

She put Guido on a drip of penicillin and cortisone to expand the efficiency of the lungs until he could get to the surgeon who would deal with the growth. The next step was to call an ambulance. The phone lines at the ambulance centre were down, so she ordered a private ambulance. Neither Guido nor Precious had cash. With Guido still gasping for breath, the doctor went around the entire trauma unit getting a tenner here, a twenty there, from members of staff and guards to get together a total of one thousand two hundred rand.

The ambulance, no bigger than a parcel van, drove so fast that he could see out of the back window that Precious was struggling to keep up despite jumping red lights. He was linked up to a heart monitor, blood pressure monitor, drip and other equipment. Each time they hurtled round a bend, tyres squealing, the two paramedics were thrown from one side of the van to the other, falling over him, falling over each other – wires, tubes everywhere, like a spaghetti fight. After a terrifying journey, an hour later, he was in a bed in the intensive care unit, his heart palpitating, his blood pressure dangerously high.

Precious was not allowed to stay longer than a few minutes. Guido marvelled at her composure. Her patient strength was consoling, her squeeze of Christian's shoulder and a pat on the back were maternal and protective, but as she turned to go her warm smile was edged with an almost imperceptible uncertainty.

The male senior nurse assigned to Guido was Kenneth from the Cameroon – a man with a sense of humour.

'How old are you?' he asked Guido.

Sixty-five.'

'Ha! You should be dead by now.'

'Eh?' Guido gasped.

'According to South Africa's lifespan statistics.' He smiled a lopsided smile. 'And if you'd come from Zimbabwe you'd have been dead for the last 20 years!' he laughed, holding his nose and pulling a face.

Guido, now sitting up in bed with tubes and wires linked to various items of apparatus at his bedside, smiled as he read a text message from Innocent telling him that the angels were working on a miracle for him. It was a smile, not a laugh. Guido understood that it's easy to ridicule that kind of belief, but it enriched Innocent's life and reflected a need to believe in something supernatural or metaphysical.

Guido would ask his philosopher cousin what harm there is. If it turns out there is no God or no angels or no afterlife, Innocent will never know. If atheist philosophers are right, there will be nothing of him surviving that can know or that can be disappointed. Religious belief is a human need that gave meaning to Innocent's life. Atheist zealots were right when they said it can go wrong when it imposes itself as a fundamental authority on moral behaviour. But that aspect of institutionalised religions had little to do with Innocent's belief in angels.

It was a government hospital, and considerably down market from the clinic. The place was like a field hospital, calmly coping with the near dead from traffic accidents and knife fights. Although it was an intensive care ward there was no bustle, no self-important matrons strutting up and down the ward aisles barking out their orders. It was all done with a certain rhythm, as though to the slow, steady beat of an African drum. There was just a relaxed ebb and flow of activity, accompanied by wide smiles and human kindness.

A lovely Zulu nurse came to his bedside to give him a blood test. His bed had already been screened off as though to shield his sensitive, blue eyes from the bloody, messy afflictions of ordinary people around him. He looked the other way, while she did it, and stared at a gap in the curtain just behind her. He thought about what Precious would be doing at that moment, and how he could protect her from events to come.

'What's the matter with him?' he asked the nurse, pointing to the bed opposite.

'Herb poisoning.'

'Eh?'

'The government told us that people with Aids can be cured by eating lots of garlic and beetroot. Now lots of people go to traditional healers, *sangomas*. For five hundred rand they get herbs. But they try to get better quickly and get back to work to pay for them by taking too much all at once and get very ill. Then they end up here in intensive care, still with Aids and also with herb poisoning. The healers never take responsibility. They always say you didn't take them properly. That poor man will probably die.'

'Where do you come from?'

'KwaZulu-Natal. I live in the hospital. My mama and papa are in London. They live in a flat with their brothers and sisters and my mama's cousins. My mama works at a hospital. They are living badly so that they can send money back to us.'

Guido nodded.

'Why have you got no arms and legs?' she asked with a cheeky grin. 'What do you do for work?'

'I paint pictures,' he croaked.

'Look at me,' she said, showing him her biceps. 'Feel.' He squeezed her upper arm, which was muscled like that of a boxer. 'When you must carry children and fetch water and the mealy pap and do all the cooking you get nice arms and legs like me, *ne*.'

She playfully slapped him on the shoulder on the one spot on his entire sixty-five-year-old body that had a touch of arthritis and laughed her husky laugh. Not for the first time with African women, he was lost for words. He just had to bravely force a smile.

A Rwandan dinner lady with her trolley rattled up to his bedside, handed him a tray, and lifted the lid revealing a bowl of thin soup and a kind of porridge. He thanked her with a smile, but a crushing sense of urgency had taken a toll of his appetite. He wasn't too concerned about the police whose possible revenge he now regarded as relatively theoretical. And, although the picture would already have arrived in Amsterdam, the art dealer-cum-nightclub owner wouldn't know for quite some time that the artist with the foreign accent – the man he had trusted for several deals – had fleeced him to the tune of seven figures.

And Christian and Saskya would be around for at least a couple more weeks. An extra pair of hands would be useful.

A plan was already taking shape in his mind. He just needed to get back soonest.

24

'Just our luck,' Christian muttered.

Leaving Innocent to look after Saskya and guard the house, Precious drove Christian to the hospital in the shiny black Mercedes. She jumped a red light at a junction as they headed east towards the freeway. If she hadn't, the taxi behind would have piled into them. But the policeman at the side of the road didn't see it that way. He pulled them over. She produced her licence.

'I have to fine you,' he said, wagging his finger. 'Six hundred.' Then in a low voice between teeth clenched into a smile. 'How much do you like to pay?'

'Little as possible.' She continued to look straight ahead.

'It's up to you.'

She looked at Christian and mouthed 'one hundred'. He hesitatingly produced a one hundred rand note from his wallet, shook hands with the policeman, and they were on their way again.

'I really don't agree with this,' he told Precious. 'It makes us just as corrupt as he is. In fact, we are corrupting him.'

She took her eyes off the road for a second to glance at him with a look of utter disbelief and then continued with a silent concentration on getting them to the hospital.

Precious hugged Guido avoiding the thin tube hanging from his nose and handed him a bag of fruit, a portable DVD player and a DVD of *The English Patient*. She found two chairs and sat down in suffering silence. Guido looked her up and down with the air of someone contemplating a work of art. She was squeezed into a black t-shirt and skin-tight, flowered slacks, and he thought that if the term 'dressed to kill' was taken literally, he would gladly die a thousand glorious deaths.

Christian turned to face Guido. 'Just to say how sorry I am,' he said. 'Your bravery is admirable.'

'Thanks, but you've no cause to worry.' He told Christian about Innocent's message, and how he would benefit from the healing powers of angelic intervention.

'If I had someone to pray to myself, I probably would,' Christian responded. 'All I can do is hope that this episode has a relatively good outcome.'

Guido thought that despite its reflection of a fantasy world of angels and gods, Innocent's text message seemed so much more authentic than Christian's words of sympathy, however well-meant.

'It does seem a coincidence your coming down with this at the very moment you're having to face a possible comeuppance,' Christian commented. 'As a philosopher, I'm not allowed to believe in coincidences. As a non-philosopher, it probably seems to you that everything is random coincidence, including this. But I'm not so sure.'

How does he know what 'seems to me'? Guido thought with some irritation. He decided that to make the best of this situation he would let his cousin witter on about his theories while Guido, hardly able to speak, could daydream about how to deal with an almost certain revenge attack by either the kidnappers, the police, or friends of the police coming after Christian, or the art dealer's underworld friends coming after Guido himself.

Precious saved Guido from having to reply by suddenly getting to her feet. 'I have to do some shopping,' she announced, with a note of desperation. If she'd been white, she'd have looked sickly pale. Instead, she had turned grey.

'Just come back when you're ready,' he told her gently in a rasping voice she'd never heard before. 'Christian and I have a lot to talk about. Or rather he does.'

She bravely smiled her lovely smile and left as though on a mission.

'How's Saskya?' Guido asked.

'Quietly processing it all. She sleeps most of the time.'

'Time is exactly what she needs.'

'Got stopped by the cops on the way here,' Christian said, scraping his chair closer to the edge of the bed. 'Precious jumped the lights. We had to pay a bribe.'

'You *had* to?'

'No. But… Anyway. It's simply not right.'

'Sorry, Man,' Guido rasped, looking beyond Christian at another patient being wheeled in. 'I've done all the talking I can manage. Why don't you entertain me with the Kettermann solution to police corruption?' There was no hint of sarcasm.

'Okay. I'll be right back.'

Guido picked up his cellphone. Another text from Innocent. He'd ordered a mass to be said for Guido at the church in Soweto, with dancing and gospel singing. He said that Guido's survival had absolutely nothing to do with South Africa's supreme health service but was due to a miracle. Each member of the congregation, he told Guido, has an angel, and angels gathered together in a group of over one hundred are extremely powerful, as evidenced by his survival so far.

Christian returned with two coffees. 'Right. If the public no longer trusts the police, faith in the justice system goes out the window,' he began. 'Restoring integrity instils pride in being a policeman and boosts public trust and confidence. Then people are willing to help the police, to report crime and to come forward as witnesses. Trust is essential, right?'

Guido's throat made a gurgling sound.

'To fight corruption, you target the police and you target the public. You stop people from paying bribes. You prosecute them and publicise the prosecutions. And you deal with police integrity. Internalising distaste for corruption is the only effective way to help them resist. You identify subculture habits, such as a *code of silence* where officers lie to protect each other, and the illusion that you can't beat crime without bending the rules. You make them examine the sort of issues you mentioned yourself - accepting gifts, leaking information, demands for discounts from businesses, free services of prostitutes and so on. They then analyse and resolve dilemmas specific to these issues. They try to work out the core values involved, and how to apply them in real life situations where they must act under pressure. Also, recruitment excludes applicants who might be an integrity risk.'

Christian paused for breath. 'I tell you, Guido. This is the answer.' He leant forward, his voice rising in enthusiasm. 'We've got to make policemen better people.'

'That would be lovely.'

'And make soldiers better soldiers. Ah, there's Precious.' He grabbed his stick, pushed back his chair and stood up. 'See you tomorrow,' he said jauntily, shaking Guido's left hand to avoid the drip needle in his right. 'Don't worry about a thing. Innocent seems to have everything covered.'

He made way for Precious who, still looking a sickly colour, bent over the bed, stroked Guido's hair, and kissed him on the lips.

'What will happen now?' she asked.

'There's an abscess,' he whispered. 'They'll remove it in the morning. Wish me luck.'

196

He watched them leave through the sprung double doors and slumped back onto the pillows with a sigh of relief, exhausted by Christian's mere presence and in-your-face enthusiasm. It wasn't that he didn't find his cousin's lectures interesting, it was just that that's what they were – lectures. Tiring, and for some inexplicable reason, annoying.

As though by default, his mind drifted to trouble ahead. What would those two innocents do if the dealer's men came while he was still laid up? Innocent could be terrifying, but there was only one of him. It didn't bear thinking about. He reached for *The English Patient* and slipped it into his DVD player.

His favourite nurse shuffled in at the start of the night shift. She looked dead on her feet. Muttering a brief 'Hello, how are you feeling?' she sat down in the armchair next to his bed, her tired eyes staring at the monitors. Almost immediately her head drooped. She snored and woke up with a start.

'Get some sleep,' he said gently. 'I'm wide awake.'

Keeping watch on the monitors gave him a delicious sense of empowerment over his own life. *I shall not die like my wife. I shall not die in a hospital bed. I shall decide where, when and how.*

25

Christian was warming himself in the shade of a pine tree next to the pool while Saskya slept. Precious brought him oranges and tea that came 'all the way from China', which she said reminded her of a song by Guido's favourite folk singer from Canada. She placed the cup and bowl on a camping table. Innocent was mowing the lawn beyond the pool. The heady scent of freshly-cut grass, musty, moist and herbal, blended with the smell of smoke from a bonfire of grass cuttings.

'How long have you lived here, Precious?' Christian asked, to break the silence.

'A long time,' she replied cagily, out of habit rather than suspicion. Guido had warned her that people who ask direct questions should always be given the vaguest possible of answers.

'Guido never got around to telling me how the two of you met.' He put down his cup, and leant forward, catching her scent. 'Why don't you sit down?'

She pulled up a chair. 'At an art gallery reception,' she told him. 'He was with a girlfriend. A Dutch woman. She was even taller than me, but skinny and had a big nose.' She pulled a face. 'He called her Duchess. I won him from her. For Mr Guido, Duchess was not precious.' She laughed her deep laugh and slapped him on the thigh as though she'd momentarily got the two cousins mixed up. 'Sorry,' she giggled, holding up her palms in front of her. She smoothed down the front of her white satin dress.

Christian inexplicably started to feel uncomfortable. He felt as though her presence – her aura – was overwhelming him. He took a deep breath, and asked, 'You said you come from Polokwane?'

'A village about two hours away from town.'

'Why did you move here?'

She adjusted her headband of vulture and peacock feathers as though to give her time to think about her response.

'I didn't belong anymore. The community elders wanted me to get a good education so that I could earn a good living. When I returned they shunned me because I had changed – not for the better in their view, but spoiled by the outside world.'

Christian nodded. 'Go on.'

'School does not make us ready for the outside world, so everything remains strange to us unless we have further education. But when we enter university we are strangers. The students from the cities, especially white ones, were inward looking. They did a lot of thinking about themselves. But we don't like to think too much in case we bring to life painful memories of horrible things. And knowledge is passed on through books rather than the spoken words and stories we were used to. It all seemed too strange.'

Christian leant back in his chair. 'I can well imagine.'

'I was torn between the culture of the university and my own culture. I was in no man's land. We had to learn in languages that are foreign to us. They are not African. They belong to the colonial masters. They say Afrikaans is a South African language. Yet it contains European values such as rights to property, materialism and so on. It is colonial. On top of that, the university itself is in a strange place, a place we don't know. It's all too strange.'

She reached for an orange and dug her nails into the peel. Juice oozed along her finger.

'When I finally returned to Limpopo years later, I found the culture there was also strange. It took me months to love my roots again, but even then I was regarded as an outcast. I had become strange to them. There was the river between us.'

Christian raised his eyebrows questioningly.

She smiled. 'It reminds me of a poem I learned by heart before I left the village. From a book called *The River Between* by Ngugi. It's about the separation of people torn between the old ways and the new ways. You must read it.

He nodded. Her deep voice held a range of sensuous modulations. Despite her playful sexiness, she had a dignity that appeared to run deep. He thought this woman would be unstoppable if she took up a mission. She might lack the skills to always choose the right path, but whatever path she did choose would be travelled with unfathomable courage. He felt pitifully small beside her and he started to brood about all that seemed mundane and commonplace about himself. She seemed to represent an entire world of which he knew nothing, and of which he could never know anything, no matter how hard he tried.

He broke the silence. 'What do you think about Guido, Precious?'

'I don't know,' she replied placidly, her serene exterior masking what must have been immense inner turmoil. 'He was ill before. The doctors cured it, but he was in much pain. He was given morphine for a long time. I'm afraid he got used to it.'

'What, you mean he got hooked on – '

'I'm afraid to lose him,' she interrupted, her voice faltering. 'Mr Guido is a real man. A real man makes his woman feel safe. And I can laugh with him. We make each other laugh. And we teach each other things. We learn together. We are meant for each other. He is my other half.

200

We are like doves. We kill doves. We eat doves. But you must kill both. They are meant for each other. Otherwise one is sad for the rest of her life. We understand what we mean to each other, but we use different words. He says I am a child of mother earth, and he is from the heavens, and that we join on the earth's surface. That we are yin and yang, which comes from his fighting art. My own culture tells me I am half – one arm, one leg and so on, in front of a waterfall, and he is the other half inside the waterfall. We join in the middle and get swept off our feet. The feeling is difficult to describe. It is like feeling whole. It is a very nice feeling,' she giggled.

'Isn't polygamy still tolerated here?' he asked rhetorically, changing the subject.

'Our male politicians have many other halves.' Only her mouth laughed. Her eyes were steady and gazed straight into his. Her expression remained unchanged, but without warning her feelings had erupted in the form of heavy tears that streamed over her cheekbones. He pulled out his linen handkerchief and handed it to her. When she handed it back it was sodden. He carefully placed it in his trouser pocket with such care it could have been a pet mouse. She wiped the last tear away carefully with her forefinger as though she wanted to save it, and lowered her voice. 'He is losing his strength. I would like him to see a traditional healer.'

Christian was astonished to feel sharp, swift pangs of jealousy. This beautiful woman was too good to be the mistress of his thoroughly corrupt cousin. Was her love for Guido really just for the security and protection he offered her? If so, he could have offered her the same – perhaps more, as Guido's days could be numbered. But from what she said, her love was profoundly more than that. Although their different cultures condemned them to be forever strangers, somehow one of them appeared to have crossed 'the river between'.

'A *sangoma*? You believe in them?'

'I believe in the power of the spirits – of our ancestors. I believe that some herbal medicines can make you much stronger than doctors' pills that poison you. But I do not believe in many of the *sangoma*'s traditional ways.'

'Such as?'

She smoothed her skirt over her thighs and leant forward to slide a hand along her shin and massage the ankle. 'What they wanted to do with one of my babies,' she said, her eyes, still wet, looking into the far distance. 'I am proud to be an African woman but when I was pregnant the *sangoma* told me to drink herbal medicine called *Isihlambheso*. She said it would make my birth easy and call up the spirits to protect my baby. But I felt the spirits were already with me. I didn't take the medicine. My birth was easy, and my baby healthy. Then the healer told me to take out the *inyoni*, the first green poo. In white and Indian babies green poo is normal, so I didn't do it. Also, my baby had an *ibala* which is a red birthmark on the head. *Sangomas* say it makes the baby open to evil spirits and must be cut out, and that the baby will die if it reaches the fontanelle. Again, I trusted in the good spirits, and the *ibala* disappeared.'

'Would Guido agree to go to a *sangoma*?'

'No!' She giggled as though impatient to shake off her sorrow, and clapped her hands. 'He wouldn't dare. But I would persuade him.'

The intimate drift of the conversation left him alarmingly aroused and flustered. He leant back on his chair affecting nonchalance, but it failed to put him beyond the reach of the musky, herbal perfume that seemed to emanate from between her breasts. With a supreme effort, he turned his mind to the safer subject of nutrition, and the puzzle of how the typical

African diet of maize and meat could sustain such a perfectly proportioned body that exuded such strength and wellness. It was a warmth and strength and gentleness that radiated from her unconsciously.

He felt he could almost breathe in her pheromones, her airborne hormones, deep into the bottom of his lungs. She seemed completely oblivious to her sheer animal magnetism, and he was again inexplicably uncomfortable at being so close to her. For one awful moment, he experienced a vertiginous urge to throw himself at her feet and declare how much he adored her. He was relieved to feel the conversation start to wind down.

'There is no other man in the world,' she sighed conclusively and smiled. It was a smile he hadn't seen before, a sad smile in a shadow of grief reflecting profound despair. His desire to hug her verged on deep hunger, even though her remark expressed so little concern for the preposterous feelings of this apparently lovesick fool. He inwardly bristled, and silently cursed her and himself, his downcast face reflecting a fretful melancholia.

It was all too much suddenly. He got up, accidentally knocking over his chair, and blushed for the first time in years. She got to her feet to help him, handed him his stick, and smoothed down her skirt that had ridden up to her thigh, white satin on deep brown skin. He coughed and looked away, and tucking in his shirt, turned to go, then hesitated as though remembering something. Abruptly and clumsily he moved to kiss her on the cheek, but she backed away in surprise, leaving the gesture to wither halfway. She threw him an amused glance and turned to stroll down to the pool.

He watched the way her hips swayed casually, as though her lower body had yet to register the turmoil in her heart, and he felt a sense of complete emptiness and irretrievable loss.

He looked back in time to see her start to peel off her skirt, but she apparently remembered that he was still around, and waited, presumably until he was out of sight.

Despite the traditional belief in water spirits, including the famous African goddess Mami Wata, most African people Christian had encountered had little affinity with water. Precious was an exception. She dived into Guido's crystalline salt-water pool every afternoon and dried herself in the sun. She swam with the grace of a mermaid and looked more at home in water than on dry land. When Christian watched her walking through the garden in one of her ankle-length hobble dresses he thought she had that mermaid-like fluidity in any element, air or water.

His appreciation of her hitherto had been innocently aesthetic. Now it was something else. He felt a crushing sense of shame, which he sensed was quite different from guilt, which would be even more difficult to live with, and in a class of its own in terms of emotional torment. In a state of complete discomposure, he headed back to his room. It briefly entered his muddled mind that he might have fallen in love, in a hopeless, distant way. He shook his head violently as if to dispel the thought.

He guiltily reflected on his feelings for his ex-wife. In the aftermath of his parents' death, Christian's bouts of melancholia had started to chip away at the foundations of his marriage. And a brief lapse of faithfulness finally closed the book on it. One small extra-marital affair is not usually enough to destroy a strong relationship. But Christian's cold, rainy night of loveless congress at a conference on 'the moral vacuum' in the depressed Belgian coal-mining town of Charleroi, with a Geordie woman he'd never met before or since, came at a high price.

He was still not sure why he did it. He knew it wasn't the usual male reasons or vanity. He wasn't the type. And he loved his wife. He loved her still. In one of the detached, fully-fledged debates he often conducted inside his own head, he thought that it was perhaps because, unusually, the woman didn't seem to feel sorry for him. He took it at the time as a demonstration of complete acceptance for what he was, limp and all.

Sometime later he changed his mind, concluding that it was because she was too embroiled in her own concerns to be sympathetic to his; and that she needed affirmation that she was everything her husband told her she wasn't – attractive and worth listening to. For Christian, it felt like an act of charity. He *did* feel sorry for *her*, and for the bruises on her plump, unattractive body that bore witness to the brutal nature of her own husband's 'love'.

Step by tiny step love for his wife became anything but mutual. It hadn't been since the cataclysmic moment of his confession when a cold curtain descended, and a clammy, forbidding stone wall built up between them. She could never have found out, but he'd had no choice but to confess. He believed it was the right thing to do. He loved his ardently devoted wife too much to deceive her. And perhaps at the back of his mind, he thought that honesty would count in his favour. It didn't. It might have counted if his wife hadn't already grown wary and weary of his rational ways in matters of the heart, and if she had felt that his support could have been relied upon out of love or some other passion, instead of via the dictates of duty and reason.

She was a woman with a strong sense of right and wrong, and of what she wanted in life. She was older than him, and what she wanted was another child. The clock was ticking, but Christian kept urging her to wait until 'the time was right', meaning an even better-paid job and a fatter savings account.

Christian still achingly missed his wife, a remarkably short woman for a Scandinavian, whom the more vicious of his competitive colleagues called 'Plain Dane'. This straw-haired, sweet-natured woman told him she needed a soulmate, not a disembodied intellect. If there was still love, it had drifted beyond reach to the point where they no longer knew how to talk and touch. Finally, she concluded that what she wanted from life no longer included poor old Christian. He came home one day to find her wardrobe bare, her cases gone.

Saskya, who had just left home, hardly ever kept in touch. Christian was abandoned. He felt so bad about the way he had conducted his life, he devoted the rest of it to trying to be good. His meteoric rise to the top of his profession was fuelled not merely by hard work and native ability, but because he was determined to make his subject, ethics, a way of life and his career a mission. It wasn't easy. It was a common theme among colleagues that he would probably be considered attractive if only he could sort out his social skills and dress sense. He was often mocked for his fastidious ways, for his predilection for sermonising, and the neat way he dressed, which in the late 20th century's craze for psychologising, tempted his unkinder colleagues to diagnose him as 'anal' in the extreme.

Christian had long ago admitted to himself that he had become a lecturer because he enjoyed lecturing. Debating was a different matter, especially when it became heated, as with young students it so often did – or would, if he let it get that far. But he rarely ever did, having cultivated various techniques to ensure that he never strayed beyond the borders of a lecture, and never risked the unknown, chaotic and random territory of an emotionally charged debate, where early experience had taught him that he would get flustered, his voice would rise a few semitones, his face would redden, and measured, logical thought processes would take flight. In the same way that he would never stray into any areas where rule of law was compromised, Debatenland was a distant, forbidden country for which he'd never qualify for a visa.

And now he was a 'here today, gone tomorrow' ethics missionary in Africa. Not that his character had changed that much. His basic instincts to do the right thing remained intact throughout. Apart from being worth doing in themselves, his good works also lent him the hope that his disproportionately heavy burden of guilt – more appropriate to that of a child abuser, or serial killer, than to a basically decent man – might one day be lifted from his shoulders. However, the older he got, the more convinced he became that the long-anticipated 'one day' would probably coincide with his *last*.

And now there was this new setback to overcome – the struggle with a desperate desire for the woman of the man who had just saved his precious Saskya.

26

The next day Christian appeared at Guido's hospital bedside just before lunch.

'Where's Precious?' Guido asked.

'Shopping. She'll pick me up in an hour.' He avoided Guido's eyes. 'She bought you these.'

He put a bunch of tulips in a glass vase on the bedside cabinet. 'She said they'd remind you of Amsterdam. She said you once played her the song *Tulips from Amsterdam*.'

A shadow of a self-mocking smile crossed Guido's lips as he stared at the flowers. 'She started to call me *Two Lips from Amsterdam* after that.' He turned to Christian. 'Saskya okay?'

'All's fine.'

'And Innocent?'

'Taking care of us. A real trooper.' Christian lowered himself into the nurse's armchair and hung his stick on the bedrail.

'How did the operation go last night?'

'Fine. Just an abscess. A bit sore, but not bad.'

Guido eased himself up onto his elbows to show him another text from Innocent – more angelic intervention.

'You can't help loving him, eh?'

'Poor deluded soul. *Opium for the people* is what Karl Marx called religion, as you probably know.'

Guido did know. *Who didn't?*

'Pipe dreams and illusions preventing people from facing up to reality,' Christian continued, crossing his good leg over the bad one. He was back in his blue shirt and fawn slacks. 'It offers certainties. Yet the reality is that certainty is an illusion. As Voltaire put it, *doubt is not a pleasant position, but certainty is*

208

absurd.'

'They might say the same about you, and your certainty about all this stuff to do with atoms and molecules and big bangs and no afterlife?'

'Scientific truth.'

'Truth? You can never escape the human point of view.'

'But – '

Guido lifted his hand. 'I prefer people's beliefs,' he continued, hoarsely. 'Your scientific truth is just another story. Some stories are more believable than others but not one of them is more realistic or superior to another story, or *narrative* as you academics call them. A story that gets you through life is a good story. If it doesn't, it's a bad story. Innocent might believe things that are nonsense to you, but all in all, despite the hardships, he's living well. Are you? Always critical, always exhausted in your drive to do well as a perfect, rational being living out your Calvinistic work ethic.'

'The point I'm making,' Christian continued to argue, 'is that when you believe your actions are determined by a higher authority, you can avoid personal responsibility.'

Guido maintained silence.

'No matter what *The Bible*, *The Koran* or any other scripture prescribes, if you can't answer yes to the question *is what I am doing morally correct?* then you need to treat it with scepticism,' Christian concluded, removing his glasses, breathing on the lenses and polishing them with his neatly-ironed handkerchief. He focused on Guido. 'You okay? Still with us?'

'Just about.' He recalled the words of his business partner in Uganda, a man who had survived the Nazi camps: 'When the bombing starts even the atheists start praying,' he countered painfully, in a voice that had become almost inaudible.

Christian had to admit to himself that even he had prayed for Saskya's safe return and offered up the complete *Paternoster* that he could still remember in Latin thanks to pious parenting by his Irish mother. But it was an incident that he preferred to ignore as a brief and regrettable lapse of reason.

Guido had already become bored with what he thought of as Christian's flat-earth attitude to the human condition. His mind drifted back to a conversation with Innocent, whom he'd found standing next to the bin. He was holding up one of Guido's old shoes. He looked uncomprehending. Guido threw him a puzzled look.

'I found it sticking out of the dustbin bag, Mr Guido.'

'Yes. And?'

'Is there another one?'

'Yes.'

'Could I have it please?'

'They're worn.'

'They are good shoes. The women at church will make them better.'

'Throw them away. I'll buy you a pair.'

'No, Mr Guido. We are rich, but to throw things away is a sin.'

He'd learned a lot from Innocent about the apparent wrong-headedness of some of his own ways of doing things. Not that Innocent preached in the way that Christian did. He taught by example, just by being himself.

Meanwhile, Guido's voice had given up. He would have liked to have said that, like many people with a religious upbringing, no matter how hard they tried, it could never be completely exorcised. He himself was corrupted by religion.

Even though in a permanent state of reformation, its whisperings could never be ignored. Despite his obsession with autonomy, a small part of him still needed to serve. *The church is empty, but the candles are still burning*, he thought.

Once he regained his voice, he vowed to tell his self-satisfied cousin that belief in a god, angels, spirits and ancestors gets a lot of people through some very tough times, and that you can believe whatever you want if it gives life meaning and makes every day a bit easier and it doesn't harm you or other people, because at the end of the day, from a purely human perspective, no one really knows what 'reality' is. He would tell Christian that the only thing people really know about metaphysical matters is that they know nothing. They can't say there is a god or gods or there is no such thing, or there was a big bang, or no beginning, or no creation, or that they can ever objectively know reality. Guido was an agnostic. He didn't know, and because he was only human, he could never know.

He knew already how Christian would reply. He would typically find a diplomatic golden middle way along the lines of, *By all means refer to authorities for guidance, but consistent with a sense of proportion the final choice of action should be yours and yours alone.*

One thing Guido was sure about – reality was not to be found in material acquisition. He didn't want to possess, either people or things. Both were predatory. And in both directions – the possessor and the possessed, predatory upon each other. He preferred to hire than to own. Yet, alongside madness and pain, ironically his greatest fear was poverty. For Guido, money was liberating. This was why he was shackled by the need to acquire so much of it. He understood that it's easy to sneer at money, but he believed that those who do so would be wise to reserve judgement until they had been forced to do without it. Really do without it. Not play at it with safety nets, but to know you have nothing and that there is no one to help and no one to care, and that begging on the streets is the next, inevitable step.

The next day he would hear about the nature of the lump underlying his abscess. The sentence would be pronounced. Would he or wouldn't he be on death row, and if so, for how long? It would be Sunday tomorrow, so he wouldn't hear in the morning as he'd hoped because the consultant, strictly Greek Orthodox, would be in church all morning. If it weren't for the fact that he believed he already knew the answer, Sunday afternoon would be one of the most defining moments of his life.

27

'The results of your blood tests have come in. We have dealt with the abscess in your throat. But the news is not good. All organs are functioning well, your blood pressure is fine and the heart has returned to normal.' The consultant stood up and removed his suit jacket, revealing scarlet braces that clashed sickeningly with his green and white striped shirt. He sat down again, resting his folded arms on the desk.

'So, what's the news that's *not* good?' Guido whispered hoarsely.

'While lying around in bed there's been some muscle wastage and we have to return your cardiovascular fitness to standard. I'll book you into a gym and provide you with a schedule of exercises.'

'The muscle isn't wasted. It was never there in the first place.' Guido scanned the man's face for a glimmer of amusement but found none. 'Is that the only bad news?'

'I'm afraid not. As we suspected, the abscess had established itself on an existing tumour which has been there quite some time. Do you smoke?'

Guido nodded.

'Some of its cells might have migrated to other parts of your body. We call this metastasis, which, I'm sorry to say, is usually associated with a poor prognosis. So, we need to keep an eye on it.'

Several times in his long life he'd wondered how much more he could take before mind and body simply gave up? Now he knew. The doctor told him that he might eventually have to have chemotherapy. He handed Guido a business card.

'Ring for an appointment in my rooms in Jo'burg,' he said. It's closer to you. Don't leave it too long.'

Guido couldn't say he hadn't been warned. The cells of a disease can patiently lie in wait for years before revealing themselves. He cast his mind back to his motorcycling accident in the late nineteen sixties, and how the doctors had insensitively told him what could be in store for him later in life. How many beautiful sunrises and sunsets was it going to cost him? He'd loved the open road, the wind in his hair, a girl's arms clutching his waist and shrieking with delicious intoxication as they leaned heavily into the bends and throttled hard into the straights.

Since then, he'd come a lot further than the doctors expected. But had it really been worth it? He had lived over four decades in the conviction that he would die sooner rather than later from the effects of organ damage and had therefore felt justified in ignoring the health warnings on cigarette packets and booze bottles. After a lifetime of worry, it turned out that it was the little white sticks that had made his tomorrows even more uncertain and accelerated his journey deathward.

He returned to his bed, drew the curtains around him and forced himself to focus on what he had just been told. He knew he quickly had to overcome the initial blow, disbelief, quiet inner rage and self-pity, and make the mammoth effort needed to turn his mind to an appropriate attitude towards death. For most of his life, he had expected it sooner than most, but it had still felt too abstract to deal with.

He knew that the tragedy is not in dying but failing to really live. He felt he'd done reasonably well in that respect. Yet there have been people with wonderfully satisfactory lives who still appear to be *half in love with easeful death; to cease upon the midnight with no pain* as Keats had put it.

Yet, for most people, no matter how awful life is, death seems to be an even worse alternative. Unlike those who maintain that suicide is a coward's way out, Guido had long considered it a brave, honourable and dignified finale. It also gave death the possibility of being a purposeful act, rather than ending up as the passive victim of disease and decrepitude. And if it's true that death gives meaning to life, and that immortality would be a curse removing all meaning, then a good death, at the right moment chosen in a careful and considered way, must be preferable to leaving the messy, painful, prolonged period of undignified humiliation to an indifferent whim of fate.

By a 'good death' he hoped that virtue would have its reward in the end if he had as few moral regrets as possible and if he could be remembered with fondness by those he left behind.

His only anticipated grief would be for their sadness and bitterness. He counted himself lucky that they were so few. Precious and Innocent would be devastated, but their tough resilience born out of a life of tragedy, would buoy them up. They had all the skills necessary to survive in the harshest of environments, and especially with the money Guido would bequeath to them. He wouldn't be forgotten, but the effect of his life on theirs would diminish very quickly. And there was no one else. Christian and Saskya were just visitors passing through. And at least there would be no guilt or remorse, unless the dead carry it with them.

He was not religious, but he had religion in him. Would he see his wife again? The possibility made the thought of death that much more attractive. He would not be dying alone. Not that it would be quite like dying on the battlefield, where death is shared in the brotherhood of fellow comrades, but still…

Death might be a stage on the path to another realm of life somewhere nice like Paradise, or somewhere much hotter and less comfortable. The sins of his past did put the chips on his landing in the hot place. And reincarnation could hold some nasty surprises. He wouldn't want to come back as an animal, not even one with Tsotsi's kindness and dignity. And being reabsorbed into the cosmos as a bunch of subatomic particles didn't appeal either. Short of coming back as himself – Guido II – he couldn't think of any suitable long-term outlook. And the thought worried him deeply.

Christian was wearing a black shirt tucked tightly into a pair of Guido's jeans. Guido laid his book on the bedside cabinet. 'Nice clothes.'

'Mine are in the wash. You've got your voice back.'

Guido nodded. He too was dressed in black, sitting on the edge of his bed, ready to go.

Christian let his eyes catch Guido's for a second. 'What did the consultant say?' he asked.

'All clear,' Guido lied. 'They did an endoscopy and the abscess wasn't hiding anything.'

'Great news, Man,' said Christian slapping Guido's knee. 'Great news!'

Guido shrugged.

Christian grabbed a chair and sat next to the bed. 'You know, for an intensive care unit, this place is remarkably relaxed,' he commented.

'Yeah. It reminds me of African music, which often has only two or three chords repeated over and over and over. It's mesmerising. It gets dancers into that slow rhythm into which they can relax and forget about their worries. It's like that with these wonderful doctors and nurses,' he concluded.

'You've been very lucky.'

If he only knew! Guido thought. 'Grab a couple of coffees, Man,' he croaked. 'While I wait to be checked out.'

Christian returned with two paper cups and a packet of biscuits.

'What's happening back home?' Guido asked.

'No sign of visitors so far. Innocent stays up all night on watch. Precious takes over during the day.'

'And Saskya?'

'She sleeps most of the time. It's like convalescence. We missed you, standing on one leg.' Christian looked away. 'We were wondering why you do it.'

'It's a form of meditation. On one leg you improve your structure and there's no chance of falling asleep or needing a Zen monk to whack you with a stick,' he smiled. 'The meditation helps develop the power to act intuitively. Circumstances constantly change, so there's not one right way of doing things. Prepared moves and responses are left behind. You learn to be flexible. It's beyond ordinary knowledge. It's all in the ancient Chinese scriptures like *I-Ching*, the *Book of Changes*.'

'It sounds rather like what the ancient Greek philosophers called *Phronesis,* meaning practical wisdom.'

'Possibly. And contemplation of nature emphasises the ancient Taoist wisdom that we are all one, and it improves patience. Impatient workers have accidents; professionals are propped up by various pills. Eastern philosophies rarely distinguish between the mental and the physical. Fitness of an integrated mind and body means being fit for right action, *kung fu,* intuitively knowing the right thing to do.'

'Sounds good. How do they do it?'

'Exercises increase your energy and structure the body to enable it to flow efficiently. Like standing on one leg with your arms sticking out,' he wheezed with a grin. 'Your intuition is awakened. You detect imminent problems and deal with them almost before they arrive. Also, it gives access to memories and dreams usually beyond reach in the dark corners. Furthermore – '

At that moment a nurse entered carrying a clipboard. Guido signed some papers and asked for his favourite nurse so that he could say goodbye, but she was on a different shift.

It had been thanks to the determination of the trauma doctor, under extreme pressure, to trace the underlying cause of Guido's abscess, and her access to scanning equipment and blood analysis in the middle of the night, that he was still alive. The same could be said of the lovely nurse whose job it was to sit next to him all night every night watching the monitors because they would have had only a few minutes to react if the abscess had burst. He was going to miss the place; not enough to want to revisit, but enough to retain good memories of the easy-going but caring people who looked after him, and who in so many ways could have done with being looked after themselves.

They headed for reception to wait for Precious. On their way out of the ward, he passed the bed allocation board in the corridor. His name had been wiped away and replaced by somebody the spelling of whose name was as obscure as some Welsh place names.

Relieved to be home, the first thing he wanted was a shower before discussing with Innocent their defence plans. As the fresh water bubbled over his head, he felt a relaxation he'd almost forgotten was possible. He shaved and was startled by the lean, intense look in the eyes of the reflection in front of him. Since the hospital, he felt as though he hadn't quite come down to earth. He told himself it was the effect of the anaesthetic and the massive dose of antibiotics. He didn't mind. In fact, he welcomed it. Practical and physical concerns seemed to have slipped out of focus and more metaphysical matters had come into sharper relief.

Sitting on a rock wall, near a jacaranda, he drank his first decent cup of coffee since leaving home and let the remains of the sun warm his bones. He cast his mind back to the short conversation he'd had with Precious after she had driven them home.

He had told her straight away what the consultant had told him, but to keep it to herself. There was no need to spare someone like her. She'd seen it all – rape, throat-slitting, necklacing, shack burning. It hadn't dehumanised her in any way. On the contrary, it gave her a profound understanding of the human condition in a way that could not be intellectualised, or even put into words. Precious had a deep well of sympathy, but her solid sense of self couldn't be shaken.

'Must I get you herbs?' she asked bravely, her eyes wet. 'You could see a *sangoma*.'

He thought back to what the nurse had told him about herb poisoning.

'I've looked on the net, but nothing useful. Of course, a healthy lifestyle – no smoking, good sleep, no stress – might help. And standing on one leg. But there's no magic bullet. I can't buy my way out of this one.'

She squeezed his hand and ran her thumb down the inside of his forearm causing a pleasant tingling sensation at the centre of his palm.

'Could you tell Innocent? Not a word to the other two just yet, Precious.'

She nodded. 'You must take one day at a time, Mr Guido.'

'Indeed. The past weighs heavily, Precious, but the future is now the concern of others.'

'Not yet.' She held his wrist. 'We need you to make sure there is a tomorrow for us. And a day after, and a day after that.'

He kissed her high cheekbone and stroked her curly hair. A salty tear wet his lips.

'Do you feel sick now?' she asked.

'No Precious. My throat is better, and I feel fine.'

'You see! Remember doctors don't know everything. Only the angels know. Your angel must speak to mine, and then I'll know what is really wrong with you. My angel will tell me you must not take the doctor's poison. Doctors are good for treating an accident or when you have been knifed. But our ancient traditions are better for diseases.'

His eyebrows lifted as he thought of garlic and beetroot, prescribed for Aids.

'You must wait,' she urged. 'Innocent will ask the angels at church to help you. They have hundreds of them. Our angels and my body will make you better. That I promise.'

'Thank you.' He squeezed her hand.

'I feel you can hear your inner voice. Do not forget, it took you a long, long time to become so quiet inside. Nothing can take that away now, Mr Guido, not even death.'

He shuffled outside to the *stoep*, where it was slightly cooler. As he passed the herb patch, he broke off a sprig of mint, and held it to his nose, breathing deeply. He could hardly stand from tiredness. He threw his head back, stared up at the stars, and felt himself being lifted off the ground and drawn irresistibly toward the full moon suspended above the city. Precious caught him just in time to stop him from tumbling backwards.

28

The next morning, Guido helped himself to a cup of coffee in the kitchen, grabbed the biscuit tin and stacked up a whole pile of biscuits, which he then dipped into his coffee, one after the other, filling his cheeks to bursting. He didn't notice Precious in the doorway. She had never seen him do such a thing. That moment might have brought home to her in stark reality how ill he was; that he wasn't himself. 'Himself' was modest in his eating habits, careful about what he ate and always offered it to others first. She stood perfectly still, watching him replace the biscuit tin, and his gaunt figure shuffle across the polished pine floor to the French windows, hesitate, rummage for his pack of cigarettes and light one before stepping outside. She followed him out.

'*Dumela*, Mr Guido.'

'Precious! *O kae*?' He was caught unawares, but hugely pleased to see her, as always.

'*Ngiyaphila*, I am alive,' she replied, mixing Zulu and Sepedi. 'How are you? Your voice is still sick. You must get peppermint root and throw away those cigarettes. I also am not good. Please – look at my body.' She showed him her bare forearms and pointed to the goose pimples. 'They are covered in lumps. I am cold, Mr Guido. Warm me up.'

'Take a break outside for a few minutes. Sit in the sun, and warm up,' he suggested, gesturing to beyond the *stoep* to where the flowerbeds were swarming with orange and black butterflies, dancing in and out of the pink roses and blazing yellow dragon flowers.

'The sun? The sun makes you sick. If you are cold you must snuggle up in bed.' She gave him one of her

221

mischievous smiles and moved towards him. She stood by his side and slipped her warm, dry hand into his. He turned to face her. Her eyes rested on his as though she were able to see straight through him and beyond to some point on the other side of the universe.

'You are changing,' she whispered. 'Is it only because you are sick?'

He stared at the tiled floor and watched a file of ants take the long way round along the rough grouting of each tile rather than risk a short-cut across the smooth surface.

'There wasn't one moment of change, Precious. It was a series of moments. There are always events after which nothing is ever the same again.'

'Recently?'

'I guess it was the night I couldn't breathe. That night a police check would have changed everything forever. But there's more. When you come to somewhere like this it's hard not to get involved – to remain an impartial observer, to remain disengaged. I didn't tell you, but the day before I went to hospital I was threatened with involvement – with engagement. I visited the home for Aids orphans up the road to see if I could help them with money now that I've sold the picture. The next day I couldn't breathe. Was it a coincidence or was there more going on?'

'What do you mean?'

'Something beyond our understanding.'

The two of them wandered back inside. She lit some incense. He knew she could sense in him a desperate need to satisfy a spiritual hunger. She had no knowledge of the spirituality of his religious upbringing, but she understood at a deep level his suffering, and that she was capable of helping him. This extraordinary woman, for whom the alien occupying forces of her country would have shown no

222

respect, understood him and others in ways the rational mind could never explain.

She turned and gave him a beautifully warm hug that almost completely enveloped his skinny frame, and he had a floating sensation as if her energy were lifting him up, her life force flowing through his veins and nourishing his organs. She gently released her grip and gave him one of her smiles that involved her whole being – creased oval eyes, full mouth, perfect teeth, and a body that seemed to open up to him.

'I might come up later.' He tried to grin, but he was afraid it might look like a grimace. Her face clouded over as she turned away, and he watched her long neck, straight back and flowing, relaxed stride as she headed down the garden to swim.

He went back to the living room, quietly closed the door behind him and put on Donizetti's *Lucia di Lammermoor*. Music always helped him regain his centre point – a form of meditation that allowed him to keep his head when all about him were losing theirs.

Upstairs the ecstatic aria stroked Saskya's skin like angelic hands, warming the surface, but leaving the blood chilled, suspending her in a foggy state of ambivalence. She stepped to the window, and stared critically at the reflection of her pale, drawn face in the dusty pane, and the white top she'd chosen a lifetime ago for the flight to South Africa. Extending her gaze beyond her own ghostly image, she focused on Tsotsi down at the side of the house, as though hiding away while he chewed through a long, thick bone with the disquieting strength of a hyena. She wondered briefly what he would make of a human meal but reminded herself that Tsotsi was not like that. He'd never been trained to be vicious and so was just his natural self – a gentle giant. She closed her eyes, and again let the majestic music caress her skin once more before joining the others. She went downstairs and sat outside with her legs curled beneath her, and her head resting against the sandstone wall at the edge of a raised flower bed. A gecko froze on the wall, then seemed to change its mind and scrambled to higher ground, loosening a tiny shower of dust and grit.

Hearing a splash, she walked in bare feet on the springy grass to the pool. Precious waved, stepped out of the pool and dried herself.

'Please sit with me,' she pleaded. She suddenly looked distraught.

'What's the matter? Saskya asked, lowering herself into one of the deckchairs.

'I'm so worried about Mr Guido. He's getting weaker.'

Saskya nodded.

'And there's something else.'

'Oh?'

Precious wrapped her towel around her waist and sat next to Saskya. 'I have secrets I must tell him before it's too late, but I can't. '

'What secrets?'

'Lots of them. Only Inno knows, and he would never tell.'

'Go on,' Saskya urged.

'Like I told him I have two children.'

'Dad told me. What's so bad about that?'

'It was a lie. I told so many lies.' There was a catch at the back of her throat, and then a long hesitation. 'White ghosts are different from ours. If he dies, I might not be able to talk to him.'

'You mean you haven't got two children?'

'I told him so many lies because I wanted him to think well of me. Not know the kind of girl I'm really like. And

224

think me worth having. And…' She stared at her fingernails.

'Yes?' Saskya prompted.

Stranded in her memory Precious seemed not to hear, and sorrow flooded across her face like dark waters, tears leaving salt tracks down her cheeks. She seemed afraid to offer an explanation. Saskya became uncomfortable and reluctant to press the point.

At last Precious whispered, 'I did have two children. I lie because I feel so guilty about what happened to them. They were called Thabo and Crocus. Thabo means *joy*. He used to pull her pigtails and she'd laugh with her no teeth.' She looked away and then sobbed. 'But they died.'

She grabbed Saskya's hand and steadied herself as though the memory had triggered a wave of vertigo.

'I left them to help a friend,' she continued, glancing back towards the house. 'She was sick. She would have died. When I came home, there was nothing left.'

She explained that her children had been roasted alive in a shack fire when the babysitter had left them alone to fetch water from the communal tap and had locked them in for safety.

'It wasn't my fault. After that, I never saw their father again.' She started to weep for her children, for Guido, for herself, for all abandoned and brutalised children.

Unable to face Precious' stricken expression of utter gut-wrenching grief, Saskya looked away and said nothing.

'Feeling guilty is the only thing Crocus and Thabo have left me. I even feel guilty that I'm still alive. Where are they now?' She looked up as though expecting their faces to appear in the branches of the jacaranda. 'They never came back. Their ghosts are gone a long time. They're angry with me.'

Saskya squeezed her hand. Her brain felt so rattled by this

outpouring and the unexpected intimacy of it, that she found it difficult to think straight. She could have done without someone else's troubles after such extreme ones of her own, but at the same time, she admonished herself for such uncharitable thoughts.

Precious said nothing for a few moments, her head buried in her hands. She looked up. 'It wasn't my fault. And there are other secrets.'

Although Saskya couldn't begin to imagine what Precious was referring to, a shiver rippled down her spine vertebra by vertebra.

'I wanted to tell him, but with each lie, I sank deeper and deeper until I couldn't get out.'

She slumped forward, her elbows on her knees.

'I – '

'Saskya!' It was Christian.

Saskya squeezed Precious' arm. 'Sorry. We'll talk soon. But just to say that whatever it is, Uncle Guido has seen it all. He won't judge you.'

29

Without warning the weather suddenly changed. The rain started with a few drops the size of Krugerrands, leading to a heavy downpour, pounding the hard ground. A row of pied crows perched on a cable, preened themselves in ecstasy, ruffling their wet feathers, cawing with delight. Precious went off to get changed.

Christian and Saskya moved a couple of chairs out of the rain under the overhang on the *stoep*. Still stunned by Precious' confession, she smiled at him suddenly with a defiant glint in her eyes. She'd been looking tired, but her large, greyish green eyes now held their usual brightness and greenness.

'Have you been around the garden, Dad?'

He nodded. 'Beautiful, isn't it? A tiny patch of tropical Africa.'

'Sure. But a lot of these plants are not nice,' she stated, showing him scratches on her arm for emphasis. 'They either poke you in the eye, impale you, cut you, or ooze a liquid that either burns or brings out a rash or makes you want to scratch all night. Those cycads are a perfect example.' She pointed to a short tree with a thick trunk crowned by glossy green leaves, on the path to the pool. 'They're vicious. It's like they're here to defend the place.'

He turned to look. 'Knowing Guido, they probably are.'

'So much viciousness.'

He nodded and drew a breath to reply.

'I'm not going back, Dad.' A statement out of the blue, in a steady voice, and with a tone of finality. He turned to face her. She was staring at him, lips slightly parted.

'I'm not going home. I can't. I've changed my mind. By a fortuitous accident of birth, I was born in Northern Europe where I was cared for, brought up properly, fed good food, given love and a good education. But having got those basics right, I can live anywhere. I've done my time in the drizzle and cold. There's no way I'll ever go back to be rained on and frozen for half the year. I want the sun on my back, and I want people with sunny dispositions. More importantly, I want to help children here have the benefits I enjoyed. There's too much that needs to be done out here. It's the brutality. I have to do something.'

Christian nodded. She kissed his cheek. He put his hand on her back and rubbed between her shoulder blades. He couldn't remember the last time he'd felt so completely at ease with her. He'd concluded long ago that he would never be able to relax because of his sense of responsibility towards her. His fears for her safety and for her future put him in a permanent state of tension. Somehow the rescue had cast a spell, magically dissolving such concerns and demolishing the walls between them.

'Remember all those gymkhanas I used to drag you to, Dad?' she asked. 'The bacon and beans you made me while you tucked into your free-range boiled egg?'

'Yep. And you erecting a circuit of jumps in the garden, and jumping over them for hours in a one-person, horseless gymkhana. *Come on Horsey!*'

He thought of the times at home when she'd got up from a meal and gone outside, her impatience palpable, enveloping her like an aura. He remembered when he first realised she was smoking, was certain she was drinking, and was worried about the possibility of other things she might have been experimenting with. She'd been equally impatient to leave home – eager to leave, and just as eager to stay. Eventually,

228

she did leave – all on her own – to Edinburgh to do a humanities degree. He was glad to see her go – the sort of relief he would feel at releasing a caged bird. At the same time, he was gutted, and fearful that a caged bird would be injured in the wild, torn apart by stronger birds, or simply caged again by someone well-meaning or someone malicious.

'You were a bit over-protective, though,' she told him. 'It used to make me angrier than a constipated giraffe.' She burst out laughing. 'And you didn't like my friends. They were a really important part of my life. You couldn't even make the effort to be civil to them.'

'You know I'm not very – '

'Sociable? When did you develop your anti-social side, Dad? Was it before Mum left?'

'I'm not anti-social. I'm unsociable. I couldn't stand being trapped in groups of people with their boring small talk, rudeness, prejudices about immigrants on benefits, petty concerns about food and the state of their health and hating a government that gives more handouts than most other countries on earth. I get a panic attack just thinking about it. With my few old friends I'm really quite, well, quite friendly.'

'Maybe. But I was ashamed of you when my friends came round. Not because of your limp, but because you were so different from other dads – not interested in sport, or outdoor hobbies. I had the feeling you looked down on other dads who went fishing at the weekend, or were into motorcycling, or loved the Grand Prix or rugby. It was like being the only Muslim in a street of Christians. Everything we did seemed different from everyone else. Even the vegetarian food. It was embarrassing. And then I'd feel awful. I even felt guilty about you being lame. But at the same time, I loved you for the way you were. Oh Dad, you used to tear me in two!'

She paused for a second and fiddled with her fingers as if

rolling an invisible cigarette. 'You never once told me you were proud of me, though.' She stood up and turned her back to him. 'A lot of the time I thought you didn't like me. And I used to feel crushed by the need to look after you when Mum left, what with your foot and everything. That's why I left.'

'Come off it, Sas.' He tried not to appear hurt. 'Look at all the times we spent together with the horses, camping. And that time I drove to Edinburgh to help you move rooms, and we went out for a meal. It was like being with an adult. Momentarily I forgot who I was, or what I was, rather. I shed the weight of responsibility and experienced a rare moment of feeling equal with you.'

'That was much later. It's because you're a bloke. You didn't seem to want to talk about serious or personal things with me. Or if you did, it was one of your bloody lectures, judging, advising.'

'Come back and sit down. Please.' She sat next to him again, but the distance between them had become that of oceans or continents.

'Sometimes, for whatever reason, dads are stand-offish with their daughters. It's normal. Come and give me a hug.'

She kissed him on the cheek. 'You'll have to make do with that for now,' she teased as he took her hand.

'Sas, you did come to me for advice and comfort about personal things. And you used to ask me about my life, my feelings and my ideas.'

'Yes, *your* ideas and stuff. You sometimes acted as if I were prying or interfering. On your birthday cards, I always tried to show how much I appreciated you as a dad, but you're difficult to be close to in a direct way. Even your presents were a kind of lecturing – books you thought I *should* read.'

'You don't think I was too ambitious for you?'

'No. But you're a hard act to follow.'

'Did you feel protected?'

'Yes. Remember when I confided in you about that boy in grade nine? Did you ever tell Mum?'

'No. It was a confidence.'

His heart was pumping fast in anticipation of what he thought was an inevitable question – did she feel abandoned when he left the country to take up his post in Lisbon? She'd been deserted and left to her own devices to make a whole new life in a new city and with no friends or relations. Her mother was in Denmark, and although prepared to return for any emergency, she was still remote. And there was no social media. Only lately had it dawned on him what he'd done. But the shadows were starting to lengthen, and he sensed a sudden restlessness in her.

'I'm too inhibited to tell you how beautiful you are,' he said out of the blue. 'You only need a looking glass to tell you that. But I can say you've always had an inner beauty, Sas.' He coughed and looked away. 'And I've always been extremely proud of you.'

'You still can be. I've learned more about myself in the past few weeks here than I learned in years at home. And I'm desperate for a fresh Cape sea breeze on my face. I really have left my old life far, far behind. I have a very rich and beautiful one ahead of me. And you, Dad?'

He picked up the half-full glass of what he assumed to be soya milk and took a gulp. It was fresh dairy milk, and the taste took him back to a holiday with his parents on a farm on the English west coast. He would have been seven or eight years old. He suddenly felt terribly homesick for the past.

'The university won't extend my visiting scholarship,' he struggled to tell her. 'It's a matter of work permits. I have to start work in Lisbon in a couple of weeks.'

'Before you go off and leave me again, you must tell me what you would do to put a stop to corporal punishment. Remember the poor kid with the skinned hand?'

'You need to help people think about how their behaviour affects others. That's morality in a nutshell. You need empathy – putting yourself in other people's shoes. And that needs imagination.'

'I can feel a lecture coming on, Dad. I just want to know what to do in simple terms – not a bloody course in moral philosophy.' She seemed to shrink within herself. A shiver racked her tense body. 'You've got a lot of grey matter up there, Dad' she said, thrusting a finger at his head. 'But it's action we need.'

Christian shook his head and shrugged. He felt an unease settling over him, and he shifted slightly on his seat, avoiding her gaze. 'Fair enough,' he said. He would have liked to have offered her a quick fix, but there are none, and the atmosphere was suddenly so highly charged that he momentarily found it difficult to find the right words and string them together. 'I need time to think,' he said with a dismissive wave of his hand. He grabbed his stick and struggled to his feet. Changing his mind, he sat down and placed his stick in front of him as though ready to defend himself with it.

'Why don't we start with your own solutions, Sas? You must have some?'

She drew in her upper lip nervously. 'My solution? I've thought long about it. My own school on my own tropical island will use *consequences*, not bloody barbaric punishments.'

'Like most schools back home?' There was no sarcasm in his voice, but he immediately felt he should have left it.

'Sort of.' She searched his eyes for irony. 'Instead of

causing pain, discomfort or deprivation to a kid for doing something wrong, I'll rely on direct adverse results.'

'Example?'

'The child that steals gets ostracised. The child that drinks his dad's brandy gets a hangover. Punishments only teach kids that the parent or teacher disapproves of what they did, not that what they did is simply wrong. Punishment is an outside threat. If the threat's removed the child's got no reason to behave. The threat of punishment doesn't make kids behave well when no one's looking. But if they're presented with the direct nasty consequences of their actions, they have good reason to avoid repeating the behaviour.'

'Sure, but truly natural consequences can be too harsh,' he countered, putting his slim hands together, his fingers interlocking as though in prayer. 'And some might even be *rewarding*, as in the case of undetected theft. This means it's again left to the parent or the teacher to make sure the act delivers suitable consequences. Surely, mild punishments would also work well when *natural* consequences would be inappropriate?'

'Point taken. So, there's a compromise here, right? – consequences where they would be effective; appropriate punishment in other cases.' She leant back in her chair so far, he thought she would tip over backwards. 'The aim is to avoid this bloody brutality, not to exploit fear.'

He let out a slow sigh of weariness and closed his eyes. 'Furthermore, stooping to badly hurting a child corrupts the punisher,' he added.

'Yep,' she agreed, taking a long pull at her glass. 'And it's illegal.'

He nodded. 'That's separate from morality. Being illegal doesn't necessarily make something wrong. There are good laws and bad laws.'

He rubbed his eyes with his left fist and pushed his fingers through his grey hair. His back was already aching. 'When natural consequences are unlikely to change behaviour, punishment should aim to mimic natural consequences, and corporal punishment should be prohibited, if only for the fact that it can get out of hand, do serious harm and look like revenge or venting anger. Agreed?'

'Agreed. For now...' She took a breath as though about to continue, but he interrupted her before she could speak.

'It's getting late Sas.' He pushed down on the table with the palms of his hands, and stood up stiffly, reaching for his stick. He tucked in his shirt.

She got to her feet with such athletic ease it could have been taken for teasing him.

30

Guido was in a state of complete introspection but was soon shaken out of it. Saskya came bouncing through the French windows onto the *stoep* and dropped herself on the chair next to him. Christian hobbled behind.

'Morning Uncle Guido.' She looked radiant in jeans and a cotton blouse in her favourite colours – black and white. 'You look a lot better. Just as well. You couldn't have looked much worse!'

Unless she was covering up, her spirits seemed to have been remarkably restored.

'Yep. All clear,' Guido lied for the second time that day.

'Great news, Uncle Guido,' she said, flinging her arms round his neck. 'The sun is out. Feels like a sign from God. It's time to pull myself out of self-pity and get back to those gorgeous kids in Cape Town. I'm in a big hug mood.'

Her enthusiasm was unstoppable and infectious. Guido would have liked to have thrown his arms around her but contented himself with grasping her hand. 'I'll leave you to it,' he muttered as he started getting to his feet.

'Stay Uncle Guido. Please!'

He sat down again.

'I was up at six to do some work. Now that's what I call commitment.'

'That's not like you!' Christian teased.

'I had an exciting and inspiring morning, and I've hardly started,' she beamed. 'I'm so excited I feel like I'm on drugs, my brain is buzzing, and my heart is singing. I no longer feel the need to scream. I feel centred again. I've got the answer.'

'To what?'

'To tackling education. To making kids think for themselves and remember what they learn.'

'Making them? Do what I say, and think for yourself.' Christian's mocking smile quickly withered as she flashed him a look.

She drew in her upper lip nervously 'I'll do it through religion.' She stated it as though out of the blue in a way that declared the subject closed, but quickly followed it with one of her smiles that wrinkled her eyes. She paused for effect, directing her large greyish green eyes at the ceiling.

You could have heard a pin drop. The silence felt like minutes before Christian managed, 'What?'

'I got to know those guys who abducted me. They're deeply religious. The church of Zion.'

'I brought you up to reject that mumbo jumbo. How could you possibly contemplate – ?'

'Because unlike you I'm open-minded to it, and I'm open-minded because you, as a philosopher, brought me up to be.'

'But – ' he spluttered.

'Philosophers are open-minded; I'm a philosopher's daughter; therefore, I'm open-minded. It's a silly-gism.'

Christian looked away in despair. 'It's neither valid nor – '

'Dad. Lighten up, please!' She sprang to her feet. 'To change people, you must work through their existing belief systems, otherwise they don't listen, or if they do, they don't believe you.'

'But – '

'Let her speak,' said Guido gently.

'Dad has always had this instinctive drive for didacticism, Uncle Guido. You've no idea.' Her jokey tone failed to mask a deep-rooted frustration. 'My jaw aches from years of suppressing a yawn, and my eyelid muscles have had tougher workouts than a gym junkie's biceps. It's only love that kept me from hiding when he was gearing up to spout forth the encyclopaedic knowledge on his subject of the day. Yet, if I wanted his attention when he was reading one of his professional journals he'd shoo me away. Then, when he was ready for a long-winded regurgitation of useless facts and stats, he'd cling to me like a limpet.'

'Sas, please, there's no need – '

'To get back to what I was saying, it's also a matter of terminology – using their language, which is suffused with religious references, just like European languages used to be. *Godspeed, angels watch over you.* That kind of thing.'

'Which religion are you going to use?' Christian asked, hardly managing to keep the sarcasm out of his voice. 'This country's got just about every faith under the sun.'

'You're always so negative, Dad. Unless it's one of your ideas. Then we're all mad or stupid if we don't believe in it.' She looked exasperated. 'It would depend on the school's ethnic makeup, but Christianity, Hinduism or Islam will be obvious favourites.'

'What would your ideal school look like, a seminary?' He flashed a smug grin that he hoped would say *come on, snap out of it.*

Her gaze met his, but she frowned and looked away. 'I have every right to be what you'd call irrational, Dad. I can do without cold analysis by the great Kettermann brain for once.' Turning her back to him, she shifted her chair towards Guido. 'Uncle Guido, let's make Dad redundant. Pension him off. Then I'll sack the government, get an ark, put all the kids on it, and just drift far across the ocean to become stranded on an uninhabited island, live off seafood barbeques, sleep under the stars, and only half-heartedly write *help!* in the sand. I'll teach that focusing on differences causes cruelty; and that our commonalities are the foundations for a global community, humans, animals, trees and plants alike. Look at dogs. Except for posh pedigrees, they're all different, yet they're quite happy to play together and sniff each other's bums.

'My teaching methods will draw on the Catholic mass or Muslim and Jewish services,' she continued, her voice rising. 'Sermons of short bite-sized chunks repeated over and over, rather than lengthy slices of knowledge lectured monotonously in obscure languages in stuffy classrooms well beyond most students' concentration span, and never to be repeated. One-off linear learning is a total failure. I'll repeat that: *one-off linear learning is a total failure.* I'll use rhetoric and repetition. Ideas will be presented with eloquence and passion – old-fashioned oratory – repeated again and again, using aphorisms and call and response in a Pentecostal atmosphere. I'll have scrolls on the walls with the virtues from all major moral philosophies as well as Africa's uBuntu – *I am because we are.*'

She pressed on, striding back and forth, wildly gesticulating.

'We never remember what we don't see or hear again and again. Or we recall the theory but forget to put it into practice. Ideas need to be repeated again and again to sink in. I'll do this through a sort of liturgical calendar like Muslims, Jews and Christians have. I'll draw up a schedule of holy days and rituals, devoted to basic immutable truths and ideas like the importance of charity and compassion so that the emotional experiences sink in for good. We'll use books that express moral and spiritual values, but only those that are objects of aesthetic beauty – exquisite picture books by the world's best illustrators. And the San stories about oneness with everything there is. To help the values find their way into our souls.'

She took a deep breath, her eyes focused on some distant

object. 'My Utopian island will be stateless, classless and moneyless, with common ownership of everything. My school building will be modelled on a temple, church, synagogue or mosque, or combination of all four. Its heavenly spires will inspire. They'll have high ceilings, with inspirational paintings to give an atmosphere of meditation and contemplation, just like places of worship. Meals will be vegetarian – not just for health's sake, but as a way of putting into practice care for living beings. We'll have our own organic garden where the kids can grow their own fruit and veg. Physical exercise will be a vehicle for spiritual exercise – dancing and meditation in movement. Think about it, Dad,' she said in an American accent imitating an evangelical pastor. She pointed a finger at each of them in turn. 'Take account of other people, creatures and trees. Don't follow the crowd. Think for yourself. I said think for yourself! What did I say?'

Christian sat stony-faced.

'You said *think for yourself*!' Guido responded, springing to his feet, and waving his hands in the air. 'That's right!' he sang in a deep, croaky voice. 'You said *think for yourself*! Praise be on high! Amen!'

Guido and Saskya started clapping a steady rhythm, and both subsided into a fit of giggles just as Precious appeared. She let out a hoot, and her body picked up a syncopated rhythm where her lower body seemed to dance to a different beat from her upper half. Palms outstretched, waving, she could have been about to enter a trance.

Saskya did a little dance, executed a perfect cartwheel, and headed barefoot across the garden towards the ethereal luminescence of the pool.

Christian turned to Guido who was still chuckling. 'I'm worried about that girl,' he said in a serious tone, shaking his head. 'She's either manic or depressed. I hope she's not bipolar.'

'She's alive, Christian. That's all. Alive in every sense,' Guido replied, turning his whole body towards him, as though to shake him. 'Where are the ghosts of your life? Your angels, your ancestors from the spirit world, where are they?'

He took a deep breath to calm himself and swallowed hard to relieve the pain in his throat. 'It's not as if you haven't got any. It's just that you can't open your eyes wide enough to see them. Why can't people like you accept most people's urge to believe in something divine?'

'Because none of it's true, and – '

'Knowledge that looks like absolute truth today doesn't always look that way tomorrow. In the name of humility, perhaps you should extend respect even to people whose ideas you think are currently wrong-headed. You don't have to join the rack and fire atheist inquisition just because you're an intellectual. You're living a very grey life in a barren, academic, disembodied, black and white world, my friend.'

Christian was stopped in his tracks. Memories of arguments with his wife flooded back. And he suddenly thought of old photos of his father – black and white photos he had studied time and time again in the hope that they would reveal more about the man who was a wonderful father, but who had remained largely unknown to him. *Black and white.* Why did it hurt like a kick to the groin? Why care about what this absurd, half-crazed cousin said or thought? His opinions and irrational beliefs were founded on ignorant mysticism and superstition. If it were the Middle Ages, this ridiculous man who stands on one leg would be casting spells and burning witches. It was impossible to take him seriously. Yet...

He reached for his stick and carefully got to his feet, his

shoulders hunched as though he'd been caught in a cloudburst. He tucked in his pale-blue shirt, turned and shuffled off to his room without another word.

Guido went back to the lounge still replete with the warmth of the fragrant air and put on a sumptuous piece of choral music by 17th century Dutch composer, Jan Pieterszoon Sweelinck entitled *De Profundis*. Saskya, wrapped in a fluffy bath towel, her wet hair hanging in waves and ringlets, joined him. They sat in companionable contemplation of the beauty permeating each and every one of their senses. Neither uttered a word.

31

Guido came in from the garden where he had been standing on one leg again. Christian was not the type to ridicule others. He despised those who did so, but he couldn't help chuckling to himself. The man looked ridiculous. Standing on one leg his other leg and his arms stuck out like branches of a small tree, his eyes closed. Meditation, he'd said. Why couldn't he sit cross-legged like other people who feel the need for that kind of thing? It was the kind of quirky behaviour of people who spend too much time alone. Sometimes he thought that Guido's eccentricity verged on mental illness, or was it some exhibitionist streak? The two cousins might share similar blood, but he felt that they shared little else.

Guido briefly acknowledged Christian's presence and told him there was a pot of coffee on the *stoep*. Guido needed a break from Christian. He went inside and sat listening to the gorgeously sombre jazz ballad *After the Rain* by saxophonist John Coltrane while Precious lay with her head snuggled into his lap. He stroked her hair absent-mindedly, his head full of thoughts of guns and gin traps and the possibility of an even earlier death than the one that had just been pronounced.

'What will Saskya do now?' she asked.

'She wants to go back to Cape Town and teach in the township schools there.'

'Can she speak isiXhosa?'

'No. Most parents want their children to be taught in English.'

'That is too hard. In the villages, Mr Guido, we learn slowly. We are not like people in Johannesburg where everybody speaks different languages. We only hear our own language, so we learn English very slowly. In 1994 we were promised an education. Everyone was promised an education. But when we do go to university, to school, very often we don't pass whereas white people do pass. It's not fair, all this education that's meant for us is done in English. This is a broken promise.'

'It's not a broken promise; it's what many parents want,' Guido pointed out. 'And education doesn't just arrive in the post. Even during apartheid, white people had to work very, very hard for it. Black people now must do the same thing. If they expect to get their degrees automatically, they're in for a shock. They should earn them according to the same standards that apply to white people.'

She looked up. 'I like it when you beat me with words,' she said huskily, her hand squeezing his knee.

'Precious, please! I have to work.'

He was halfway to his feet when Saskya strode up to him. She stood before him, thumbs looped into the belt of her black jeans. She was in a bright-red blouse. 'How are you feeling Uncle Guido?' she asked evenly, sitting next to him on the edge of the sofa.

'Fine. Much better.'

'I'm happy for you.'

'Me too. I've no time left to be unhappy. At your age, you've plenty of time to be unhappy. And melancholia is great for creativity.'

She smiled hesitantly as though afraid he was going to get embarrassingly maudlin like elderly people sometimes do. She was leaning forward, hands pressed down on her knees, perhaps in readiness for a quick exit.

'Mr Guido, you are looking so nice!' Innocent beamed. 'I

love your shoes.'

Surely Precious must have told her brother about his health. As if he'd read Guido's mind, Innocent's face clouded over, his bottom lip sticking out. 'I'm sorry, Mr Guido. Precious told me,' he whispered. 'I'm still praying for you to get well. My angel will sort you out.'

'Inno, I've lived twice as long as I expected, and the doctors aren't certain.' He grinned, and added, 'Anyway, my shoes would be too small for your clown's feet.'

Innocent gave a loud burst of deep laughter, doubled up as though caught by stomach cramps, and slapped his thin thighs. 'That's not what I meant,' he said. 'But, Mr Guido, I would cut off my toes for shoes like that!'

'Take a seat,' Guido told him. 'We need to make a plan. To deal with unwelcome visitors.'

Innocent shrugged his shoulders and draped his gangly body over a chair at a respectful distance, a few feet away from Guido. He bent his long legs beneath him and straightened his back to attention.

'Any visitors will have to break in or convince us to let them in,' Guido pointed out. 'The dealer's men will want revenge and whatever they can lay their hands on. Most likely they'll plan to force me to tell them where the safe is and to kill anyone else in the house, and then kill me.'

'Instead, we kill them, *ne*?'

'No. If we did, more would follow. We let them in. They'll be expecting ordinary unarmed householders, not the likes of you and me, right?'

Innocent grinned and nodded.

'I forge my own death – with makeup and red paint on one of the walls in the back room,' Guido continued. 'There's paint in the studio. Remember, dried blood is almost black.'

'I have seen a lot of dried blood, Mr Guido.'

'At gunpoint we make them phone their boss to say the job is done. He's bound to ask them to take pictures on their cellphone to prove it. You will take their phone and take pics of me apparently dead from a bullet wound to the head.'

'Then we kill them,' Innocent repeated, marching his fingers over the table.

'No, we let them go.'

'But they tell their boss.'

'Exactly! They'll never admit to failing. Why would they? This way they appear to have done the job, they get their payment, they keep their reputation, and we throw in a few battle scars to help them prove their bravery.'

'Scars like this?' said Innocent, lifting his t-shirt, revealing an ugly line with dots running parallel either side of it, stretching across his stomach diagonally.

Guido had never seen Innocent without a shirt. 'How the hell did you get that?'

'I tried to subdue a mugger. I didn't know he had a knife. If I'd known I would have shot him. If they fight me I cut them. If they cut me I shoot them,' he said, his right hand in the shape of a pistol. 'Those are the rules. Everybody knows.'

'You're lucky to be alive.' Guido said.

'A car came along. I stopped the car. The driver wouldn't take me to hospital. He didn't want blood in his car. I subdue him as well. I pull him out of the car and I drive to hospital myself. The man was stupid. There was even more blood on the car than if I had been a passenger.'

Guido shook his head and told him to concentrate on doing the front garden from now on, and to look out for cars stopping outside, or that keep coming back. He also warned him not go to the gate to see any callers but to use the intercom inside the house to speak to them.

'How long?'

'A day. A month.' A surge of excitement swept through him. 'But they *will* come.'

'How will they find us?'

'They'll find us one way or another. Mark my words.'

'I'll be ready for them,' he said, clicking his fingers. Then, jerking to his feet, he clumsily shoved his chair against a huge cactus pot, shattering it. 'Sorry Boss. I'll clear it up.' He bowed and bounced off in the direction of the house.

Guido decided to postpone Tsotsi's walk. Usually at this time of day, once a week, Innocent would take Tsotsi to Emmarentia Park on the other side of town. It was a twenty-minute drive, but, although the dog had plenty of exercise chasing around the garden, Guido liked him to socialise with other dogs. Emmarentia was the only large park where they could roam free off the lead. In most other parks where people like to picnic or barbecue, the temptation to steal the food from under their noses was too great for Tsotsi.

Unusually for a German Shepherd, Tsotsi was black, which, together with his amazing sense of smell and hearing, made him an even more effective guard dog. If dogs in general were feared, black dogs were feared the most, and struck terror into the hearts of the bravest of African men. Although Guido suspected that Tsotsi, a gentleman with a childlike zest for life, probably wouldn't harm a fly.

Guido was aware that Alsatians are vicious only when they've been trained to be. That's because whatever they're trained to do – sniff out drugs, sniff out trapped people or the enemy, carry messages – they are exceptionally good at it. If they're trained to be vicious, they will perform the task with exceptional ability. Tsotsi hadn't been trained to be anything apart from sociable, but he still had the air of a dog that meant business.

Occasionally Guido would take him to Emmarentia himself. With his wolfish smile, Tsotsi was a gentle giant as his muscular form bounded round the park with smaller playmates, although always prepared to stand his ground against the likes of Rottweilers and Dobermanns.

The days that Innocent took Tsotsi were the one moment in the week that Guido felt insecure – abandoned by both of his guards. Most planned house-breaking took place in the rich northern suburbs, but opportunistic crime could happen anywhere, anytime, and could be vicious. He often thought of the eighty-year-old lady down the road who was tortured to death with a clothes iron because she didn't tell them where she kept her savings. She couldn't; she had none. Another householder had most of his teeth removed before the thieves believed he had nothing to hide. Then they shot him in the head for good measure.

The next best crime repellent was a snake. They are widely believed to cast deadly magic spells as well as deadly venom. Guido had put a sign next to the front door warning visitors of the presence of snakes and other reptiles and had hung rubber replicas from the branches of shrubs and trees at strategic points.

Yet, when Tsotsi and Innocent were away, Guido was on high alert.

32

Christian asked Guido if he could borrow the Merc to see if the freeway to the airport was open, and, if so, to visit the airline office, and see if there was a chance of getting any refund for their lost flights, and perhaps some news about the strike.

'Innocent will take you.'

'I'd like to drive on my own for once.'

'Sure. Ask Inno for the key.'

'I don't want Sas with me,' he said. 'Keep an eye on her for me.'

'Eh? How long will you be?'

'An hour or so.'

'No problem, cousin,' Guido smiled ruefully.

Christian didn't get far. He hadn't even reached the freeway before he was stopped by a police check. Remembering Innocent's advice, he reversed slightly, wound down the window, and greeted the policeman with a smile and a 'how are you, Officer?' The policeman asked him for his driving licence and hearing his accent asked for his passport. Christian handed him his British licence and explained that he never carried his passport for security reasons.

'Why? You think this country is dangerous?' the policeman asked with a note of menace in his voice. He looked at the licence with exaggerated concentration, turning it over and over. 'It's expired,' he stated at last. 'Last month. Look.' Holding it tightly between figure and thumb he held it up for Christian to see. The policeman was right.

'I don't understand. There's a paper licence with this. I checked. It expires in another few years' time.'

He thanked the cop for his trouble and promised to renew

it as soon as he got home.

The officer slowly shook his head. 'You are driving immediately. I must arrest you for invalid licence and no ID. You must park your car over there. Lock it. You will spend the night with us and appear in court tomorrow.'

Christian, who until that point had been ordinarily worried, was now just plain scared. He cast his mind back to Innocent's story of police hospitality in overnight holding cells, and the kind of intimate attention he would receive from other prisoners.

'In my country policemen impose a fine on the spot rather than troubling the courts,' Christian told him, desperately trying to control a tremor in his voice and sound authoritative. 'Doesn't that happen in this country?'

Whereas the eyes of a British policeman could be expected to be full of censure, the dark eyes of many African traffic cops express a perpetual desire for money, nurtured by a perception of being underpaid and undervalued, and by a compulsive craving to exercise power. This cop was no exception.

'What are you suggesting?'

'I just wondered how we could make it simpler and save you time and trouble,' Christian managed, reaching for his wallet. 'If South Africa had on the spot fines, what do you think it would be?'

'I don't know what you are suggesting,' the officer replied, looking around. 'Whatever it is, you must make the suggestion.' He looked across at his colleagues who were busy dealing with other motorists.

'It would have to be something we both feel comfortable with, but in the circumstances, I would think one hundred would be appropriate.'

'More,' he grunted sourly.

Christian shakily opened his wallet which contained only a single, blue one hundred note. His pulse thumped a steady rhythm inside his skull.

'It's okay,' the cop muttered, reaching through the window and grabbing the note.

Once it became clear that a deal was possible, it was almost as if a friendship had been struck up. They were colluding, playing a game. He said, 'I am supposed to examine your boot. Open the boot.' Christian pulled the boot catch, opened the door, struggled to his feet, and nervously stooped to retrieve the phone that had fallen out of his trouser pocket. As he did so, he dropped his wallet at the officer's feet. He bent to pick it up, and a sharp pain shot through his lower back, making him wince. The cop looked on and led him to the rear of the car. Christian lifted the boot lid.

'Everything is in order, isn't it?'

'Of course.' The cop pretended to look and then ordered him to shut the boot.

They both acted a role and in their separate ways seemed to be relieved that it had worked out successfully. The policeman handed Christian the licence and with a sardonic smile wished him a good day.

The look of relief on Christian's face gave way almost immediately to a shame-faced expression that revealed disgust with himself as though he were the one who had been bought off, as though he had become a receiver of bribes. He found himself irrationally trying to remember whether the word 'bribee' existed to describe the cop and whether it was a briber-bribee relationship? He was briefly overcome by a sense of irrelevance, as though smart questions and smart answers were constructed from yesterday's words fading dimly into a past life. He felt that if he were one of Guido's plants, he would need urgent re-potting and relocating to a sunnier spot.

The events of the last few days had reminded him that he was not as brave as he would like to think. Brave enough when it came to speaking out, expressing opinions, defending arguments about a nicety of philosophical theory in civilised, highly regulated dinner-party chatter. On the less cerebral sides of life, he was clearly found wanting.

He had the nagging sense that the awful experience of Saskya's abduction, like a parasite, had wormed its way into his blood and infected his character – his values and the fundamental ways of behaving that he had for so long held sacred. Many of his principles seemed to be on the brink of subsiding into an amorphous mass of uncertainty, where, if he were not vigilant, 'anything goes'. He had now reached the stage where he could no longer think of one single principle that he would hold up no matter what the circumstances and the consequences.

He experienced embarrassment and hypocrisy, as though he'd been exposed as a phoney. *There must be another way!* His thoughts screamed at him. He noticed he'd broken out in a sweat. His skin was itching, and he felt a desperate need to run and run until he dropped.

He concluded that his nerves couldn't stand another round of ethical examination. There was little chance that the airline would refund anything, and he didn't even know if the airport could be reached because of the strikes. He could always go some other time once life had returned to something like normal.

He turned the Merc around, and headed back the way he came, scared stiff he might not remember the way, and be caught in another road block – this time with no cash to buy his way out.

He stopped at the traffic lights and glanced down to his

251

right. There was an elderly woman slumped with her back resting against the traffic light pole, her head drooped, her eyes closed and her shrunken mouth wide open. She was skin and bone, worse than he'd ever seen in pictures of refugee camps, and she could have been taken for dead. Next to her, within inches of the traffic, was a little toddler. The child nearly stumbled under a passing truck, but the woman looked as though she was past caring.

Christian looked the other way. He had already firmly decided not to give to beggars – not one rand. Back in Cape Town, he'd read a council pamphlet discouraging help of any kind. 'A handout is not a hand up', it said, claiming that charity could be used to buy drugs or cigarettes.

When Christian got back, he mentioned this to Guido. His cousin just smiled ironically and looked away. *It's the grand theories, the 'big picture', that cause the suffering,* Guido had thought to himself. *Why feed that particular beggar at those particular traffic lights when there are thousands of them? Why? Because you can!*

Christian was also desperate to talk to someone about the police check. Innocent told him they are always looking for bribes. 'You should not give them one hundred,' he advised, shaking his head as though picturing in his mind's eye the amount of basic food it could buy. 'Twenty is okay next time.'

Guido's response was that he was lucky to get away with a hundred and that most people carry a two hundred note in their ID book or passport. You hand it over with the note in it, and when he hands it back the note is gone. 'This means that when there's a queue of traffic at a police checkpoint, the policeman's eyes are on you,' Guido told Christian. 'If you protest it just gets worse. You can almost smell the malodorous smog that hangs over their mendacious little minds.'

The attitude of these two temporary Jo'burgers did nothing to soothe Christian's overheated conscience. It had cast a painfully sharp light into the dark recesses of his mind where his weaknesses had long lain hidden, and seemed to nibble inexorably at his self-confidence and his self-righteousness.

33

Christian awoke from a siesta to the sound of his heart thudding in his ears, his soaked t-shirt stuck to his itchy torso. Still half asleep, convinced he was smothered in tiny insects, he scratched frantically. He blinked to clear his vision that was misted up like a windscreen on a wet winter's day. He lay in bed a little longer, staring at the patches of sunlight on the wall, and listening to the sound of the birds. Then, easing his tired frame out of bed, he gently lowered his feet to the floor and reached for his stick.

The shadows were already long. Still unsteady, he went downstairs to join Guido. As he lumbered down the hall, he paused to take in his own reflection in a mirror cracked down the middle. Two half faces stared back – one a perfect reflection; the other a distorted image that made him shudder and feel a chill crawl across the hairs on his neck.

He found Guido in the lounge, where the front of the room by the French windows was still suffused with shafts of warm, deep yellow sunlight. An Elgar cello sonata filled the air with deep melancholic rumblings of fear and hope. Guido looked up, gave him a welcoming smile, and waved him to a chair.

The two of them, their profiles silhouetted against the back window, looked amazingly alike physically and in their facial features. But in the light, there was a depth to the lines on Guido's face that Christian did not have. Although Christian had suffered, particularly during his parents' death and his divorce, his features seemed to have remained largely untouched, whereas Guido's face wore the scars of a long, difficult life, and experiences probably beyond Christian's imagination.

Guido opened his mouth to greet Christian when the gate intercom vigorously burst into its Mozart ringtone. He hesitated for a moment before pressing the answer button. There was silence at the other end. Then it disconnected.

'Innocent!' he shouted. 'Who's at the gate?'

'No one.'

'Have you seen anything?'

'Only a JoPower van. Driving up and down. Twice. I was coming to tell you.'

'I told you to alert me immediately!' Guido barked, the blood rushing to his face.

'What's wrong?' Christian asked, struggling to his feet. 'Where's Sas?'

'Upstairs. I think she should move into a hotel for the time being,' he told him. 'I've got a nasty feeling about this.'

Christian nodded thoughtfully. 'I'll take her. I'm not letting her out of my sight again.'

Guido shook his head. 'Sorry man. I need you to stay and help.'

'No chance. I'm looking after Sas.'

'Precious will look after her. Inno's half-brother is a guard up there. You have to stay here.'

'What's involved?'

Guido retold a brief outline of the plan he had agreed with Innocent.

'What happens if they don't go along with your plan?'

'They will. If they don't bite the carrot, we'll use the stick. *Simple comme bonjour.*'

'What could I possibly do? I've no experience of this kind of thing.'

'You had no experience of anything until you did it.'

Guido kept his voice cool and level, deliberately avoiding

any sign of disapproval, encouragement, discouragement or any other judgemental attitude that might threaten to dilute the autonomy of Christian's decision.

'You're the philosopher,' he said. 'There's always a choice. As you would say, choose to do the right thing.'

'I've got a feeling that doing the right thing will involve doing several wrong things.'

'I'll shield you from as many as possible.' Guido leant forward and patted him on the back.

'Inno, get Precious.'

She was already behind him. She moved next to him and put her arm round his waist.

'Precious, I want you to stay away for a while and look after Saskya. Innocent will drive you both to a hotel in Highlands North. She's in danger here. She'll want to stick with you, Christian, so you must go with them. When you get there, say you've forgotten your wallet. It's not far. Come straight back. Then ring her to say the car's broken down.'

She turned around to face him and stared into his eyes with an intensity that made him look away. 'Why do old people make us afraid of everything?' she sighed, with a slightly anxious edge to her voice. 'If you are in danger I will fight by your side.' He turned towards her, but she moved back. 'I am a mother. I have given birth. I have seen death. I can fight like a man.'

He let his eyes roam over the breasts that had nourished her children, and the hands clasped in front of the wide hips that had given them an easy passage into the world.

'Being a mother to Saskya *is* fighting with me,' he told her, the impatience in his voice due more to nervousness than to annoyance.

Her eyes settled on him again with some unfathomable emotion, and she tenderly took his hand. Built for motherhood and for love, it seemed to Guido that she wanted to mother him now, to slip a breast into his mouth, and let him suckle until he fell into a deep, carefree sleep, forgetting all this nonsense about fighting – these stupid, big boys' games. Her thoughts had given her eyes a misty look, as though she were regarding Guido like a cloud gradually changing form and drifting higher and higher and further and further towards the horizon to be absorbed into the light-blue sky.

'As you wish,' she whispered. The tenderness of her husky voice hung on the air.

He turned to Innocent and told him to leave with Christian and the two women 'pronto'.

'Be careful, Mr Guido.' Precious hugged him tight with a sudden passion that expressed a wealth of emotion. 'My angel will be by your side.'

Innocent took her by the arm and went with Christian to fetch Saskya from her room, and briefly explained the situation. He handed her a cellphone.

Minutes later they were gone.

The hotel lounge was almost empty except for those at the bar. Saskya and Precious squeezed next to each other on a red, imitation-leather bench seat so that they could hear themselves above the convivial murmur of voices. A waiter brought their order – a beer for Saskya and bubbling mineral water for Precious.

Precious took a breath deep into her stomach. 'Saskya, I must tell you something,' she whispered, her face puckered with concern. 'Another secret. You promise never to tell anyone?'

Saskya threw her a quizzical look and nodded.

She hesitated for a few seconds, holding her breath. 'Mr

Guido has cancer.'

'What? He said he was clear.'

'He lied. He hates causing a fuss.'

'How bad?'

'He has death in his bones. I should have told you when I told you my secret.'

'I'm so, so sorry Precious,' Saskya murmured, squeezing Precious' hand.

Saskya grabbed her cellphone. It was Christian. She nodded, thanked him and hung up.

'The car's broken down at home,' she said. 'Innocent is trying to fix it while they wait for the AA, and then he'll bring Dad back. He said we should eat without them.' She pocketed the phone and turned towards Precious. 'Sorry. Uncle Guido's got cancer?'

Precious nodded and wiped the dampness from her eyes.

'Did you tell Guido your secret?' Saskya asked.

'No. I can't. I want you to tell him.'

Saskya felt exhausted, already weighed down with worry about events that might be happening at the house.

'I couldn't eat. How about you?'

Precious shook her head, turned away, and bravely composed herself. There was something detached about her as she sleepwalked to the bar for a packet of cigarettes. She returned, sat next to Saskya and gave her a wan smile. Saskya hesitated and rested her hand on Precious' arm.

'I can't do it, Precious,' she said. 'I can't be the one to tell him. You must tell him. You've really done nothing wrong. It'll help him understand you better. He's basically a very caring, sympathetic man. And from what you told me, there's nothing to be ashamed of.'

'There's much more.' Precious looked away.

'I even lied about my husband.'

She hesitated.

'What about him?' Saskya asked.

'I haven't got one!' She suddenly burst into a fit of giggles, and abruptly stopped, clamping her hand over her mouth. 'I told everyone I was married after my man left me. I even wore this ring. I didn't want other men thinking they could get up my skirt.'

Saskya stroked her smooth upper back.

Precious shook her head, and whispered, 'And I lied to Mr Guido about my father.' She took a deep breath. 'I said he was an activist, a hero who had been shot by the secret police. I wanted him to think I come from a good family. But it was a lie. He was a collaborator. He was responsible for the detainment, torture and death of hundreds of anti-apartheid activists. He knew exactly what his betrayal meant.'

'What happened to him?'

She lit a cigarette with a plastic lighter and cleared her throat. 'Just before my tenth birthday, people found out. The police had no more use for him. *They* betrayed *him*.'

She beat her breastbone with a tight fist in an unconscious reaction to the wave of grief that had just slammed into her heart.

'I told Mr Guido that no one could have had nicer parents than me and that my father was kind and loving and cared about others.'

Precious bit her lips as for the first time in years she struggled to replace fiction with fact, while probably aware that in some respects she could no longer tell the difference. The faded portrait she had carried with her all that time was of a man prepared to risk his life to fight for justice for his people. The focused image now in her mind was of a man who dominated his household with an inflexible, iron will, subjecting his wife and children to absolute subservience.

Even though she regularly recalled the sharp stomach pains that accompanied her fear of upsetting him, and her fear of his belt, she told Saskya that she never questioned his behaviour, let alone resented it.

Her almost obsequious veneration for her father was ritualistic within her culture. It was 'normal'. *Right or wrong, my father* – and might was right. She and Innocent had kept themselves busy from sunrise till bedtime with domestic chores, walking to school, surviving school, walking home again, and more domestic chores five days a week, with some time off to play on the dusty dirt streets at the weekend.

She stopped abruptly and grabbed Saskya's hand. 'You must stay and help our children,' she pleaded. 'Our schools must be made safe.'

It took an inordinate length of time for what she knew deep down to come heaving to the surface, and for a daughter's unconditional love for her father to mutate into pure hatred. Her feelings for her father caused her more distress than the reasons for them.

'How could I love him one day and hate him the next – a hate that hurt me like a sharp knife to my stomach?'

Life at home had become even more unbearable. Not that her father was at home often, but when he was she had managed to slip past him and stay out of his reach, never having learned to judge with any accuracy the mood he might bring home with him, and keen to hide from him the fact that she now absolutely loathed him.

She had pushed away her feelings into the dark recesses of her mind to lie festering with all her other unendurable memories. And now the news of Guido's sickness had caused them to rise again and suffuse her at a completely cellular level.

'It's not fair to say I hid these things from Mr Guido,' she said, looking straight into Saskya's eyes. 'I love him. I had already hidden them from myself. I buried those images as deep as possible a long time ago.'

Her head dropped as though she had nodded off.

Saskya was still too anaesthetised to be able to muster a reassuring smile in return. But she could tell that the flood gates were wide open and wouldn't shut until all the 'secrets' had been released in this strange intimacy with a stranger too far removed to stand in judgement. She interrupted Precious to ask her if she would like another drink and looked for messages on the phone Innocent had given her. Nothing. She sat silent for a minute or so, brooding over what advice she could offer Precious.

Precious lifted her head, opened her eyes and continued to reveal the awful minutiae of those apartheid days. Her desperate need to confess before it was too late had given her access to memories that had long seemed impenetrable.

'I was my father's flesh and blood. I felt guilty for what he'd done. I was his accomplice. I kept quiet about him. I lied. I was as bad as he was.'

Saskya knew that no consoling words would help and that all she could do was listen. 'Is he still alive?' she asked.

The clock had been inexorably ticking down for her father. Eventually, he was found out. And suddenly everyone knew. An angry lynch mob from the community in the township where they had lived most of their lives, among them their good neighbours and friends, those they would eat, drink and share stories with, dragged him out into the street and 'necklaced' him.

'They put a tyre round his neck, filled it with petrol and set it alight.' She blew hard into a tissue.

Her mother was gang-raped by some of the younger, more enthusiastic members of the pack. A faithful, submissive, unthinking woman, still grieving for her husband, she died of Aids a year later. Precious and Innocent were raised by an auntie who dished out beatings for the slightest of offences or perceived wrongdoings. By the time Precious had reached the age of sixteen they had both left school, left the auntie and were on the streets until they were taken in by a local preacher from the Zion Christian Church.

'I told Mr Guido that I loved my father and that I was so proud of him.' Her voice broke, sounding childlike before returning to its usual huskiness. 'It was true and a lie. I did love him when he was nice. But I also hated him. I even told Mr Guido my matric marks were so high I got a scholarship to university. I didn't. The preacher got us home tutoring and arranged a community bursary for me while Innocent went out to work. There are so many lies! Will Mr Guido ever forgive me, Saskya?' Her voice faltered.

Saskya replied with a nod and a squeeze of the hand. 'He'll be sad you didn't dare tell him. He's a kind man. And none of this was your fault. It was outside your control. Tell him. He would understand you better and love you more.'

'But they say bad things happen to bad people. I wanted him to think I was better than his clever Duchess.' She held Saskya's eyes for a moment. 'Don't tell your dad,' she pleaded. 'Don't tell anyone else.'

Saskya nodded and glanced again at her cellphone, her imagination flooding her with intestinal apprehension. She started to feel unusually hungry and her bottom ached. Once Precious had finished talking, she would ring Christian.

'You must tell Guido. Especially because he's ill. He'll understand,' she advised. 'Please don't stop. I'm sorry. I am listening, but I can only think of Dad now,' she said, staring at the phone.

When Innocent and Christian got back from dropping off Saskya and Precious they helped Guido prepare everything, including splashing dark-red paint on the wall of the back room to look like the blood from an exit wound from the head of someone sitting with their back to the wall. Christian sat at the poolside reflecting on the lies he had just told his daughter – unquestioningly, as though this cousin of his had seized complete control of his moral compass. Guido whistled, and Tsotsi came bounding up to him, tail wagging. Guido shut him in the shed.

A group of ephemeral clouds rose above the trees only to be absorbed into the azure sky before reaching the opposite horizon. From one of the rooms, a tragic aria from *Lucia di Lammermoor* came to an abrupt halt on a high note. Guido tried the lights. 'Inno. Power's off!' he shouted. He looked at his watch. Four o' clock. It would be dark in another couple of hours.

34

The intercom broke the silence.

'Hello,' Guido answered. Turning to Innocent, he whispered, 'Electric engineers.' He covered the mouthpiece with one hand. 'They say it's an emergency. See how many there are.'

Guido spoke 'One moment please' into the phone, while Innocent ran to fetch binoculars.

'Two. It's the van that was parked on the other side of the road this afternoon. They are big and very black. I don't trust it, Mr Guido.'

Guido spoke again into the phone: 'One moment. I'm looking for the remote for the gate.'

'But there's a power cut,' Innocent reminded him.

'The gate's on battery.'

Guido rushed upstairs and hurriedly threw on the jacket with the double-edged sheath knife stitched into the sleeve. He ran back, two steps at a time.

'Christian! Come here.' He handed Christian a Springfield rifle. 'It's not loaded. Once they're inside, keep them covered from over there in the corner.' He gestured to the darkest corner of the room beneath a 'Rembrandt' in a heavy frame. 'Point it at them as if you mean business.'

Christian looked at the gun with disbelief as though it would bite him. He gathered himself and held it like he'd seen in the movies.

'You ready?' Guido asked Innocent, who replied with a giggle. 'Let them in.'

Innocent used the remote to open the sliding gate. From inside they watched the two men climb back into the van, and swing round into the drive. Innocent pressed the remote again to close the gate behind them. The two men slammed the van doors behind them, looked behind nervously, and walked up the drive to the front door, each carrying an identical toolbox in their left hand, their right hand in the bulging pockets of their blue overalls. One of them put down his toolbox and knocked on the front door. Innocent opened the judas window and asked them for their identification. One pushed through a photo card.

'One moment.' Innocent handed the card to Guido, who nodded and handed it back. 'Tell them you'll get the *baas*,' he whispered.

Christian stood the gun behind the door. Innocent and Guido stood next to each other on the hinged side of the door which opened inwards. Guido nodded to Christian to open it.

Christian fought to keep his voice and expression steady. 'Hi guys,' he greeted them in a friendly manner. 'You come to fix the power? Come on in.'

As they stepped inside onto the mat, Christian kept the door open, hiding Guido and Innocent. Then Guido kicked it so hard Christian lost his grip and the door slammed shut. Guido and Innocent pointed their pistols at the visitors and sharply ordered them to put their hands on their heads.

'Keep this guy covered,' Guido ordered Christian, who pointed the rifle as menacingly as his aesthetic features would allow. Guido covered the other man with his pistol while Innocent handcuffed their hands behind their backs. He searched them. They both had police-issue pistols like his own, which Guido thought vindicated press reports of a thriving market in police weapons and other equipment useful to Jo'burg's burgeoning criminal community. Innocent led them into the study and sat them side by side against the wall next to the one splashed with 'blood'. He squatted next to them. Christian stood against the far wall, still pointing the empty rifle. Guido followed them in, shut the door behind him and towered over the two engineers.

'This isn't quite how you planned your evening, is it?' he smirked. 'What were you going to do, pistol whip us, rip out our fingernails, rape anyone you could lay your filthy hands on? What did you have in mind? The usual party tricks?'

They stared at the floor as though terrified of meeting his gaze.

'This is our party now,' Guido told them in a measured, menacing tone. 'We decide on the entertainment. Sit back and enjoy the show.'

One of them squirmed, looking left and right as though still convinced that there had to be a way out.

Guido asked them their names.

Charles,' said one. 'Dignity,' said the other, in a whimpering tone of voice.

'Dignity!' Guido choked. 'How many women have you raped, Dignity?'

'None *Baas*. We do a job.'

'And you, Charles. How many people have you tortured to death?'

Charles stared in terror, his voice gone.

'Who are you working for?'

They looked at each other and shrugged in sullen silence.

'You wanna be the strong, silent types?' Guido asked. 'Inno, fetch Tsotsi!'

Innocent returned with Tsotsi, who barked loudly, exposing his long fangs. The two froze. Tsotsi obediently squatted next to Christian on the far side of the room, sizing up the two cowering before him, and licking his lips as though considering their suitability for dinner. His erect ears twitched, adding to the impression of complete predatory

266

concentration.

'The dog can be part of the entertainment,' Guido warned. 'He knows lots of nice tricks. He loves to play with little bits he can bite off.'

One of them crossed his legs tightly. The other mumbled unintelligible words of supplication to his god or gods, a trickle of spit oozing from the corner of his tense mouth.

'Let's start again,' said Guido patiently. 'Who are you working for?'

'We don't know. I tell the truth,' Charles blurted, his eyes bulging. 'We meet in a car park. Different each time.'

'Is he police?'

'No!' Charles snorted. Guido believed him.

'How did you get this address?'

'The boss gave it.'

'Did he have me followed?'

'I don't know – honest.'

'What instructions did you have for reporting to your boss?'

Tsotsi, South Africa's most loyal, reliable and incorruptible policeman, kept his bright eyes focused on the two of them, his tongue lolling over his lower teeth, while he panted as though in expectation of a new game.

'We ring the *baas*,' Charles replied, his voice shrill. 'We send him pictures of your body, and the safe and any money and stuff.'

'Who rings him?'

'Me,' he squeaked.

'Good. Now listen carefully. This is how it goes. You do exactly what you were supposed to do.'

Their eyebrows lifted in unison as though at the command of a conductor's baton.

At that moment, the door creaked. A man dressed in

similar overalls, stood, using the door as a shield. He was pointing a pistol at Guido. You could almost smell the man's fear. Christian still had sight only of the man's arm and the silenced barrel of a Vektor pistol. He was no more scared than he had been already. He froze with indecision.

It was Tsotsi who instinctively knew what was required. The magnificent animal skirted the door, his paws sliding on the polished floor, and launched himself at the man who recoiled in terror and fired a shot with a spitting sound that hit the ceiling. The door swung wide open. As though abruptly waking from a trance, Christian swung the rifle by the barrel using all his strength to crash the butt into the man's head like splitting wood with a long-handled axe.

At the same moment, in one deft movement, Innocent sliced the man from throat to groin, his overalls and shirt parting in the middle like a pair of curtains. If he had lived, the scar would have borne an uncanny resemblance to Innocent's own. But he was probably dead before he hit the floor. The rifle butt had smashed straight through the skull.

Christian had lost his balance, and fallen to his knees, caught in a fit of squeaky giggling. His heart was pounding so furiously it made him feel sick. He groped for his stick and his glasses that had slid across the floor. Innocent helped him struggle to his feet. Christian rubbed the dust from his eyes with his sweaty fist and looked at Guido who was staring at him in amazement, as though seeing him for the first time.

Guido turned to Innocent. 'Where the hell did he come from?'

Innocent shrugged. 'The back of the van?'

'Put him next to the paint on the wall,' Guido ordered.

'Does your boss know this guy?'

'No. He deals with me.'

Innocent dragged the man feet first. 'Now we have real

blood, Mr Guido.'

'Exactly!'

Guido left the room and returned about a quarter of an hour later with his face made up with heavy bruising around one eye, and blood dripping from a fake gunshot wound in the temple. The wound was surrounded by black powder marks. His shirt was bloody and torn. Guido had forged his own death.

He took up a prone position against the wall splattered with red paint. Guido handed the gun to Innocent who stuck it in his belt. 'Get a pic with his phone.'

Innocent grabbed Charles' phone and took a photo of Guido who was now lying down, playing dead. Christian kept his rifle pointed at them.

Guido then told Innocent to take a photo of the third man. For the third photo, Guido commanded Tsotsi, whose fur was soaked in blood, to lie still next to him. The dog's high forehead frowned slightly as though even his enormous intelligence couldn't quite take in what was happening.

'I'm giving you thirty thousand rand,' Guido told them. 'You tell your boss that the pic of your friend is the body of my guard and that you tortured him until he gave you the keys to the safe. Tell him the other pics are of me, Guido van Rensburg, and the dead guard dog. You tell him that thirty big ones were all there was in the safe. *Klaar*?'

They looked at each other and nodded. '*Klaar Baas.*'

Thirty thousand! Innocent looked at Guido as if he'd gone mad.

'Inno, cuff his hands in front of him so he can use the phone,' he barked.

'Send the pics now.' He handed Charles the phone.

He took back the phone and checked that the pictures had gone through. He put it on speakerphone.

'Ring him now,' Guido told Charles. 'Any funny stuff and the dog will deal with you.'

'Well?' said the voice at the other end. Guido recognised the transatlantic accent.

'Job done, *Baas*.'

'And the safe?'

'Thirty grand.'

'Fuck! Is that all?' The voice was angry.

'I'm sure.'

'Is there another safe?'

'No *Baas*. We hurt them bad. Look at the pics. They were singing like birds.'

'Stay away for a few days till I contact you. Keep that money safe, or else...' The phone went dead.

Guido took the phone and made a note of the last number dialled and the number of the phone itself. He handed it back.

'You both understand the deal,' Guido said. 'If your boss finds out you screwed up, he'll have you killed slowly. This way you've done a good job. He'll be pleased with you. He'll give you more jobs.'

He told Innocent to take the keys, to bring the van into the garage, and to come straight back.

'Put your friend in the back,' Guido told the two engineers. Christian still had them covered with the unloaded, blood-stained rifle. Innocent switched cuffs on the second man to his hands in front of him. The two of them struggled to carry their colleague, whose body was already starting to stiffen. By the time he was loaded in the back they were gasping for breath. Guido handed them a wad of notes. Innocent opened the garage doors, then opened the gate with the remote, and kept the van covered with his pistol. Guido unlocked the cuffs.

A few minutes later, they were gone, and a silent peace

270

descended with no one knowing quite what to say.

There was no hi-fiving like a winning basketball team. Nor tears of euphoria. Just a tremendous, glorious, sense of being alive and sober reflection on what might have been if it had gone wrong.

The three of them spent the next couple of hours cleaning up the mess. They burned the clothes in the garden incinerator and scrubbed the blood off the floor. Innocent shampooed Tsotsi. The most difficult job was getting the paint off the wall. When they were satisfied that there was no more to be done, they celebrated with a stiff drink on the *stoep* – Dutch gin for Guido and Christian, and a litre of *Inkomazi* for Innocent, who had picked up a swollen lip, giving him a sulky look. In a single gulp, Guido polished off the small glass filled to the brim, savouring the burning sensation as it burst into his stomach. It was good. In fact, it was *damned good*. He grinned at Christian and raised his glass. 'One more for the cardiac?'

Feeling that his nerves had been stretched almost to breaking point, relief had sent warmth through every muscle and sinew of Guido's body. He felt the urge to giggle. He lit a cigarette, and let it hang from the corner of his mouth, his nonchalant pose a picture of studied equanimity. He looked at Christian and smiled, but seeing the look on his face the smile withered halfway, and his expression turned to one of patient weariness as though finding himself in circumstances that had become tiresomely familiar.

Christian's bliss had been short-lived. His hand shook so much he could hardly get the glass to his lips. A lump had hit the pit of his stomach, making him gag for breath. This sort of thing happened in fiction, not to real people, and not to real people like him. Struggling to cope with what felt like an attack of vertigo, he nodded at Guido and forced a grin. Relief had visibly made space for other feelings. Guilt and pride were vying for first place. But, as always, guilt was ahead by a mile. He had killed someone. Not by accident. Not by mowing down a pedestrian. Not even as the result of jealousy or anger. In his entire life he'd never knowingly met anyone who'd done such a thing. It wasn't even out of duty. He had acted instinctively. On one level he felt it was the right thing to do. But the 'right thing' had been terribly wrong.

'So, Professor of Ethics, you can add *killer* to your CV,' Guido said, raising his glass. 'Welcome to the club. How does it feel?'

Guido immediately regretted the remark which had meant to lighten up the gloom. Christian leant forward on his walking stick, staring at the scrubbed backs of his delicate hands, and noticed that the palms still had traces of black grease from the gun barrel. He tried to rub it off with his handkerchief but couldn't. He briefly wore a look that was rare for him – a thorough disgust with life, and perhaps even with himself whom he failed to recognise.

His mind had refused to let go of his complicity in police corruption, and especially his distant infatuation with his cousin's woman. *Thou shalt not covet thy neighbour's wife.* And now this! He wouldn't know how to begin to describe how it felt. There was no defining line that he had crossed, but tiny unconscious tentative steps had led him across a barren no man's land stretched between the trenches of good and bad. He felt a blinding revulsion for what he'd done and yearned for what he imagined having been a suspended weightlessness in the benign depths of the amniotic fluid of his bosomy, generous-hearted, Irish mother, with her unconditional love and protection and infinite forgiveness.

He shook his head, and gave Guido a look which said, 'How has it come to this?'

Both men sat in contemplative silence for a while before Guido abruptly interrupted by ringing Saskya.

She sounded breathless. 'You all okay?'

'Everything's fine.' He steadied his voice. 'You needn't stay longer. Innocent will fetch you.'

Christian turned to Guido and shook his head. 'Please don't tell Saskya about all this,' he pleaded. 'She wouldn't understand.'

'Fine by me,' Guido replied abruptly, as though waking from a reverie. 'So, what should we tell them?'

'I don't know.' Christian felt woefully inadequate at spinning a web of deceit. 'Say it was a false alarm?'

'Then they'd still continue to worry.' Guido threw a rueful glance across the table, his eyes resting on Christian with a look of almost paternal concern. 'We'll tell them it was a bloodless coup. That we paid them off. It's close enough to the truth. Agreed?'

Christian nodded.

Guido shrugged and got to his feet. 'Let's go inside.' His voice had dropped to a murmur. He guided Christian into the dining room.

Christian felt his heart thumping nervously. He felt dizzy and lost in a numb, anticlimactic sense of despondency. Weighed down by this unknown, darkest breed of gloom, he couldn't even bring himself to look in the cracked mirror.

'You can be proud of yourself.' Guido's deep voice caught his attention. 'You did what was necessary.' He gave an appreciative glance.

Christian looked away. He sat staring into space in a state of emotionless inertia, feeling grimy and contaminated.

Innocent, who had been observing the exchange with detached amusement, had jumped to his feet and followed them in. 'I'll get the women, Boss. Sorry! Mr Guido.'

Guido nodded. 'Not a word to them about what really happened. Tell 'em we bought our way out of trouble.'

He rang JoPower to get the electricity supply restored, and made an appointment for the next day. He told Innocent to connect the petrol generator to power the lights and to leave Tsotsi out all night to patrol the fence. When the generator kicked in, the burglar alarm went off automatically and Tsotsi ran up and down the fence snarling at imagined intruders, while Guido went through the house, resetting the alarm and the electric clocks.

Innocent took the car to fetch Precious and Saskya.

Guido took off his shirt and stretched out on the bed while Precious lit the lamp, her eyes bright as she bent over the flame, concentrating hard as though tending to a sick patient. Two pipes usually relaxed him to the somnolent point where his ghosts made way for angels, but still left some of the potency he kept for her. But that gift would have to wait for another time. He looked at her but could barely focus.

'Precious,' he whispered.

'Yes?' She took his hand.

'Just precious…'

'Are you scared, Mr Guido?'

'My mind is ready to depart, but the rest of me shows some reluctance.'

'Your mind lies to you.'

'Yes, Precious. It lies.'

Peace at last. All worry dissolved into serene, endless, empty space, devoid of meaning, where belief in reality is exposed as vanity, and where it makes way for all there was – successive waves of contemplation. This was as close as he believed he would ever come to a state of grace – guiltless, remorseless, contemplating the goodness in himself, and the fundamental goodness of most other beings. Already her physical nearness had become indifferent to him. The pipe provided the serenity of a little death – *une petite mort* – in which his obsessive thoughts of real death floated away beyond the horizons of his mind. The act of love tonight would be love without the act. This seemed to suit them both, a blessing he was grateful for.

Guido's dreams nearly always followed the same theme – getting lost, and not being able to find his way home. This time he found a friend's baby lying on the floor gulping from an upended bottle of brandy. He grabs the child and searches everywhere for the mother. But wherever he looks he can't find his way back again. A young hippie holding a reefer asks him for a light. He gives him a box of matches and the man warns him that in Africa birds of prey can easily lift a baby. He continues to search frantically until he awoke drenched in perspiration. Precious was wiping his forehead with a damp flannel.

He turned over and shuddered under the sheet, chilled by something more than just skin deep. His head seemed to ring with mocking laughter. Was there really anything else he could have done – a different path to reach this point in his life?

'Shall I make another pipe?' she asked soothingly.

He always took two; never more, never less.

'No thank you, Precious.'

'Mr Guido!'

He gave a lopsided smile. 'I've come a long way standing on one leg,' he whispered. 'After all those years, the dreams and visions in meditation have become almost as good as pipe dreams.' He thought again of his wife. 'And they're free and they're legal.' He gave her an ironic smile. 'They're all I need from now on. They might even save me.'

He shuddered, and a look of fear passed briefly over Precious' face as she stroked his hair.

'I'll have a pipe myself, Mr Guido. You will be my pipe. I'll give you nice dreams, *ne*?'

He kissed her forehead and sensed that her need for him was just for *her* this time. It was often like that – she for him; he for her. She wasn't his mistress; he wasn't her master. They were for each other, 'to each according to their needs' as Christian would say. This time, he sensed her need for him was driven by fear – fear for the changes she sensed in him; fear of losing him. She seemed to need him to make her feel safe. This time he thought she wanted *him* to suckle *her*. He sensed in her a need to unburden herself of something profound – perhaps replacing pieces of fiction with snippets of fact. Should he ask her to marry him? She would shout 'yes!' so loudly they'd hear it in Cape Town.

35

The next day, a ghostly sense of peace had descended on the household. Even the street seemed quiet as though it had been snowing invisibly. Precious decided to go for an early swim while Guido pottered around in the studio. She headed for the pool, stopped in her tracks, remembering again that there were guests, and retraced her steps to fetch a bathing costume. On her way back to the pool she met Saskya, sitting with her back to a sandstone wall, soaking up the heat.

'You haven't told Mr Guido what I said?'

'No, Precious. I told you. You must tell him yourself.'

'Please tell him *now-now*.' She squeezed Saskya's shoulder. 'I'm scared.'

Saskya firmly shook her head.

Guido was back in the lounge playing the music to the opening song of Shostakovich's Fourteenth Symphony, the profoundly moving adagio *De Profundis* with its theme of unjust and premature death in the Spanish civil war. The lyrics were the Russian translation of a poem of the same name by Spanish author Federico García Lorca.

Guido decided that when Precious had finished swimming, he would play to her Leonard Cohen's English translation of Lorca's poem *Pequeño vals vienés*, and watch her body sway subtly to the rhythm, her lovely features relax, and her eyes turn their focus inwards towards unfathomable depths. He reminded himself to ask her for a lock of her hair when she got back from the pool. Just in case.

Africa had transformed Guido into a resilient and mentally strong individual, but he knew he would never escape his conscience or the ghosts that never stop their whispering. There was nowhere within reach that he could exorcise them and lay them to rest. The towering cathedrals of France and Spain, with their sublime Gregorian chant and the ethereal fragrance of incense, where he could have consulted the religious icons by candlelight and unburdened his heart in the intimacy of the confessional, were far beyond reach.

Would guilt's insidious stamina outlast him? He ached to celebrate Corpus Christi and absorb through his skin the choir and congregation's rapturous voices soaring to the vaulted ceilings and beyond. Or lie on his back on a prayer mat in the Nasīr al-Mulk Mosque in Persia's Shiraz, meditating on the love poems of Omar Khayyam, and feel a sense of heavenly transcendence as his soul was drawn up towards the gold and blue and red mosaic dome as a taste of what may lie ahead.

That sense of spirituality, awe and mystery – *mysterium tremendum et fascinans* – had been absent from his life for too long, starving his soul and shrivelling it to splinters and dust, to be scattered on the Highveld winds. His forged documents would never pass the scrutiny of border control outside southern Africa. He was exiled, excommunicated, trapped in a form of purgatory. The world's obsession with terrorism and security had severed any possibility of returning to those old and ancient sanctuaries.

He went to his room and consulted the *I-Ching*. The resultant hexagram confirmed his sense of a turning point ahead. He carefully replaced the gold coins in the safe.

Guido stood sipping his coffee, while soaking up the heat from the morning's sunshine. A pair of Go-Away birds strutted up and down, their pale beaks occasionally pecking at the bare ground, their crested heads bobbing back and forth.

He lifted his eyes to the cloudless, blue sky, and fixed his gaze on a black dot moving in wide circles. An eagle at that height could study miles of the earth below with the accuracy of a spy satellite. With regal detachment, the bird seemed to scorn the fuss and concern of the human dots hundreds of feet below. It continued to circle in a downward spiral until Guido could pick out the white and black feathers before it soared out of sight with no perceptible movement of its majestic wings.

Guido looked away as he heard footsteps behind him. He could almost tell from Innocent's face what he was going to say.

'The cops are at the gate, Mr Guido.' He looked down at Guido with an unusual depth of feeling in his wide, oval eyes.

'How many?'

'Four.'

'What do they want?' Guido asked him.

'To see Mr Christian.'

'Where is he?'

'The shops. With my sister and the girl.'

'I thought Precious was swimming.' His stomach somersaulted. 'How do you know they're real cops?'

'I know one of them. From Central Police Station. This is not good, Mr Guido.'

Guido handed him a wad of notes. 'Deal with them.'

'I can't, Mr Guido. One is wearing a nice suit.'

'Thank you Innocent. I'll get changed and meet them.'

'No. They want Mr Christian.' He stiffened, and then seemed to shrink back within himself.

'I *am* Mr Christian. Guido van Rensburg is dead, shot through the head, remember? Look.' Guido reached into his

279

back pocket and flashed Innocent the forged copy of Christian's passport with Guido's photo.

Innocent's silent gaze was transfixed for what seemed like an age, his face clouded by a fog of perplexity, his tongue clicking. 'You can't. This is not right.' He stared down at the light palms of his hands with stricken eyes. 'You are very, very old. You will die. Your mind is still young. You must find another way.' He shrugged violently as if to shake off some dreadful image from his mind's eye. His swollen lip added to his tragic expression.

'You're all in danger,' Guido urged. He narrowed his eyes against the glare of the sun. The eagle had returned and was hovering directly above. 'Look after him and his daughter. I'll take his clothes. Give him mine. They can't use an SA airport. Drive them to Botswana. They must fly home from there via Namibia and Germany. Christian must never return.'

'But Mr Guido – '

'*I am Christian Kettermann*. Understand? Remember, we must do whatever's necessary.' He let out a giggle. 'Empty both safes. Give Tsotsi to your brother. I trust you, Inno. Close the house. Leave tonight.'

'No, Mr Guido!' He sank to his knees, his hands pressed together in supplication.

'Get up, Man. Before they break down the gate. Let them in.'

'Please, Mr Guido!' His stricken face exuded undiluted anguish.

'We'll meet again. This is a land of miracles and magic. Tell Precious. There's nothing that can't be arranged. Tell them Mr Christian is on his way.'